D0618191

DUE

The Drowning House

The Drowning House

A Novel

ELIZABETH BLACK

NAN A. TALESE | DOUBLEDAY
New York London Toronto Sydney Auckland

Copyright © 2013 by Elizabeth Black Garrett

All rights reserved. Published in the United States by Nan A. Talese / Doubleday, a division of Random House, Inc., New York, and in Canada by Random House of Canada, Toronto.

www.nanatalese.com

DOUBLEDAY is a registered trademark of Random House, Inc. Nan A. Talese and the colophon are trademarks of Random House, Inc.

Book design by Pei Loi Koay
Map illustration by Genevra Collier
Jacket design by Emily Mahon
Jacket photograph © Ben Stockley/Gallery Stock

Library of Congress Cataloging-in-Publication Data
Black, Elizabeth, 1950–
The drowning house : a novel / Elizabeth Black. — 1st ed.
p. cm.
1. Women photographers—Fiction. 2. Galveston (Tex.)—Fiction.
3. Family secrets—Fiction. 4. Domestic fiction. I. Title.
PS3602.L275D76 2013
813'.6—dc23   2011046222

ISBN 978-0-385-53586-1

MANUFACTURED IN THE UNITED STATES OF AMERICA

1 3 5 7 9 10 8 6 4 2

First Edition

To Marie, with love

Galveston . . . died in 1900. What remains in my memory is . . .
a place of the mind . . .

—*Dallas Times Herald*, JANUARY 2, 1966

Stare, pry, listen, eavesdrop. Die knowing something. You are
not here long.

—WALKER EVANS

The Drowning House

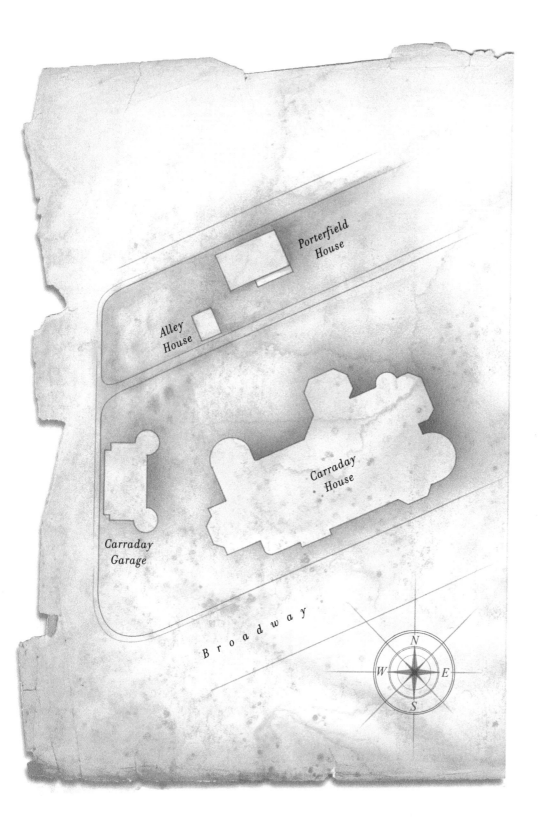

Porterfield
House

Alley
House

Carraday
House

Carraday
Garage

B r o a d w a y

N

W   E

S

Chapter 1

IF THERE WAS A SIGN, I MISSED IT. But I knew I was in Texas when I swerved to avoid a shape by the side of the road. It must have been around six in the morning, the first thin light just visible through the pines, when I crossed over the state line.

I stopped and backed up to confirm that the shape was a chest of drawers. Or rather the skeleton of one, since the drawers themselves were gone and the empty spaces where they should have been gaped open. I'd lived away long enough to find the sight incongruous. But it came back to me all at once, the things I'd seen abandoned at the side of the road in Texas. Not just on rural blacktops but along the busiest superhighways—gut-ripped mattresses, clothing, suitcases, and once, a velvet rocking chair.

It was what you might expect in a country at war—personal belongings strewn along the side of the road, as though their owners' lives had exploded, sending them flying. Or on the frontier, when travelers came this way as a last resort. In the days when "Gone to Texas" meant you were desperate.

It was May 1990, and still cool enough at night to leave the car windows open. I heard a bobwhite whistle, and I whistled back, but the only response was a quick flurry of wings. Bobwhites have different calls—for assembly, for food sharing, calls of alarm and flight. Probably I had said the wrong thing.

I had been driving for several days. Early on, I'd left the route Michael had drawn for me on the map. It was a route as unlikely as the map itself, where the entire continent was an uninterrupted expanse of green. As I drove up the ramp onto my first stretch of freeway, the map blew into the backseat, and I let it lie there.

Before I left, Michael and I had argued. He couldn't get away, he had a case coming up for trial. "I'll put you on a plane if you want," he said.

"You'll put me?"

"Clare, it's just a phrase."

"You know I can't fly."

We'd had the same exchange before. What usually happened next was that Michael would shrug and go back to his desk, with its shifting piles of papers and stacks of books on torts and civil procedure, and I would wander the apartment, picking things up and replacing them like someone seeing it all for the first time.

Instead I said, "I'll drive." Saying it made it seem like something I could do.

"You're going to drive to Texas from D.C.? By yourself?" Now I had his full attention. "You haven't driven anywhere in months."

I had tried. I'd gone out to the garage, keys in hand. I'd seen through the window Bailey's blue parka lying on the backseat, one arm flung out in a gesture so vividly like her that for a moment I could almost believe she was alive. Then the truth washed over me. Bright spots swam up from the concrete floor and my legs began to shake. I went back into the house.

Michael had even suggested selling the station wagon, but I'd resisted.

"Well." Michael is tall, and when he concentrates, he looks down and frowns. I had once found it attractive, the way he would focus his energy on a problem only to forget it completely a moment later, raising his head and gazing out again at his own serene world. That was before I'd ever supposed I could be the problem. "If it will make you happy."

I didn't tell him that happiness had always seemed to me to descend suddenly, when you least expected it, like a sun shower. That often it wasn't until much later you could look back and say, then, on that ordinary morning, with a car full of six-year-olds squirming and kicking, as the station wagon flashed through the dappled light of the tree-lined streets, then I was truly happy.

"Michael, don't," I said.

"Don't what?"

"Don't deal with me. I'm not a client." In the end, he tried to give me the keys to his car, the BMW. The offer was real. Still, he was visibly relieved when I declined. He did give me the map and a judicious kiss on the cheek. Our bodies didn't touch. We had not been good together in bed for some time.

After about an hour, I exited the freeway, pulled over, and buried my face in my sleeve. There were so many trucks and trailers, and even the compact cars whizzed by so fast that the station wagon seemed to shift in their wake. I took a few deep breaths. There were other routes. I would find a secondary road and keep heading south, the way travelers did when America was truly new and green.

I slept in snatches. I showered twice—at a campground, where a raccoon watched from the edge of the wooden deck, and at a women's shelter, where the sad-faced desk clerk asked no questions. I ate while I drove, littering the back of the station wagon with fast-food wrappers. I passed any number of motels and restaurants. But I was afraid to make a real stop, afraid that if I did, I might reconsider. Once I was in Texas, I knew the Gulf would draw me. Its pull was stronger than anything I'd left behind.

If I had been asked, I would have said that I'd lost my daughter a year ago—two months and three days after her sixth birthday. *I lost Bailey.* That was the way I thought of it, and the thought was both hopeful and damning. *Lost* suggested that she might someday be found, as if she had wandered into the next aisle at the grocery store or been forgotten by the car pool, that she might reappear, absently twirling a damp strand of hair around one finger. Still, anyone listening carefully would understand that it was an admission of guilt. *I lost her.*

I also lost the person I was then, the person I was becoming. The new Clare I saw reflected in Michael's eyes—listless and unresponsive, she spent too many hours sleeping, too many hours in the twilight of the darkroom working from old negatives.

Of course, Michael's was not the only perspective. Jules, my agent, would have said more positive things. That I was a young photographer whose star had risen suddenly. That I had been invited to Galveston to choose material for an exhibition. And it was true. In my camera bag I had the letter confirming everything.

It had arrived late one afternoon. I was lying on the bed, still wearing the leggings and frayed T-shirt I'd slept in. Soon Michael would call from his office and ask if I were dressed. I would say yes and he would pretend to believe me. Then he would remind me of the upcoming partners' dinner. *You should get out more,* he would say. But when I thought of the hotel dining room where the dinners took place, of the bleak expanse of white linen, the tightly wired flower arrangements, the recirculated air that smelled faintly of cleaning fluid—all of it so like one of the nicer funeral homes—I knew it was impossible.

Then an image came to me. I was still holding the phone, answering Michael's questions—*Yes I remember, yes of course I have something that isn't black*—when it presented itself, a face in partial shadow. I hung up and went back to bed, pulling the covers over me, but the face followed. Finally I got up again and went to look for a book.

In a cardboard box, still unpacked, I found the Cartier-Bresson volume and turned the pages until I came to a photo showing the interior of a once grand Galveston hotel. A sign tacked to the wall reminded boarders to pay their rent in advance. On the landing was an elderly woman, her body shapeless in a flowered housecoat. Darkness poured out of the doorway behind her and rose up from the baseboards, so that her face and body were split into light and shadow.

It was one of several images of Galveston looking sad and shabby, images that had caused controversy when the book was first published. Others were different. Cartier-Bresson had also captured in his photographs the sensuality, the drowsy, self-indulgent beauty of the Island.

That was when I began to think about Patrick. And the Carradays.

The big house where I'd spent so many hours. The questions I'd left unanswered.

I grew up watching the tides, and I know it's only after change is under way that we recognize it, when the incoming rush catches us unaware, and we hurry to gather our things and move up the beach. Still I ask myself, when? When was there no longer any going back? Suppose I had stayed with Michael, attended the dinner. Could I have become again the woman he loved and married, the Clare who was Bailey's mother? Could I have made myself give up those other thoughts? And if I had, would everything else have been different?

AT A GAS STATION NEXT TO A PRODUCE STAND, I parked and waited for sleep, hoping I wouldn't dream. My dreams were always about falling. Things dropped around me—branches snapped, walls and roofs collapsed, objects of all kinds plunged from the sky. Sometimes I fell—down stairs, off bridges.

When I woke I went to the restroom, splashed my arms and face with water, and drank from the faucet. I dried myself with brown paper towels. I realized I was hungry, and I bought a pint basket of blackberries and ate a few. I'd stashed a half-eaten package of crackers under the front seat, and as I drove south, I finished what was left, swallowing hard and coughing up crumbs.

Past Houston the landscape began to flatten and simplify. There were no more pipe yards or feed stores, no more roadside chapels or ice houses advertising beer and pool. I saw white smoke drifting from the Texas City refineries. An egret lifting itself on leisurely wings. I could feel the presence of the bay and the deeper water beyond.

I thought of Bailey and told myself that the pain of losing her would diminish. That someday I would have the memory without the hurt. And while the sun glinted off passing cars and the breeze whipped around my ears, it seemed possible. I drove faster. Soon I came to the shallow rise that offers the first glimpse of Galveston.

Below was the old causeway, a series of sand-colored arches that skimmed the water next to the higher, modern road. The approaches at either end had been washed away, so that only the middle stood, rising abruptly from the water, like the spine of some ancient animal whose submerged skeleton had unexpectedly shifted.

Probably there were practical reasons why the old causeway had never been torn down. To me it said something about the Island, marked it as a place where the ideal of progress was complicated by stubborn survivals. A place where you could sometimes see the past running alongside the present.

The surface of the bay was broken only by the creamy trails of pleasure boats. Overhead, clouds hung huge and motionless as mountains. I saw nothing that would have been out of place in a travel brochure. Nothing to explain the feeling I had, like the one you get when the roller coaster leaves the loading platform and starts to move slowly, inexorably, up the first incline. For this was the Texas Gulf coast, the soft, sinking-down edge of the continent, and there wasn't a real hill for miles.

Chapter 2

NATIVES CALL GALVESTON "the Island," as if there were no other. Those who are BOI, born on the Island, take pride in the fact.

My name is Clare Porterfield, but the house I grew up in is known as the Hayes-Giraud house, for the families who lived in it a hundred years ago. Warren Hayes was a successful cotton factor, a man with a barrel chest and sideburns that sprouted in thick tufts. He gave the house to his only child, Lavinia, when she married a doctor, Phillip Giraud, from Louisiana. When my father, also a doctor, acquired it, I think he saw it as his special responsibility.

It was late afternoon when I arrived. The metal plaque was still there by the front gate, displaying the Hayes-Giraud names and the date of construction, 1887. I parked next to the carriage block at the front curb.

Growing up, my older sister, Frankie, and I understood that the house had a life of its own, imperatives that weighed equally with ours. I remember her asking my father when we would replace our ten-year-old Buick.

"Some people buy a new car every year. We paint the house," my father said with satisfaction. His teeth were stained brown from the pipe he smoked, and he never showed them when he smiled.

My mother, Eleanor, raised her head and gazed out across the garden. "Some people travel."

Anything found in or around the house was said to belong to it, and the Hayes-Giraud possessions mingled with our own. Sober, homely portraits of Warren Hayes and his wife, Belle, painted when they were both in late middle age, hung in my father's first-floor study. When I was small, I tended to confuse them with my grandparents who lived in Ohio. A sightless, vaguely classical, marble bust of a woman discovered in the attic and said to be Lavinia Giraud presided over the front hall. At Christmas, when my parents hosted a gathering for my father's students, someone invariably penciled in Lavinia's eyes, giving her a startled look, as though she had come suddenly to life and was dismayed to find things changed.

There was also the chamber pot decorated with cabbage roses that occupied a stand in our bedroom, never, we were warned, to be used.

"Why can't we use it?" I asked.

Frankie groaned. "Why would you want to pee in a pot?"

I didn't want to tell her I was afraid to leave our room at night.

When I was growing up, the house was white, with black shutters and a black cast-iron fence in front. My father's choices. Now I saw that the clapboard walls had been painted a soft green, and the porches, with their pierced-wood trim, stood out in a way they hadn't before. Delicate patterns of light and shade played over the whole outside. It was now unmistakably an Island house.

I wondered what my father, Anson Porterfield, would have thought of the change. He had been an internist at the local hospital. He did his best to ignore the annual influx of visitors, both the summer people who built costly houses on the beach and the tourist crowds who cruised the seawall. I often asked myself why he had chosen to live on the Island, since he so disliked the seasonal ebb and flow. He had died the previous summer, suddenly, of a stroke. I didn't return for the funeral. In fact, I hadn't been back to the Island at all. Not since I'd graduated from high school more than ten years earlier.

It was easy to find excuses—a summer job when I was in college, later a series of opportunities too good to turn down. My mother didn't press the issue. She visited me occasionally. My father didn't like to travel.

The front door was unlocked, so I let myself in.

Every old house has its own complex smell—a distinctive combination of aged woods, of generations of stain and varnish, of furniture polish and floor wax. In Galveston, there is also the smell of salt. In 1900, during the Great Hurricane, the flood waters rose to the second story. Whole families drowned together amid the floating furniture.

The bust on its pedestal was still in the front hall, but someone had tossed a crumpled canvas fishing hat onto Lavinia's head where it rested at an angle, hiding one of her sightless eyes. I stood listening. The house was quiet. I crossed the hall and opened the door to the back lawn.

My mother was kneeling at a flower bed. She wore a man's white button-down shirt over white jeans—her idea of work clothes. Her hair was twisted up off her neck. As always, she looked cool and unwrinkled, as though she lived in a climate of her own making. I couldn't remember ever seeing her sweat.

I stopped to watch her, as I used to do when I was small.

Eleanor was different when she thought she was alone. Her face softened and her shoulders settled, as though she had put down something she was carrying. The woman I glimpsed then was a stranger, preoccupied with ideas and feelings she didn't share with us children, and I wondered what it would be like to know her.

Because the habit was an old one, I waited for a moment in the shade of the overhang. I saw Eleanor sit back on her heels, arch her back, and raise her arms to stretch. She removed a comb, then shook her head, slowly, deliberately, so that her hair fell down over her shoulders and swung back and forth, thick and blond and abundantly streaked with ash.

Why is it we are so reluctant to think of our parents as sexual beings? Even as adults, even when the evidence is in front of us? I reached back to close the door, hard.

At the sound she rose quickly and became her usual brisk self. I saw her glance at the camera I carried on a strap over my shoulder. "Sweetheart," she said, "you're here at last." She leaned down, put her cheek next to mine, and held it there for a moment. It was what she had always done, not quite a kiss. I felt her breath in my ear and the crisp surface of her shirt. I thought, as I had so many times before, how dissimilar we were.

I am slight, blue-eyed, with unruly hair that reacts strongly to weather. Aunt Syvvie, my mother's sister, once said that I reminded her of an actress she had seen. "Susan Cabot. She was in the original *Gunsmoke* with Audie Murphy. She played the daughter."

"Sylvia, no wonder you look exhausted," Eleanor said. "You've been up watching those old movies again."

"*Gunsmoke* is a classic," Aunt Syvvie protested. "And it's true, what I said about her." She turned to me. "You have such beautiful eyes."

My mother banged the watering can down on the porch. "Don't be ridiculous. You'll give her ideas." Aunt Syvvie was plump and easily moved to tears. Her small indulgences—movies, magazines with lots of pictures, a bottle of Shalimar with a blue glass stopper—were regularly held up for mild ridicule. Nobody took her seriously.

Eleanor brushed my hair back with both hands and held it while she searched my face. "Such a long drive," she said. "Are you all right?"

I nodded.

"Frances called."

My sister, Frankie, was everything I wasn't—tall, athletic, unafraid.

"Come inside, it's hot." Eleanor looked me up and down, and I wondered for the first time in days about my appearance. "You must want a bath," she said. "But first, something cool to drink."

She took a green glass pitcher from the kitchen windowsill and snapped off two stems of mint. She cut a lemon into wedges. From a drawer she removed long-handled ice-tea spoons.

She was so precise, her movements so full of intention, that her hands seemed to draw everything in around her. The pitcher of mint, the room with its high ceiling, the garden hastening toward summer all seemed to exist only as the setting for her task. It was deeply restful watching her, like falling under a brief spell of hypnosis.

"You saw they're remodeling next door?" Eleanor asked. "They must think they're in the Caribbean. The colors. Sugar?" I nodded and she set the bowl on the table.

This was a familiar topic. My parents followed the dramas of the old houses—their trials by weather and insects, their prolonged rehabilitations—the way Aunt Syvvie followed the fortunes of movie stars.

Eleanor said, "I should let Will know you've arrived."

It took me a minute to realize who she meant. When I was growing up, he had been Mr. Carraday. In family conversations his last name was always invoked. *They want Will Carraday to back the building restrictions. Will Carraday has bought a new plane.* I knew all about him. Anyone who lived on the Island did. As a child I had spent many hours in the big house across the alley with Patrick Carraday, Will's son.

Patrick, who had been the brother I never had, then later, something more.

But knowing about Will Carraday was not the same as knowing him. I pulled off a mint leaf and rolled it between my fingers, and as the smell rose up, green and pungent, I was flooded with a familiar ache.

"He wants to talk to you, of course."

"About the exhibition?"

Eleanor paused. "I suppose."

It was only after the formal arrangements had been made that my mother had raised the possibility of a visit. She'd chosen her words carefully, never mentioning how long I'd been away from the Island. Never calling it *home*.

"What does Mr. Carraday want to know?" I asked.

Eleanor set her glass down carefully. "Clare, don't begin this way."

"What way?"

"Looking for trouble."

"I'm not," I said, although it wasn't really true. Something quivered inside me, like the pivoting needle of a compass. We both knew where it would point.

"He could have found someone here, you know," Eleanor said. She wiped her mouth deliberately, and I noticed a splotch of color on the napkin. I didn't recall her wearing lipstick. "He asked for you."

I picked a chunk of ice out of my glass with my fingers and put it in my mouth, but not before it had dripped down the front of my shirt.

"I gave you a spoon," Eleanor said.

I swallowed and pushed my chair back. It grated against the floor. "*Will*. Does he expect me to call him that?"

"Of course. You're an adult now."

"That's right. They can't send me away."

Eleanor sighed. "Clare, we've talked about this. Your leaving the Island was something we agreed on together, both families. It was a serious situation. The girl died."

"That wasn't our fault!"

"I'm not blaming you. I've never blamed you. But you shouldn't have been there. And people were upset. Your presence would have been . . ."

I spoke before she could find the word. "Was that the reason?"

She hesitated for a moment. Just long enough to suggest she'd considered her answer. "Of course." Eleanor regarded me steadily. "And you came back. Once things had settled down."

"Patrick didn't come back. What's he doing now? What's he driving these days?"

Patrick was a couple of years older than I was. He had wrecked three cars, spectacularly, before he was seventeen. The last had gone over the seawall and into the Gulf at four in the morning. Patrick survived and was discovered naked, drunk, and laughing on the beach.

"Patrick spent some time in Europe. College was not really an option for him. Then he came back. He has a place of his own. He's working for his father."

I tried to hide my astonishment. A host of images assailed me—Patrick fighting with another boy, rolling in the dirt. Patrick at the beach, shirtless, a brown bottle balanced on his head. I couldn't imagine Patrick in an office, sitting behind a desk.

"He is?"

"There. You see?" Eleanor suppressed a smile, but I could tell she was pleased at my reaction. "In fact, Patrick is doing very well." She took a slow sip of tea. "I hope you won't bring all that up with Will. It was a long time ago. Here, on the Island, the whole thing's been forgotten." She wiped her mouth again carefully. "Frances is looking forward to seeing you," she said.

All families have their enduring fictions, repeated so often that they are accepted without question although they have no basis in fact. Ours featured Frankie and me as equals and friends. The truth was that Frankie was my parents' favorite. We had never been close.

Frankie was always busy. Around her, I felt as though every minute was already full, that all the air in any room that contained us both had already been used up. I kept to myself. When I was small, I hid in the shade under the lattice-covered porch, where the ground was damp and sandy, strewn with bits of broken shell.

When I was older, I retreated across the lawn to the alley house, a two-room cottage at the back corner of our property. I slept a lot. I was accused of doing nothing, of daydreaming. I knew what was meant—a momentary thought often dilated into several minutes of reverie, while I stood motionless. In time I came to understand that I was not like the rest of my family. So I became someone who watched more than she spoke. As Frankie put it, a snoop.

She accused me regularly. "You've been in my top drawer. I left it open exactly half an inch and now it's closed."

"She did laundry this morning. Have you got clean socks?"

Reluctantly, Frankie looked and saw them, rolled and sorted by color. "I don't care," she said, "I know you've been in there." I shrugged. I had been in her drawer, and I knew she was keeping two hundred dollars and several condoms in a Band-Aid box. But she couldn't prove it.

Eleanor spoke. "Frances and Stephen will be down for the weekend." My sister and her husband were both doctors with practices in Houston. "They can't make the party."

"Party?"

Eleanor regarded the mint in her glass. "Tomorrow. It's Will's birthday. We're celebrating. Of course we hoped you'd be here."

I wondered who that "we" included. "Is Patrick coming?"

"He's been invited. More tea?" I shook my head. "And Michael?" Eleanor asked pointedly. "How is he?"

"Michael is fine." To my surprise, it was true. I knew Michael had suffered. I'd seen him, shoulders hunched, sobbing in the shower. But he had completed his task, delivered his burden to wherever it is old sorrows go. While I had barely started. I was beginning to think that grieving the loss of my child would be my real life's work. Michael's ease—one of the traits I'd loved and married him for—was now the principal thing dividing us.

"He called last night. He said he hadn't heard from you in days."

I looked down at my hands. They were stained with blackberry juice.

We sat in silence for a moment, each of us aware of things unsaid. "Well. You'll want your bath." Eleanor removed our glasses and took them to the sink.

I was in the hall when I heard her call my name. "Clare?" She caught up with me at the foot of the stairs.

She came close and put one hand on the back of my neck and the other on my forehead, as she had done when I was small and she suspected a fever. Her palms were cool, her touch gentle but firm, as though by the pressure of her hands she could subdue my troubled thoughts. I smelled the lemon on her fingers. "Are you sure you're all right?" she asked. "You look so tired."

"I'm fine," I told her. I had never been able to say anything else.

"You're on the Island now. Be a little careful."

I ducked my head and stepped back, away from her.

The runner had been replaced, but the stairs gave and sighed in the old way. Out of habit I turned toward the back bedroom I had shared with Frankie, half expecting to see it divided, as it had been when we occupied it, by a frayed clothesline strung from a hook on the door to her dresser. With our miscellaneous belongings gone, the space seemed bare, the furniture smaller and oddly disconnected, like the objects in a child's drawing.

In the room where I would stay, officially recognized as an adult and a guest, was a high bed with a white canopy like a sail. The crisp linens made me aware of the berry stains on my hands. With a feeling of relief, I stripped off my clothes, dropping them on my way to the bathroom.

In the porcelain claw-foot tub, gradually I relaxed. I thought about how I had grown up taking baths, and how different a bath was from a shower. In the shower, you stood with your eyes half closed, hardly regarding yourself. You performed the necessary motions quickly, without looking, and the uprightness of your posture somehow characterized the whole process.

In the bathtub, on the other hand, your body lay before you, inescapable, close enough for critical inspection. You were obliged to face the disconcerting changes that came with adolescence. If someone walked in, you couldn't turn away quickly. You were exposed, vulnerable.

Anything that grows can be trained, over time, to take on a certain form. A young tree, splayed against a wall, extends its branches only to the sides. If a child regularly assumes a posture of vulnerability, a crouch—in the bathtub, under the house—does that determine the way she grows, the way she thinks of herself? When she marries, does it dictate the kind of man she chooses? Someone who, like Michael, seems unassailable?

Unassailable. That was the word I used to describe him to myself. I'd believed that from Michael I would learn to move through life confidently, to expect and encounter good things.

I stood and stepped out of the tub. I wiped the mirror, but the fog swam back almost at once. *Don't look,* it said. *Don't ask. Snoop.*

A dog barked, and I stepped to the open window. The world outside was fading into dusk. The noise of the cicadas rose and fell.

I stretched out on the bed. As if from far off I heard the sounds of my childhood—the metal vents on the roof spinning and pinging, the scratch of a crape myrtle against the screen. Later, I knew too when I heard something that didn't belong, a quick step that wasn't Eleanor's. A sound that said someone else, a stranger, was in the house.

I waited, tense and listening, until the footsteps faded. But all I heard was the old house shifting and settling, the breeze moving around outside, and the sound of my own breathing.

Chapter 3

IN THE MORNING, I WOKE TO FIND my cheeks wet with tears. I wondered if there were a kind of memory that belonged only to the body, that needed no conscious recollection to call up the past.

I hadn't planned to have a baby, and I was four months pregnant before I knew for certain. Then I found myself overwhelmed by fatigue. It was like standing in warm surf, letting the water move me along, imperceptibly, farther and farther from the place where I'd started. Later there were nights when I woke in a wordless panic, sweating. Hands pressed against the hard roundness of my growing belly, I wondered, *What have I done?* By then I was showing, and our friends knew. Apparently none of them saw my terror.

But once a stranger, an elegantly dressed woman with gray hair and a briefcase, stopped me on the street, patted my shoulder, and said, "It will be all right."

Jules wasn't so sure. "You of all people," he said, "to get sucked into the baby thing. I thought you were serious."

I slid off the big bed and looked around for my clothes, but they were not on the floor or in the bathroom. I wrapped myself in the towel I'd used the night before, opened the door, and listened. From downstairs came the click and sudden surge of the washer.

Eleanor must have taken my clothes. I would have to borrow something of hers.

THE TWO ROOMS AT THE FRONT of the house, overlooking the street, were my parents'. They had slept in separate bedrooms for as long as I could remember. In Eleanor's, the coverlet was taut across the bed, the pillows plumped. On her dressing table stood a glass lamp, and I remembered my mother sitting within its circle of light. It seemed then that she was the source of the soft brightness around her. She produced her own glow, and it was hard to take your eyes off her.

I found the white shirt she had been wearing the day before lying on a wicker hamper in her closet. I picked it up and held it to my face, but it was too much hers for me to put on. Her unworn clothes hung in neat rows. Their order was somehow equally overwhelming.

Then I noticed a group of things—shirts, khaki shorts, and a cotton sweater, all hung together—that I recognized because they had been mine when I was small. There were clothes of Frankie's too—a sundress, a tank suit that had once been supple as skin and was now stiff and oddly attenuated from its years in the closet.

I took a shirt off its hanger, a plaid camp shirt. I slid a hand into one of the short, square sleeves. How old had I been when I wore it? Five? Six? I'd been smaller than Bailey, whose arms and legs were surprisingly sturdy.

I heard Eleanor's voice and put the hanger back. I didn't want her to see me there. It was one thing to appear in her clothes, another for her to find me looking.

I stepped back into the hall. Through the window I saw the Kiehlers' house and their yard, where a bare-chested brown man was trimming a palm with measured swings of a machete. He wore rope sandals and a wide-brim straw hat. There was nothing to distinguish him from someone doing the same job in front of the same house a century ago.

The street was quiet. A car would have given away the year, made it clear we were approaching the twenty-first century. But there were no cars. Not even parked cars. My station wagon was gone.

I took the steps two at a time.

In the kitchen, Eleanor was standing at the sink. "I heard you get up," she said. "I could have loaned you a robe." She placed a bowl of blackberries on the table. "These were in your car. I thought you might like some for breakfast. What else? Shall I make you some eggs?"

"Where is the station wagon?" I asked.

"Otis has it. He's working on it."

"Otis?"

"Faline's Otis. They're married. For heaven's sake, Clare, it's been more than ten years. Things happen. Will came by and saw the car and offered to clean it up for you. It looked as if you'd been living in it." She paused. I knew she wanted me to explain. I met her gaze but said nothing.

She sighed. "You can go over there as soon as you're dressed. You do have a comb?" She handed me a small pile still warm from the dryer. I took the clothes from her without answering and stood to go.

"You haven't eaten. A little fruit . . ."

"No, thanks. Maybe later," I said. I didn't want to stay and discuss my attachment to the station wagon. I knew it said something about my state of mind that I would rather keep to myself.

In the front hall, I passed Lavinia with her enigmatic, blind stare. She seemed to be leaning forward on her pedestal, listening, trying to compensate for her inability to see. I noticed that the fishing hat was gone.

Chapter 4

OUTSIDE, THE SKY WAS GULF BLUE, a color you see nowhere else, intense and full of light, a color that throws ordinary things into sharp relief and turns them into sudden visions. The clouds were few and scattered. Not the conditions a photographer looks for. Too much contrast, too many shadows. But it was on a day like this that I had taken the photo of Bailey in the swing, the photo that changed everything.

Over the years, I had produced my share of ordinary scrapbook pictures—evidence of Bailey's progress, of our life as a family. And like any parent I had thrown away my share of botched shots, especially as Bailey grew and became more active.

The spring she turned five, it was clear a transformation was under way. It was not just that she had lost the plump, rounded arms and legs, the dimpled hands and elbows of her first years. As a young child, Bailey had been exceptionally fond of sitting. She would take up a location, usually a busy one, the floor in front of the dishwasher or the middle of the front steps, and dispose herself and her things— the Playskool barn, the plastic glamour dolls she forced to inhabit it— as though she planned never to move again.

Or she would sit in my lap, taking inventory of my features. She would explore my ears with her fingers, my teeth, so much larger than hers, so plain and serviceable, lacking any frilly scallop. She would touch my eyelashes with one carefully extended finger, laughing when I blinked.

After she turned five, all that changed. When Bailey came to me, it was to fling herself facedown across my legs, exhausted, speechless. Her back, which had been soft, undifferentiated flesh, had become a complicated system—a multitude of ribs, the small, distinct shoulder blades that stood out like wings. Although I knew she weighed more, she seemed lighter. She no longer possessed the specific gravity that belongs uniquely to babies and young children, that makes them—at the same time—so easy to hold and so fatiguing to carry. She seemed to be assuming a new form. Preparing herself for some astonishing and yet inevitable role.

I did a series of running, then jumping shots—Bailey with her arms pumping, Bailey with her arms and legs outstretched, hair flying. About that time, I must have taken the first shots of the swing.

It hung from an old oak in the backyard, a rope swing with a weathered wooden slat for a seat and two knots underneath where the frayed rope tied. Below the swing the grass had worn away, leaving a patch of packed earth and hardy weeds. The tree was mossy, bent, and the whole arrangement had a pleasantly rustic look that fit the haphazard, overgrown character of our backyard. Far better, I thought, than the metal swing sets I remembered from my childhood. The chains that pinched, the seats that burned on hot days. The rust. If the rope swing had to be shared, well, that was a plus for an only child.

I took some panning shots, sighting over the lens and deliberately blurring the background. Then I realized it wasn't motion I wanted to capture but stillness.

Stop-action photography had always fascinated me. Not the science, not the discoveries—I didn't care that a horse at full gallop lifts all four feet off the ground. It was the expectant silence that enclosed the runner halted in midstride, the ballplayer, one hand stretched above his head, reaching for an invisible ball.

Who wouldn't choose to remain in that moment of perfect anticipation? What outcome could measure up to the infinity of possibilities it promised? Who wouldn't choose to preserve them all forever, to remain safe and hopeful in the endless present of those images?

But the foot slaps the track, the ball hits the glove. Every instant of every day, life is streaming past, all experience—every action, word, or thought, every particle of intention—rushing toward some moment you can't foresee that is anything but safe. Toward, perhaps, one ordinary afternoon.

I set my shutter speed at 1/1000 and began again. We were in the backyard. Bailey had been to a birthday party where she had eaten a popsicle, and there was a cherry ring around her mouth. The overalls that had been clean four hours before were streaked with food and grass stains.

The northern sky was pale blue, the light diffuse. The clouds were mere fluff. When one of them covered the sun, I raised my Leica and caught Bailey just as she left the swing, in that instant when she knew herself to be weightless, flying. She climbed back into the swing, and I took another. "Again!" she said. Then the process took over, and I knew I was working well because of the way everything else thinned out around me until the yard and the street and the voices of the children seemed faint and far off. I couldn't tell yet whether the result would be good, but the feeling was there, and I gave myself up to it. I finished a roll, reloaded, and started another.

I had the best shot expensively matted and framed (that was in itself a bad sign, suggesting that I felt it needed dressing up) and gave it to Michael for his birthday. He unwrapped it cautiously, holding it in his lap. "Very expressive," he said. He kept his head down, his eyes fixed on the image, so I couldn't see what was in them.

"Michael. That sounds like something you overheard at an opening. I want to know what you think."

"Do you?"

"What do you mean?"

He looked at me then, and I saw that he was struggling with a mixture of emotions. "Do you care what I think?" I went behind his chair and put my hands on his shoulders.

"Of course I do." Gently, I massaged the place where his muscles knotted. I moved up to the back of his neck. "I want to hear your ideas. But I don't want advice." I felt him stiffen, and I dropped my hands. "I can't work that way."

"No? How do you work?" He stood and moved away to the window. The afternoon light picked out the lines that were starting in his forehead, the shadows under his eyes. Was that what made him look suddenly so sad? And so fixed in that sadness, as if the thoughts he was having were the same ones he had had many times before, the only thoughts he could have?

"Well," he said, "okay. Since you want to know. I wish her hair wasn't in her face. I wish her overalls were clean. But that's not it really. This isn't my Bailey. I don't know her. It's a beautiful picture of . . ." He shook his head. Then he turned toward me so that he was backlit, a dark figure without a countenance. "I know I'm a lousy judge. It's probably really great. So let's forget that. Let me say instead that sometimes it's as if we're just, I don't know . . . props. Interesting, but only in the context of your artistic vision. Whatever that happens to be at the moment. The Laughing Girl. The Man by the Window."

"You forgot the Snotty Lawyer." Now I was glad I couldn't make out his face. It was easier to speak my mind to that dark outline. "Do you hear yourself? Do you hear what you're saying? You, the hotshot litigator? What happens to people when you put them on the stand? I've heard you planning it. So don't tell me it isn't deliberate."

"That's different. I'm talking about us."

"I don't recognize the distinction."

"I know you don't."

"Michael, I can't keep my life in compartments. One for work and one for home. One for you and one for Bailey. I can't measure out my feelings like that. So it's true, I admit it, my work and my life overlap. What's wrong with that? I'm a mother and a photographer, for God's sake. Why can't I photograph Bailey? Oh, yes, snapshots for the album, those are fine. But if I choose to photograph my child in any other way, you think I'm exploiting her?"

I felt the blood rising to my cheeks as I went on. "You're right, the Bailey you know isn't the one I do. Your Bailey sits perfectly still. In a chair. Her hands are in her lap. She looks at you. Isn't that what you'd like? Isn't that your vision?" I couldn't have explained why the thought of it was so unbearable. But I could feel a hot whorl of anger spiraling up inside me like smoke off a smothered fire.

"Just because something's ordinary doesn't mean it's contemptible."

I hardly heard him. "You know what I think? I think it drives you crazy that what I do is something you don't understand. You don't get it. You don't see what I see. So you want me to photograph in a nice, obvious way that's easy to understand and that makes you comfortable."

He shook his head, but without conviction. In matters of taste, Michael was deeply, thoroughly conventional. I'd once taken a picture of Bailey gazing out a window with her eyes wide and one small finger up her nose. I loved its unself-consciousness. Michael hated it. Why was I still trying to win him over? When of course he would have preferred a traditional portrait—his daughter, dressed and posed, looking into the camera. *Looking at him.*

He didn't answer. To his credit, he kept the photo of Bailey on the credenza in his office. He was still trying. In those days, we both were. And one afternoon a former classmate of Michael's who worked in marketing stopped by. A client, he explained, was launching a campaign. The picture was exactly what they wanted. It captured a child's energy, her exhilaration. It didn't look posed. She wasn't a model, was she? That made a difference. She didn't look like a professional. "Your daughter?" he said. "Outstanding. Your wife took it. You must be proud."

And in fact he was. Almost immediately, for the first time, Michael was truly proud, even if he didn't entirely comprehend what it was the marketing people saw in the photo. All it needed was for Richie (and the others who came after) to endorse it.

I admit, the vindication, when it arrived, was sweet. And I made a real effort to enjoy it without gloating. At the same time, I was hurt—and angry—that the opinions of a group of relative strangers meant so much more to him than mine. If he couldn't see for himself, make his own judgment and defend it, if he was going to take it on faith from someone, why not from me?

The deal bought the two of us, as a couple, some time. There were meetings, there was a contract to be read, considered, signed—this was Michael at his best, lasering through the pages of stultifying prose, offering elegant, subtle changes. There were celebrations. There was backslapping and applause.

It was like a wave that comes in and covers everything strewn across the beach, all the small items that up until then have been the focus of much attention. The arguments we had been having, the facts we had stockpiled for the sake of having those arguments again, all the details that, a few days before, had preoccupied us, disappeared under the smooth swell of activity.

I have been tempted to blame what came afterward on Michael, to say he was the one who was ambitious for the kind of street-corner recognition that comes with commercial success. I would like to be able to claim that I had nothing to do with it. But I can't.

I wanted to sell the photo as much as he did, maybe more. It wasn't something I had anticipated. We didn't need the money, Michael was doing well, and he had never held it against me that my income, when I had any, was sporadic. But when the pieces of the transaction came together into a whole in front of me, it was like the lights going up on a stage. I saw immediately that there was a place for me on it. So Michael and I together traded away a portion of our daughter's childhood. Our reasons may have been different, but we acted together.

Don't misunderstand, Bailey adored it. This is how I defend myself in the conversations I have over and over with no one. I say that Bailey shivered with delight to find herself in window displays and on the pages of magazines. And once as a cardboard cutout, almost life-size, in a shopping mall. The image seemed to be everywhere. Sometimes we'd stop to look at it and a passerby would discover the likeness. *Oh my, is that you? It's you!* That was part of it. She was a minor celebrity.

But she was so young.

A child spends her first years in a kind of trance, an uninterrupted flow of sensation, from which she wakes into consciousness only now and then. Her sense of self begins as flashes—*this is my hair, long enough now to reach my mouth, to grind between my teeth; this is my cheek, creased from the way I slept*—realizations that are, for a child, like electric shocks that sizzle along the nerve endings. Too much, too soon is like being struck by lightning.

Bailey was not, would never be, a professional model, despite both hints and more direct offers. That was not something either Michael or I would have contemplated. The photo, after all, was the point. It was enough. And I had thought it would end there.

What neither of us had foreseen was how the campaign would change her. Not in a way that would have been apparent to a casual observer. I saw it, though, and I knew Michael did too. Bailey held herself differently. Her movements were purposeful in a way they hadn't been before. Her headlong grace was gone.

I told myself it would have happened anyway, Bailey was getting older. She was a little girl, and girls, especially those gifted with an extra measure of charm, like to practice their skills. They may go through a phase where they make up to people, especially to men. Why did I find it so disturbing? I only know that there were times when, watching Bailey pirouetting in front of Michael, trying out sideways glances and theatrical sighs, I felt sick at heart.

Michael, as the object of her new attentions, was pleased. He didn't see her looking over her shoulder, seeking an audience, when she twined her arms around his neck. So it was not something I could discuss with him. No one else appeared to notice any difference.

Bailey loved to show people how I took the shot. It became a feature of her play dates. Richie had given us one of the cardboard cutouts and it stood in Bailey's bedroom. It was worn, one corner was broken, but when I tried to throw it out, Bailey shrieked.

"Why this sudden interest in housekeeping?" Michael asked. "If you want to pick up around here, why don't you consider moving some of your stuff"—he meant my equipment, the lenses and other things I kept within easy reach—"out of the living room."

"Because it's convenient to have it here."

"Okay. You have your things around, let her have hers."

"But it's broken."

"It will fall apart soon enough."

I had no answer. And so the cutout stayed.

But when Bailey had friends over, I found myself doing things I wouldn't have ordinarily, dreaming up errands or excursions to get her out of the house, proposing games, once even making cookies from a worm of dough I'd bought at the supermarket to distract her. It rarely worked. Eventually the suggestion would be made.

"Let's play something in the yard," she would say. This was the inevitable prelude to the reenactment. It was intentionally vague and totally disingenuous. There was only one game Bailey wanted to play.

I didn't watch anymore. It was too hard to see her doing a bad imitation of herself—a performance drained of all the spontaneity the marketing people had prized. But even with the kitchen door shut, I would hear occasional fragments of dialogue, Bailey's newly complacent voice explaining the order of things. Insisting, "Now watch!"

Even her playmates tired of it, all except Phoebe, who was not popular because she had a lisp and a tendency to spit. Poor Phoebe, starved for any sense of belonging, would play the game over and over.

Like all mothers, I had tried to protect my child. From the stranger, a woman with oddly cropped hair and a shapeless coat, who talked to her in the park, who reappeared too often and seemed a little too friendly. From the dog next door, pacing and drooling behind the fence. There were more generalized worries too—poison, small objects, anything sharp, swimming pools, sash cords, traffic. There were car wrecks, plane wrecks, wrecks of all kinds. For a parent, the news was a nightly catalogue of disasters waiting to happen. But it had never occurred to me to worry about our own backyard. Even now, when I recall the worn grass, the shaggy tree and makeshift swing, nothing in that scene speaks to me of danger or gives off any alarm.

I couldn't hear everything from where I was in the kitchen. I was looking over prints. I had a dozen or so spread across the kitchen table. The rhythm of the exchanges had, I suppose, become familiar, so that what I noticed first that morning was a silence that lasted too long. And I remember that I got up slowly, slowly set down the magnifier, because I disliked what I knew Bailey was doing and didn't want to see it. It wasn't until I opened the kitchen door that I heard Phoebe's thin wail and then a sound that was like the beating of a hundred wings, a sound I knew was only in my own ears. The air that was suddenly full of fear rushed in and hit me in the face and I saw the swing in a tangle.

I have been told that my going to her sooner would have made no difference. That she died almost immediately. I think a lot about that. *Almost immediately.* What does it mean? Was there a moment when she looked up, her neck at an implausible angle, and searching for someone, saw just the gray board fence? Was she confused? Frightened? Did she call my name?

Remember, I am a doctor's daughter. I know what asphyxiation is. I know how long it takes.

"An accident," Michael said, as though that explained it. When he, more than anyone, with his experience assessing responsibility and assigning blame, should have been able to recognize the chain of evidence stretching back over months—the acquiescences, the lapses of judgment, the acts of selfishness, small and seemingly insignificant at the time, but linked, traceable, like the paper-clip chains Bailey draped around her room.

It was over in a minute. In falling, Bailey had defied gravity and taken flight, shedding the weight of the world as easily as the sweater she hadn't needed and had dropped earlier, that lay in a small pile beside her on the grass.

Michael wasn't the only one to call it an accident. That was what everyone said, "an accident" or even "a tragedy." But I had lived with him too long, listened to him and his partners preparing for too many trials. Misfortune was not a concept he believed in. How could he propose it now as a solution? He had said more than once, *Someone has to pay.* Who else was there but me?

Chapter 5

I COULD HAVE TAKEN THE SHORTCUT across the alley to the Carradays'. The alley ran like a seam down the center of the block between the big houses on Broadway and the less impressive structures in back of them. It was a strip of raw, packed sand and gravel. Wild plum trees and pomegranates grew in the alley along with dusty clumps of cannas big enough for a child to hide in.

There had been a time when Patrick and I had gone back and forth that way—across the alley and through the oleander hedge—so often we had worn a trail that was visible from the upstairs windows. What architectural planners call a desire line.

But I hesitated. Any number of memories might rise up from that earth along with the smells of salt damp and vegetable rot. Instead I followed the street around to the formal front entrance.

Before the days of air-conditioning, Galveston's grandest houses were built along Broadway, on the north side of the street. In winter the sun fell through their front windows and stretched into golden lozenges on the burnished parlor floors. In summer, the prevailing southeast breeze cooled the interiors when the temperature rose into the nineties, and even the flies sat motionless on the windowsills.

Across the back alley, facing in the opposite direction, was a series of more modest residences that didn't benefit from the sun or the breeze. Because of the climate, this arrangement played out across the East End. Which explains why my father, the small-town doctor, and his family came to live directly in back of Will Carraday, whose grandfather had made and kept a fortune.

Even this early in the season, there was a knot of tourists in front of the Carradays', some of them with cameras. A young woman in an embroidered blouse was posing at the iron gate while a man with sunburned forearms tried to take her picture. He was losing patience because she kept looking over her shoulder at the tall windows. I knew what he had in mind—the kind of vacation shot that furnishes proof: *We went to the Gulf coast, we visited the sights, we were happy.* Probably, like most tourists, he had overestimated his capacity for new experience. What he really wanted now was something familiar, even if it was only the routine of the picture taking.

"Excuse me." I moved to go around them.

"Do people actually live here?" he asked. I knew what he meant. Built to astonish, the house still achieved its purpose. He glanced at the girl, he wanted her to agree, but she was examining a blister on her heel.

According to the guidebooks, at the turn of the century the Islanders purchased twenty-three grand pianos and more than three thousand gallons of French wine in one year alone. Now the sidewalk was split in places where it had heaved and buckled. There was a row of parking meters. I opened the gate and started up the walk.

The Carraday house was famous in its own right. But the story of Stella Carraday, of what had happened to her there, gave it special fascination. I wondered if the tourists at the gate had heard it. If the young woman had lain awake, thinking about Stella, after her boyfriend had gone to sleep smelling of Solarcaine.

I stopped and looked back. The girl smiled. She had the round eyes and full cheeks of a child. Stella had been only seventeen when she drowned. If you believed the story. So many strange things were said to have been discovered in the aftermath of the storm. A horse, thirsty and disoriented in a second-floor bedroom. Dead snakes dangling from trees.

My father was skeptical. "It's quite a tale," he said. "I understand they've named a dessert for her over at the hotel."

My mother looked past him into the fireplace. She appeared to be studying the bunches of dried hydrangea that filled the unused space. "Strawberries Stella," she said.

Stella's death, her naked body—the storm waters tore the clothes off most of the drowned—had the lurid blaze of melodrama. Whether the account was true or not, its sensationalism violated my father's view of what history ought to be. For him, even reenactments and people in costume portraying historic figures betrayed an excess of enthusiasm, like wanting to use the chamber pot. Learning from the past, effortfully, as my father had once learned from a cadaver, was acceptable. Trying to revive and take foolish pleasure in it was not. But he and Eleanor were asked so often, by so many visitors, that the story had to be told.

Growing up, I'd heard it many times. I had visited Stella's room in the Carraday house too, stroked the ivory brushes on the dressing table and examined them for hairs. I would have explored further, if Patrick had been willing to wait. Sometimes I imagined her conversations, her thoughts. The events of her courtship. Given my father's disapproval, it was a subversive act.

I reached the veranda and the Carradays' front door opened.

"Faline." I stopped, overwhelmed by the pleasure of saying her name. She flew out the door and hugged me to her so suddenly I stumbled. Then she stepped back and held me at arm's length. "Look at you," she said. She smoothed my shirt. "No shoes. Clothes still all over the place. I suppose nobody at your house got an iron?"

"You look just the same," I said. It was true. She had not so much changed as become more plainly herself since I had last seen her. She had always been slender, but now the tendons showed in her hands. And what had been a streak through her black hair fanned out from her forehead like white veining in a rock.

She folded her arms. "That car you been driving. It don't look much better." She shook her head. "But you want that miserable old vehicle, go on around and talk to my Otis."

"I want to talk to you." There were things I wanted to know, questions I couldn't ask anyone else. A whole line of inquiry I had kept to myself for too long. Questions about Patrick and me that only Faline was likely to answer. *What did you tell them? And, more important, why?*

"Not now, baby. You hear that racket?" Faline tilted her head in the direction of the garden. I could make out hammering and shouted directions. "By tonight we got to have a dance floor outside. You ask me, some people go to a lot of work to entertain theirselves. Come by when it's over. I guess you know where to find me. Like always." She looked me over again and shook her head. "I hope you intend to clean up for the festivity."

I smiled. Faline favored those she cared about with a steady stream of disparagement. Even her shows of affection hurt. When I was young, she would catch me as I ran by and pull me to her so hard that my shoulder popped. I had seen her squeeze the back of Patrick's neck until his eyes watered.

"Is Patrick here?" I asked.

"Here in this house?" Faline tilted her head and looked at me slyly. "How should I know? I'm supposed to keep track of his where-about? He's a grown man, not that you'd know it." She seized the vacuum cleaner as though she expected it to resist and turned it on. She shouted above its roar, "Go on now. Unless you forgot where the garage is."

"I'll come and find you after the party," I said.

She waved, and the heavy door swung shut. I stepped out of the archway into the blinding light.

The Carradays' garage was a two-story building with corner turrets and a taller central tower. Originally, it had been the stables. Upstairs, there had been six servants' bedrooms, each about the size of one of the stalls below.

I crossed the yard and went around to the side street where the double doors stood open. A man with his back to me leaned over the engine of the station wagon. He spoke without moving. "You could get ant bit, going around with no shoes." A pair of tattoos snaked up his arms into the sleeves of his T-shirt. A rag hung out of the pocket of his work pants. He straightened, and I saw that his hair was shoulder length, pulled into a ponytail.

"I know about fire ants," I said. "I was born here." The stone floor was cool and dry under my feet.

I made out five cars, not counting mine—a Bentley, a jeep, a two-seater convertible, and several others. Vehicles of every description for Patrick to wreck. I came closer. I saw that the mess had been cleared out of the station wagon, and the whole car had been cleaned and polished. The hubcaps gleamed and even the tires had a dull sheen. I stepped closer and saw, with relief, the familiar dings, the tired upholstery. I spotted my old canvas suitcase in the back.

"It's ready." The man dropped the hood deliberately. "You might could use some brake fluid."

"I didn't ask you to do this," I said. "Where did you get my keys?"

His broad face remained impassive. Still, I got the impression he was amused. "You left them in the car."

"I wasn't expecting anyone to take an interest in it," I said.

"A kid might have gone off with it. Joyriding. It's been known to happen."

I felt my chest constrict, but I tried not to react. "What do you know about that?"

He pulled the rag from his pocket and wiped his hands deliberately. "Faline told me. About what you did. The two of you."

"It was nothing. A few blocks." *My Otis*, she'd called him. I wondered what else she might have said about Patrick and me. Faline had been my ally. She'd taken my part against Frankie, and shielded Patrick and me from the consequences of our behavior when she could. I didn't like to think of her talking about us with Otis.

"What about the fire?" he asked. "The girl that died." He seemed familiar and I wondered why. Was he an Islander? On the Island, everyone watches. *There goes that Porterfield girl again, no the other one, with the camera. Going down to the bait shop, probably.* Had he been one of those?

"Otis. Do I know you?"

"We never met." He seemed a little less comfortable now. I sensed an advantage, and when he moved away, I followed him to where a door opened into a part of the garage I had never seen before. Brackets along the walls held rows of heavy horse collars, some plain, some set with polished bells. "What's in there?"

"The tack room."

I stepped closer. Why didn't I remember any of this? There were complicated harnesses, long driving whips, and other things I couldn't identify, all of them in perfect order and smelling wonderfully of well-kept leather. But apart from the wealth of extraordinary equipment, it was a simple room. A worn Oriental rug warmed the stone floor. A round oak table held a few books and magazines. In an alcove in one corner was a bed.

"Is this a bedroom?"

"Not really." Otis hesitated, as though he were choosing what to say. Then he added, "Sometimes he has his dinner brought out."

I turned and saw the carriages. There were several, of different shapes and sizes. The spokes of their wheels were pointed up in gold. I peered into one of them. A silver flask rested on the tufted leather, as though it had just been set down and left. The carriages were beautiful, but even horseless and still, they had a top-heavy, precarious look. I had not realized what an act of faith it must have been to step up into one of them.

They looked old, but of course they couldn't be. It was silly even to think that one of them might be Stella's carriage, the one she'd tried to escape in. Surely it was gone, the wood rotted by the salt air, the springs rusted to nothing.

But looking at all those straps and buckles, it was easy to see the fingers of a groom working them. A short man, with the sleeves of his stiff-collared shirt rolled up, his eyes worried above a thick mustache. Easy to see Stella, in her white kid gloves, clutching a small reticule. To hear patches of conversation, pauses, high-pitched, nervous laughter.

Otis held out the keys to the station wagon. "Don't make trouble for Faline."

"I'm not a child," I said.

"There's all kinds of trouble." He folded his arms across his chest.

Then I knew who he was. The gesture gave him away. I had thought of it as Faline's alone, something defining, that pose with the chin tucked, the arms folded. Now I saw that, like a fleck of color in a woven blanket, it would appear and reappear within extended family. And I remembered something Faline had told me one night in the Carradays' kitchen.

"You're related, aren't you?" I asked. "You and Faline?"

There was a toolbox on the ground. Otis squatted on his heels and opened it. "Cousins," he said.

"I know about you, too. She told me."

"Nothing to tell." He closed the toolbox and snapped the metal latch as if that finished the conversation.

But I wasn't done. "I bet you never had a wedding portrait, did you?" I asked. How could they say no to a present?

In the photo, the similarities are uncanny. It's not just the dark hair, the sloe eyes, although, seen side by side, they are strikingly alike. It's in subtler things too—the flat planes of their forearms, the long, straight fingers. Their arms are folded, in the gesture characteristic of both.

Only their shoulders touch, as though that were all they needed, one point of contact. I tried to remember whether Michael and I had ever had that kind of connection, one that could flow like current through the smallest opening.

Mr. and Mrs. Otis Lagarde, First Cousins. The title was Jules's idea. When I saw the prints, I did wonder how it would feel, making love with someone who looked so much like you. Seeing yourself in him. Would the similarity be reassuring? Would you think, *Yes, I know that, and that?* Isn't that what we all want on some level? I remember once when I was small seeing Frankie kiss a mirror, and startled, rub the evidence away with her sleeve.

Otis shifted slightly and I knew he was listening. Then I heard it too—whistling, but not the usual kind, the thoughtless, under-the-breath noise that signals boredom or nervousness, three or four dry notes. These sounds were as firm and clear as birdsong.

So even before I saw him coming across the lawn, or registered the boyish air that his whistling and his jeans and his casual friendliness only underscored, he was not what I expected.

People say he was tall. In fact, he was several inches under six feet. But he moved with an easy economy and none of the stiffness most athletic men acquire as they get older. And there was an energy about him that was only partly physical, that left a sort of afterimage, so that when he had gone, you continued to feel his presence. His hair was thick, close-cropped, white. His eyes were the kind of blue you picture when you think of a summer morning.

He took my hand in both of his and held it. "Do you remember me?" he asked. There was something wistful about the way he posed the question, as though it were more than a pleasantry. As though it really mattered to him whether I remembered. When of course it was a given. Everyone knew him, or at least knew who he was. On the Island, his casual manner was set off by a sort of accompanying radiance that derived in part from his wealth, but also from his family history and its place in the local pageant. If he was aware, he gave no indication. This was it then, the famous charm. "I'm Will Carraday," he said.

When I try to recall the rest of our conversation that day, I can't remember anything specific. Will and I stood together. We talked. Otis closed and locked the garage doors and left. How long were we there? I don't know. I remember that Will expressed sorrow about Bailey, I know he welcomed me to the Island. And somehow, coming from him, these commonplace messages seemed essential and profound.

Chapter 6

LATER I HEARD WILL DESCRIBED as calculating, and I suppose in some ways he was. You'd expect someone who owned a controlling interest in several companies, as well as a bank, to be astute. But his pleasure as he greeted his guests that night was real.

They came through the door with their elbows tight against their sides, and stepped tentatively into the pool of light under the chandelier. But when Will spoke to them or took their hands, when he fixed his attention on them, they relaxed. Yes, he adjusted his manner, the way a good dancer adjusts to his partner's height and ability. He was not the same with everyone. But it seemed less a conscious choice than an instinctive move toward harmony, and his guests responded to it.

Charm. Skill. Whatever you choose to call it, Will's gift wasn't inherited from his father, a dour man with a heavy, low-slung jaw and a habit of working his back teeth that had earned him his nickname— the Grinder. Not from his grandfather, either. Ward Carraday's appearance was said to have frightened his customers into paying their bills.

While the guests were arriving, I stood in a narrow passage off the front hall where I could see everyone without seeming to watch for Patrick.

When I thought about Patrick, when I tried to imagine our meeting, there was no consistency about any of it. Sometimes I felt certain that I would know him despite any kind of change. At other times,

I thought the years must have turned him into an entirely different person. What Eleanor had said raised new doubts. Patrick behind a desk? I resolved to practice, so I could meet him and offer my hand casually without giving anything away. *Do you remember me?*

The paneled walls of the passage were filled floor to ceiling with family photos, most of them taken years before. I was only pretending to look, but every so often something caught my eye. There, for example, was Mary Liz Carraday, Patrick's mother, before her accident, field dressing a downed buck. Will, holding up a glistening fish.

The image below was painful—Patrick a scrawny seven or so, reaching awkwardly to put one arm around his sister, Catherine, who was already so much wider. Catherine was disabled. From the time she was about twelve, she had lived away, but I could always tell when she was visiting. She spoke only a few intelligible words, she made harsh squawking noises, and when a door or window opened, I could hear her.

"Are you hiding in there?" Eleanor was wearing a silk tunic that set off her eyes. Her hair was up, not coiled and pinned as I remembered, but loosely piled, so that it looked as if it might come down the way it had in the garden. I realized with a shock that her fitful incandescence was something other people could see. *My mother is a beautiful woman,* I thought.

"You said to come early so we could see the house."

"I said to come early so Will could *show* you the house," Eleanor said with careful emphasis. She touched the shoulder of a young woman standing nearby. "This is our new neighbor, Leanne." I wondered if she could hear the invisible quotation marks around her name, Eleanor's way of letting me know that what came next would be party talk, not to be taken seriously. "You've seen what they're doing next door," Eleanor went on, "such a wonderful job. Lots of repairs. Painting." She raised her eyebrows at me and was gone.

"Hi. Sorry, no hands." Leanne held up a glass and a skewered shrimp. She smiled briefly and deliberately, then her features fell back into place. Her straight blond hair was so fine I could see the pink of her scalp. She waved the shrimp. "I'm hoping if I keep my hands full I won't eat. I've still got twelve pounds to lose." There were shadows under her eyes and a not-quite-white stain on her shoulder. *She has a baby,* I thought, and felt something turn over inside me.

"You don't look as if you have any weight issues," she said.

"No."

"Lucky you." She paused. "I mean, I bet you're disciplined. What you eat."

I thought of the week's worth of junk food and the trash I'd left in the car. I shook my head.

Her smile flickered on and off. "You work out?"

"No." I wondered why she'd asked. No one had ever mistaken me for an athlete. Then all at once I understood. I had known girls like her in high school, they came around acting friendly once a year, right before the class elections. I wondered why she thought I was worth her trouble.

"I lost my daughter a year ago," I said.

"Oh. I'm sorry." The color left her face. "I'm so sorry," she said. She looked unhappily at her feet. I noticed that her heels hung out over the backs of her too-small sandals. She must have seen me looking. "My feet grew when I was pregnant," she said. "I thought they'd go back, but it doesn't look like they will. I mean, it's been four months." She smiled again, earnestly. "Now I'm going to have to get all new shoes." She stopped. "But listen to me. When you—"

"I just didn't feel like eating."

"Well. You wouldn't, would you?"

I shrugged. "Grief affects people differently. I know someone who goes out and wrecks a car when he's unhappy. It's expensive, but he can afford it. Or his parents can." A waiter offered wine on a silver tray and I turned and took a glass. As I did, my camera swung around where Leanne could see it.

"Oh," she said, exhaling, "you're the photographer."

"That's right."

"So you're not . . . I mean, I thought you were part of the family."

"Of this family? No. Thank God."

Her face flushed suddenly.

"Clare." Eleanor was back. She smiled brightly at Leanne. "Excuse us." She took me by the arm and led me into the big double drawing room—pale damask walls set off by a frieze of lilies, the ceiling painted to look like sky and clouds. I didn't need Will to give me a tour, I could have led one myself. The house was filling up, and the noise of the party eddied around us. "What did you say to her?" Eleanor demanded.

"Leanne? I guess she was disappointed. She took me for one of the Carradays and I had to disabuse her."

Eleanor looked at me closely. "Did she say why?"

"No."

"She was upset."

"She seems concerned about her weight. She did just have a baby."

"I see." Eleanor folded both hands around her glass and looked down into it. "Clare. Is this how you want the rest of your life to be? No one expects you to forget. But this . . ."

"She was only talking to me because she thought I was important. Because she thought I was one of them. And I told her I'm not."

There was a pause. Eleanor didn't move, but she seemed to withdraw. Her large green eyes grew larger. After a moment, she said, "When you were born, I thought things would be different. I thought, who wouldn't want two healthy girls, one who is—" She stopped herself. Then her nostrils flared, and I saw that she was angry. "You have never had any reason to be ashamed," she said.

I felt confused. I wondered how much she'd had to drink. "What do you mean?"

Eleanor shook her head. "You're lovely," she went on. "Or you would be if you smiled more."

I thought of Leanne and the determined way she flexed her facial muscles. "Smiling isn't something I can do for effect," I said. "I need a reason."

"You could have another child. You and Michael."

"I don't want another child."

"You say that, but . . ." She looked at me, and for once her gaze lacked the customary element of appraisal. "I want you to be happy," she said. "Why can't you believe that?" When I didn't respond, she sighed. "What will you do?"

"What I've always done, I suppose. Look around. Take photos. Try to learn something."

Eleanor straightened as though drawn by an invisible wire. "Don't be foolish." A waiter hurried in from the next room. Someone, a woman, her voice low and cracked, called after him. "Easy on the water, for Christ's sake." I heard a prolonged and complicated cough.

Leanne was making her way back toward us through the crowd. Eleanor saw her, and she moved to take my arm again, but I shook her off. "Will you come with me?" she asked.

I couldn't remember Eleanor ever asking for anything. What she did was give signals. When she stood at the end of a meal, we knew to help clear the table. If she picked up a suitcase, my father would take it from her and carry it to the car. Her request was so unexpected I followed her without protest.

Over my shoulder I saw Leanne with a plate in her hand, staring.

The adjoining room, the solarium, had been the height of fashion when the house was built, when the palaces of Long Island's North Shore set the pace for extravagant construction. It was filled with the same sort of plants that grew naturally outside—palms of different sizes, ferns, a monstrous lily in an oversize porcelain pot. Despite the air-conditioning, there was a smell of musk.

Mary Liz Carraday, Will's wife, was sitting on a wicker chaise. A throw covered her motionless legs. She held a cigarette in one hand, a ribbed gold lighter in the other.

"So it's you," she said. "Well, come over here where I can get a look at you." She squinted up at me. "Still carrying the camera." There was grudging approval in her voice. She took my wrist between her thumb and forefinger and swung my arm away from my body. "My God, you're puny. You never had much chest and now look at you. Flat as a board."

Faline appeared and placed a fresh drink on a small glass table.

"What is this," Mary Liz said, "cat pee?" She held the glass to the light. "Looks like half water."

"Well it's not. So you better make it last." Faline bent and rearranged the throw. "I told Clayborn and them not to let you be doubling up."

"So he's under your thumb now, too. I suppose no one entering this house is safe." Mary Liz turned and looked up at a stranger who was standing beside her. "I met you already," she said. "Will's new boy."

If this was meant as a dismissal, the stranger paid no attention. "We've been talking about preservation," he said, smiling.

He was compact, with the build of a wrestler. I remembered the high-school meets, the boys circling each other until I thought nothing was going to happen. Then all at once they were twisting on the floor. Maybe he was used to sudden attacks. Maybe that was why they didn't bother him. "Charlotte doesn't approve of old houses being moved, even to save them," he said. He smiled at the woman standing next to him. I wondered if I should remember her.

"Charlotte will bore you to death on that subject if you let her," said Mary Liz.

"You know you don't mean that," said Charlotte. Her features were neat and small, the kind that would have been described as "cute" when she was young but were now insufficient for her face, which had puffed up around them like a dinner roll. She had the confidence that often accompanies the ability to write large checks. "Historic houses have no meaning," she said, "once they're moved off-site."

"Jesus wept," said Mary Liz.

"You could create a site," the man persisted pleasantly.

Charlotte shook her head. "That's Epcot. Only worse, because people confuse it with the real thing. Reconstructions like that make people think that they can choose whatever they want."

There was a silence. "I'm Clare Porterfield," I said. "My family lives on the other side of the alley."

"Oh," Charlotte brightened, "the Hayes-Giraud house? Terrific.

The carriage block. It's so correct. That's the way it should be done. Respect for the original context."

The man said, "I'm sorry, I should have introduced myself. Tyler Henry. Ty. I'm with the bank." We shook hands. His palm was smooth and dry. His clothes—blue shirt, khaki pants—were casual, but in the way of an office worker on a Friday rather than a person who makes his own schedule. I was pretty sure he wasn't an Islander.

"What if a house isn't moved," I asked, "but a parking lot goes in next to it. And a high-rise. Until there's nothing left of the original context. Then what?"

"Well," Charlotte said, "it's not ideal, but at least it isn't fake." She frowned. She must have understood that I was talking about the Carraday house. It hadn't happened yet, but it could. "Things can't always be pretty, whatever the tourists want. The past wasn't always nice."

"The tourists want condos," said Mary Liz.

We heard raised voices, the sound of a number of people coming our way.

"Here comes the goddam expert," Mary Liz said.

It's interesting to watch the very rich play the role of host. Everything about them, about their lives, is already so overstated, it doesn't take much to push the situation into parody. But Will, with his air of detachment, of mild surprise, got it right.

He was wearing a white shirt with the cuffs turned back and linen trousers that were just wrinkled enough to look comfortable. As always, there was a crowd with him. Every so often, someone would get close enough to touch his arm or bump his shoulder, as if by accident. I knew what they were thinking. You can't change the circumstances of your birth, and few would be able to achieve for themselves what Will had. But he made them believe in good fortune, and they hoped a little of it would rub off.

Will took my hand in both of his, the way he had done earlier. He looked approvingly at Ty and me. "Excellent. I see you two have met." He turned to Mary Liz. "We're going to do the fireplace and the study, then we'll see how everyone's holding up."

She nodded. "You go on," she said, as though she had just then decided not to accompany them. I knew that since her accident Mary Liz couldn't move without help; surely most of the guests knew this too.

She'd been around horses from childhood, ridden in barrel races at state and county fairs, then gone on to compete against professional cowgirls and try her hand at saddle broncs. For her wedding to Will, she wore a fitted satin dress with a fishtail train. A picture in the hall showed the toes of her boots poking out in front like little brown animals. It had been almost thirty years since her horse fell on her and she lost the use of her legs.

Will turned to me. "I'm afraid this will be old hat for you." He gestured toward the drawing room in a way that managed to suggest both pride in the old house and disarming personal modesty.

"Of course not," I said. And in fact I wanted to hear him tell Stella's story, to provide the details that were missing from the guides and tourist brochures. To give substance to the scenes of Stella's courtship that I had imagined growing up.

I suppose all children dream at some time of running away. For me, the desire had been persistent, acute. Stella gave me hope. When I was small, I told myself that if Stella could escape, so could I.

It was part of the city's lore that on September 7, 1900, Stella was seen riding alone in a carriage with the young architect who had designed the Carraday house and overseen its construction. Henry Durand had wooed Stella secretly with lilies, her favorite flowers, at first carrying them to her a few discreet stems at a time, later lavishing them on the interiors, so that the house itself became a secret lover's gift.

This was the part of the story I'd focused on. What happened next was not clear. Were the lovers unable to reach the causeway? Did they lose their nerve and turn back? No one knows.

What is certain is that during the day, the weather changed. At dawn the sun rose through a bright haze and the air was still. But in the afternoon, the sky grew dark and the temperature dropped. Those in town, on Broadway, couldn't know that on the south side of the Island, waves larger than any seen before were attacking the streetcar trestle where it curved out over the Gulf.

According to the popular account, when the Great Hurricane struck, Stella was alone in the house. Her parents had already fled to the mainland. Stella's body was said to have been recovered three blocks away, her long hair still entangled in the drawing-room chandelier.

Will put his hand on my lower back and steered me gently to where the other guests were gathered. He began to talk, secure in his audience. He described the work of the craftsmen who had built the house. He talked about his grandfather, Ward Carraday, and his early days as a storekeeper, when floors were sand and his customers picked their teeth with long knives. He offered anecdotes and just enough humor to entertain even those whose only real interest was being seen at home with one of Galveston's wealthiest men.

When it was time to speak of Stella, Will's account was spare, he talked briefly about her love affair with the young architect. The story of her death he avoided entirely. Then he moved toward the fireplace. It was massive, extravagantly decorated, the opening flanked by a pair of fantastic hoofed legs. Above it, set into a panel, was the full-length figure of a girl.

Will made an L with his thumb and forefinger. "From here over," he said, resting his hand on one corner of the panel, "what you see is plaster painted to look like bronze." There were expressions of disbelief. "Plaster is easier to work and less expensive. My grandfather wasn't above saving a nickel here and there." He grinned. The guests smiled and nodded, pleased to be let in on the deception. "The figure, of course, is my aunt Stella. You can see the likeness, I think." He picked up a framed photo from the mantel, then replaced it.

I looked at the relief. The face with its upward gaze and parted lips was sweetly sentimental. But the body was plainly sensual. The folds of Stella's dress defined her rounded thighs and soft belly. The bodice had slipped so that the curves of her breasts showed clearly, and all her clothing was in disarray. On her right hip, she carried a pitcher. There were lilies crushed at her feet.

Will nodded at an older woman who leaned on an elegant, silver-headed walking stick. "Harriet," he said to her, "you know my sister, Rhetta." The woman smiled, as people did when he singled them out. He went on, "My sister, Rhetta, lives in Paris, and she tells me that this looks a lot like a painting there, in one of the museums. It seems to have been popular in the 1800s. She thinks young Henry Durand might have shown a copy of the painting to my grandfather. Maybe he even offered to reproduce it at a bargain price. Who knows? But there is a difference. The painting only shows the girl from the waist up. Stella, of course . . ." Will reached over and rested one hand on the figure's slender bare foot. As he did, I felt again his touch on my back, the precise weight and extent of it.

Did I mention that Will was especially attractive to women?

That was when I raised my camera. It wasn't a great shot. Will's mouth was half open, the figure of Stella awkwardly truncated. When the flash went off, there was an audible gasp. The guests turned. Some looked annoyed.

I didn't care what they thought. I was looking at Will. He had hosted similar groups so many times, told his stories, fielded the inevitable questions. Now something had changed. It was as though somewhere a bolt had slid back, a door opened. I felt it, and I saw that he did too.

He went on with his talk, ushering the group toward the staircase and up past a pair of stained-glass windows toward his study. He kept everyone moving. He must have understood how exhausting it was to stand and admire.

We were bunched together on the stairs, taking small, awkward steps, when I heard someone say, in the kind of raised voice you are meant to overhear, "I think it's rude to take pictures without asking." Leanne's eyes were glazed and she was breathing through her mouth. "I think it's tacky."

"My dear, she's an artist." It was the older woman with the walking stick, Harriet, who spoke. She was smiling, and I couldn't be sure if she was serious.

Leanne said, "An artist?" She looked at me. "You're a photographer, right?" Before I could answer, she went on. "Photography isn't even a craft. The camera does everything." Her voice rose. "You just push a button."

The woman in black said, "There's more to it than that." Her long-sleeved jacket was fastened all the way up, and I wondered that she wasn't hot. Her white hair was twisted into a figure eight at the nape of her neck. She turned to me. "I'm Harriet Kinkaid," she said. "You won't remember. But I live in what you children used to call 'the witch house.' Oh, it's all right. In fact, I rather like to think of myself as a witch. Better than being just another old bag." She laughed, a sound of pure delight that made her seem suddenly much younger.

That was when Leanne, stiff-legged, began to tilt backward in her too-small shoes. She must have been steadied on the way up by the presence of the crowd. Now there were just the three of us, everyone else had gone on, and there was nothing between her and the floor below but the hard angles of the stairs.

The space around us seemed to contract suddenly into tight focus. I saw Leanne's left hand fly up, saw her reach for the banister and miss. Her eyes widened and I heard the sound of something shattering and I knew her glass had flown backward and landed in the front hall. Then, as quickly as it had begun, it was over. Tyler Henry was there, his hands on her waist. He walked her down.

Harriet Kinkaid patted my arm. "Don't worry. She'll be fine. They ought to warn the unsuspecting about the planter's punch. Those old recipes are lethal. Most of us can't drink the way they did. Our ancestors."

She touched my cheek. "The hair. The eyes," she said. "I would have known you anywhere. I used to see you when you were a little thing, going around with your Brownie camera. The one Will gave you. You were an interesting child."

She turned to face the second-floor landing. "I'd better move along now if I'm going to stay with the others." She grasped the stair rail and began to work her way up, a pull on the banister, a push with the stick. She looked over her shoulder. "Maybe you'll come and visit me one day," she said. "I'll show you *my* house. I believe you'll be entertained by the contrast." She laughed again.

Alone on the landing, I thought about the way a pinhole camera reconstructs an entire scene through the smallest aperture. Trees, buildings, figures materializing out of the tiniest dot of light. *Your Brownie camera. The one Will gave you.* Harriet Kinkaid had pricked a hole in time. Through it, the past, complete and undimmed, came flooding.

Chapter 7

HAVE YOU EVER DISCOVERED YOURSELF in someone else's snapshot? Felt that small shock of surprise? You might have forgotten that the photo was ever taken. But there you are—your face unbecomingly flushed, your arm draped around the neck of a man who smiles foolishly at your breasts. Closer inspection reveals that your hem is hanging.

Some people would say that the photo shows the truth. That the camera doesn't lie. But it does—a fact I recognized from the time I looked through the viewfinder of the Brownie 127, clicked off a picture, and left my sister, Frankie, out of it.

It was Easter Sunday when I found the camera in a nest of green cellophane grass at the foot of a jelly palm in our back garden.

Typically Frankie and I each received a small gift to mark the holiday, often a crystallized sugar egg trimmed with colored icing. Through an opening in one end you could see a suite of ducklings or the profile of a rabbit. Frankie used to pry the hardened icing off her egg with a nail file until there was nothing left but its gritty skin. Then she'd go after whatever was inside. I wanted to keep mine intact so I tried to hide them from her in the chaos under my bed. She always found them.

We were not regular churchgoers, but I knew what heaven was, and in my mind it had something to do with that white stillness and the way it enclosed the tiny distant rabbit.

Of course the scene inside the egg never changed. I remember thinking that the camera was similar. I had never handled one before, and I did not understand at first that the images that streamed past the viewfinder were mine to choose.

That same year Eleanor had bought white straw purses for Frankie and me. They were made to look like baskets, with a hinged lid and wicker hasp. Frankie and I were outside, dressed and ready to leave for Easter Sunday dinner, when Eleanor saw me. "Not the camera, Clare," she said. "You might lose it."

"No, I won't."

"Ridiculous present for a child that age," said my father. "Clare, take it in the house."

It was quiet inside. I walked toward the stairs, but at the last minute, I slid around the corner into the kitchen. Standing behind the door, I opened the basket and jammed the camera in. In my hurry, I pushed the lid down too hard, and the raffia hinge broke.

The list of things I had unintentionally spoiled was already long—clothing and objects torn, stained, and broken.

I returned to the car, carrying the basket carefully in both hands, holding it closed. No one noticed anything. Not until we were seated at our table, and a waiter, thinking to be helpful, lifted it off my plate by the handle, and the purse came apart. I tensed, waiting, but my mother was oddly quiet. I wasn't punished.

At no time was there any mention of Will. Not then, not later.

My first photos were of a chair. The seat, the back slats, from in front, from the side. I discovered that the act of photography alters the most straightforward objects, perhaps permanently. That something once observed and photographed, from a certain angle, is never the same again. I was less interested in things like flowers and sunsets that grew or altered naturally. Their eventual transformation was to be expected.

No one saw any merit in what I was doing, although it was tolerated like most childish enthusiasms. "The things she photographs," my father said. "Look at this. What is it? Appears to be a manhole cover."

My mother murmured something in response.

"Well," he said, "eye of the beholder, I suppose." From under the porch, I listened and recognized myself for the first time. *The beholder.*

Eventually I moved on to more complicated subjects—tree branches, the grille of the family Buick, the pattern left by a tire tread in the sand. Then, finally, people. Faline, kneading pastry dough. Patrick, disappearing around a corner. My early shots of my mother mostly show her back—the curve of her spine, the zipper running down between her shoulder blades, a line of liquid metal.

When I was old enough to leave the house at will, I would find and observe certain Islanders—a girl my age with a clubfoot in a round black shoe, the old man who worked at the newsstand, who would sometimes take out his teeth and set them on the counter. "I can't believe they want to be photographed, not like this," Eleanor said.

"They do. They're friends," I said. It was a lie—I was not good at making friends.

The one I sought out constantly, made excuses to visit, was the cashier at the bait shop. He had the pale eyes and scorched hair of a fisherman, and he was missing a hand. I used to hang around the shop examining the lures, and sometimes I would buy mud minnows that I later released into the storm drain, just so I could observe him and the wizened knob of his stump.

Growing up, I believed I was deficient in a way that I couldn't identify precisely and that this explained my failure to fit in with my family. It was something inside, not visible, a matter of character or outlook, I thought. And for that reason, hard to come to terms with. But here was a man whose defect was plain to see, and it didn't bother him at all. I stared as he matter-of-factly measured out the bait shrimp, made change, his sleeve rolled comfortably above the elbow. I hoped that if I studied him long enough, I might learn his secret.

Chapter 8

THE NOISE OF THE PARTY FILLED the Carraday house. Outside, night was gathering in the long fingers of the oleander hedge. In the rose garden, draped tables held silver bowls heaped with glittering cracked ice and pink shrimp and silver platters of oysters. There were piles of blanched asparagus and darker green bottles of champagne. Slowly, I made my way down the buffet. Someone spoke my name and I turned. It was Tyler Henry. "What's good?" he asked.

"Everything."

He leaned over my shoulder as I served myself. "What's that?"

"Mud bugs." He looked blank. "Crawfish."

"And I thought Texans only ate steak."

"There's barbecue over there if you want it. But this isn't really Texas, it's the Free State of Galveston."

"Meaning?"

"It's different. You can see it, can't you?"

"I can hear it," he said. "You don't talk like a Texan. Will doesn't either."

"My parents are Yankees. Will went to school in Connecticut. But it's true, people here don't talk like other Texans."

"What about Mary Liz?"

"She's from Oklahoma."

Ty smiled. "Obviously, it's more complicated than I thought."

"Hollywood has a lot to answer for," I said. I lowered my voice. "I hope you won't pay too much attention to Mary Liz. To what she said."

"You mean that I'm Will's boy?" Ty winced, but it was mostly for show. "Well, it's not so far off. My title is director of special projects, but basically I handle whatever Will doesn't feel like doing."

"Is that a good thing?" I asked doubtfully.

"Yes, in fact. What he tells people is that I'm in charge of all the really exciting stuff. He's been very gracious. He's introduced me to everyone."

I took a piece of bread and put another on Ty's plate. "So how do you like the Island?" I asked. "Are you disappointed? No range, no cattle to speak of, no cowboys, no rodeos. Was that what you expected?"

"I don't know what I expected," Ty said. We walked together across the freshly mowed lawn. Ty held a white folding chair for me and we sat down. Over his shoulder I could see the terrace where Will and Eleanor stood. When Patrick arrived, he would have to come and find them.

"I did see some cattle near where I'm staying," Ty said.

"That's not a real ranching operation. It's a tax deduction. The land will be sold to a developer before long." I shook out a napkin. "There are coyotes though. You can see them on the beach at night, if you're patient."

"You're not talking about . . ."

I shook my head. "It's easier to cross the border farther south. On Padre Island, there's a visitor center that probably sees about thirty people a year. That's where the road ends. From there all the way to the Port Mansfield ship channel, sixty miles or so, there's nothing." Nothing, I thought, except the hot wind bending the sea oats. The air mysteriously charged, full of the sound you hear when you stand too close to power lines.

I realized Ty was looking at me expectantly. I was flattered. It had been a long time since anyone had shown that kind of interest in what I had to say. I went on. "It's pretty desolate. So, yes, it's a drop spot. Marine scavengers camp there. And drug runners."

"Any of that go on here?"

I shrugged. "Galveston is busier, so people are more cautious. But it's a port city. If you stay on the Island long enough, eventually you recognize the look. Guys with serious tans and the kind of clothes you'd have a hard time remembering or describing. Rubber flip-flops and two-hundred-dollar sunglasses. They're always alone. They always sit near the exit." How many times had I heard Faline tell Patrick, "You stay away from those fellas."

The breeze rustled the massed palm fronds above us. Patches of bark rose and fell too so that the whole length of each tree seemed to be moving. Ty looked up. "Coyotes and palm trees."

"Like nowhere else."

"You called it the Free State."

"That started during Prohibition. Galveston supplied about half the country with illegal liquor. After repeal, it was gambling. There's a nightclub out on one of the piers that was pretty famous then. Every so often the Rangers would try to stage a raid. But before they could get to the end of the pier, the band would strike up 'The Eyes of Texas' as a warning and the slot machines would fold back into the walls."

Ty put his fork down. "You're kidding."

"The red-light district was famous, too. The fanciest whorehouse in town was right in back of the Artillery Club. You've seen the Texas Heroes Monument?"

"I have?"

"It's in the middle of Broadway. You have to drive around it."

Ty grinned. "I seem to recall a column . . ."

"With a figure on top? It's Victory, pointing toward the San Jacinto battlefield. The old joke was that she was directing visitors to the brothels." I sat back, feeling excited and a little giddy from so much talking. A waiter offered a wrapped bottle and I raised my glass.

When I turned back, Ty's face had gone thoughtful. "And people here were okay with this?"

"There's always been a general sense that the Island makes its own rules. I guess what I'm saying is that it's a state of mind as much as anything."

"You've thought about all this."

"It's what Islanders do when they're somewhere else."

There was a crab on the plate I'd given Ty. It lay on its back, legs splayed. Ty went to work, dismantling it with precision. Between bites, he looked at me intently. "Tell me more," he said.

"Tourists used to come here, Texans, people from other parts of the mainland, when they wanted a wild time. To indulge themselves. To do the things they couldn't or wouldn't do at home. In a place without a conscience."

"And now?"

"It's a matter of local pride, what the Islanders got away with. It was partly self-preservation. When the port traffic moved to Houston, gambling and prostitution kept the city going. But . . ."

"But what?"

"I think what really mattered to them was demonstrating the Island's separateness. Showing that they could do whatever they wanted." I looked down at my plate and realized that my food was untouched.

"And now. Is there a conscience?"

"Well, visitors on vacation still do things here they wouldn't at home. The men drink too much and start fights. The women drink too much and buy revealing clothing they'll never wear again."

"But the local people?"

"Officially, the city has no vices. Unless you count the careless beach development."

"You disapprove."

"It's probably inevitable."

"But you don't like it."

"No," I said, "I don't."

"And what about unofficially?"

"Is there bad behavior? Of course. And I'm sure the Islanders know about it because they know everything. That's the way it is here. Which is not to say they'll discuss it in front of outsiders. They tend to close ranks." I gestured toward the terrace, where a small group had gathered. "Look around you. If they aren't related by blood, they're intermarried or doing business together. Or hoping to buy their way in."

"Sounds sort of incestuous."

"Absolutely." I smiled, signaling my detachment.

"You grew up here."

"Right over there." I pointed toward the oleander hedge. "But I've lived away a long time."

Ty looked up from under dark brows. "Did you miss it?"

I felt a quick pinch of anxiety and straightened in my chair. "I didn't want to come back, if that's what you're asking. I have a career I could never have had in Galveston."

"But you thought about it."

"Occasionally."

"It's a seductive place," he said. "The colors. The weather."

I swung my bare leg and nodded. I wondered when he would discover what all Islanders know—that the air and water are often so close to body temperature you sometimes feel, if it weren't for the accident of your skin, you could melt into either one.

It was agreeable being the object of Ty's interest. But I was thinking about Patrick. Where was he? I had dressed with him in mind. As the party progressed, I'd thought about how I wanted to look when he made his appearance. I wanted to seem relaxed, like someone who went out often and had a good time. Who ate and slept like other people and did not cry unexpectedly.

My skirt was blue, a sheer layer over a darker lining. I rearranged its folds. "The Island has always drawn people," I said. "Even when it was run-down. Before they started fixing things up. Rehabilitating the city and its past. Making it all into copy for a vacation flyer."

"You think it was different?"

"The reality? Well, you heard what Charlotte said."

He thought for a minute. "That the past wasn't always nice." He paused. "But isn't that what we all do? Rework our history? Most of us keep to the basic facts. But we improve on them, cast them in a better light. We back off just enough to be comfortable. I mean, who would want to remember what it was like to be an adolescent? The awful details. To live with that knowledge on a daily basis."

I wondered how long he'd been in Galveston. If he'd heard about the fire. About Patrick and me.

Ty glanced over toward the house. Had he seen me look that way? Or had I gone on too long about the Island? I had no sense anymore of how people talked in social situations. I felt deflated, the way I always did when I described Galveston that way. Everything I'd told Ty was true. And yet I'd done exactly what I'd complained about—presented the information in a way I knew would be amusing.

At the other end of the garden, the buffet tables had been quietly cleared away. Waiters were circulating with coffee and chocolates. Under the tent, a band began to play.

This was what it meant to have things done. I thought it might be the most appealing thing about being really rich—this ability to orchestrate what was going on around you for everyone's benefit, and to do it without apparent effort. I could understand how hard it might be to restrain that impulse, once it had become a habit. And that it might be misunderstood as interference. To my surprise, I realized I was expressing Will's point of view.

The group on the terrace had grown. I recognized several guests Will had introduced me to earlier. The president of an insurance company. A developer who had renovated one of the old hotels. Across the lawn I saw Leanne, her head thrown back, asleep in a lawn chair.

Will led Eleanor onto the dance floor. The band struck up a familiar number, and there was scattered applause. Will was a wonderful dancer, graceful and light on his feet. But his real gift was the way he showed off his partner. As he spun her out, a strand of hair fell down past Eleanor's cheek, and she laughed and pushed it back.

Then it came to me. Will was a fisherman. Hadn't I seen a photo of him in the foyer? On a boat, wearing a canvas hat stuck with lures? It was his urgent step I had heard in our house, his hat I had seen in our front hall.

No wonder he and Eleanor looked so much at ease together. If Mary Liz objected, she wasn't letting on. Probably everyone else understood too. Some of them, at least, applauded. Who knew what they really thought?

I took a deep breath. It seemed I needed more oxygen than the moist air provided. I looked up into the night sky and saw that what I'd thought was an especially bright star had moved. I realized that it wasn't a star but a plane, entirely silent, on its way to a destination I could only guess at.

Ty asked, "Are you all right? Can I get you something?"

I shook my head and stood up. "No, I'm sorry. I'm just tired. I've been doing a lot of driving. I think I'd better make it an early night." Ty stood too. I could see that he was disappointed, but he was too polite to ask questions.

There was no point in trying to explain. If Ty remained in Galveston, he would learn that whatever was happening between Eleanor and Will, the Islanders had already taken its measure and made the necessary social corrections. If he wanted to belong, to be part of Will's circle, he would have to be willing to adjust his responses too. He'd heard the stories. But he didn't understand yet. Things were different here.

A BARRIER ISLAND, LIKE GALVESTON, is a slim formation of loose sand, no more than five to ten feet above sea level. The sand is always moving, raising itself into long bars offshore, into dunes above the beach.

The sand becomes stable only when it is covered with vegetation. First the grasses and sea oats. Then the vining plants, low to the ground—beach morning glories with interlacing runners, doveweed, goatweed. The leaves of these plants are thick and succulent, hairy, or reduced in size—adaptations that decrease water loss. Their roots go down deep. So specific and so extreme are the requirements of the environment that many of these plants can grow nowhere else.

Everything on a barrier island is dug in or braced—the plants, the egrets in the marsh grass, even the fishermen in caps and T-shirts, squinting, waist-deep, leaning into the wind, searching for shifts and currents.

There is so little to rest the eye on. Is the emptiness too much to bear? So that without understanding why, Islanders will do anything to fill it? I don't know how it happens. But islands have a way of taking over, of seizing the imagination. So that the people who live on them become different too, become wishful thinkers, fabulists, rearrangers of facts. What those on the mainland would probably call liars. It's not surprising really in a place where survival, life itself, is the result of a kind of stubborn reinvention.

A hurricane can cause a small island to disappear in a matter of hours.

For some, the potential for catastrophe makes island life irresistible. It acts like a drug, heightening the senses. It magnifies the sound of the surf until you can hear it through heavy curtains and thick walls. It makes the breeze sweeter against your skin. It invests each day, each small decision with significance because it could be the last. You are waiting for the world to end, and part of you wants to see it happen.

The Islanders like to talk about the weather. That's how they greet each other. *There's a storm in the Gulf.*

Is it a game? Do they truly believe that they are invulnerable? Mention the laws of nature, meteorology, geological evidence, engineering, laws of any kind, and they just smile and look away. Is this where Galveston Islanders get their reputation for tolerance? *Live and let live.*

When the truth is, in a place so small, so interconnected, and so precarious, willful disregard can be a powerful form of self-interest.

Chapter 9

WHEN FINALLY WILL'S PARTY WAS OVER and most of the lights were out, I left my bedroom, crossed the alley, and stepped back through the oleander hedge.

The mass of the Carraday house rose up suddenly before me, the lighted windows bright against the black sky. It was impossible to approach it gradually, to accustom yourself to its immensity, to the welter of narrow chimneys and conical towers of different heights that bristled above it. I'd been coming and going there all my life, and still it took my breath away.

The door was open and I let myself in.

Nothing in that part of the house had changed. There was the dumbwaiter that connected the two floors. On rainy days, Patrick and I would take turns hauling each other, cramped and sweating, up and down, until Faline heard the hollow knocking of the wooden pulleys and dragged us out.

Though it was late, a light still burned downstairs. I went down the half-dozen steps and through the doorway into the kitchen. It was in a half basement at the back of the house. Because it was below ground, the kitchen was always cool and pleasantly musky, like a root cellar.

Faline sat upright in an upholstered wing chair in the corner. A low, plush-covered footstool, clearly new, stood to one side. Next to it lay a stack of newspapers. Behind her on the wall was a row of call bells for summoning a staff that no longer existed. Faline's eyes were closed, her brows drawn together as if she were focused on some chore, but her lap was empty and her hands lay at her sides. I saw her eyelids flicker. I cleared my throat. When there was no response, I spoke her name.

"No need to shout," she said. She opened her eyes. "You try my étouffée? I can tell you don't get any real food up north. You wouldn't be so skinny."

I recognized this tactic—Faline was adept at diversion. "I don't want to discuss the menu," I said. "You told me to come back later. Faline, I need to know what happened."

"What happened? What kind of question is that? What you think happened? The party's over. Everyone gone home. Except you. You always turning up. Ever since you been a small child." She pointed to the refrigerator. "I saved you some brown-sugar bread pudding."

"Maybe later. First I want to know what you told them about Patrick and me."

"You come here at this hour to ask me that? Why you still fussing about something everyone else have long forgotten? What difference it make now? Anyway, I stand by what I did. It was best for you both."

"Why was it best?"

"Why?" Faline stood abruptly, pulled a cloth off a rack and snapped it. "Why? Since when I got to justify myself to you? My conscience clean, is all you need to know." She turned her back and began to polish the stove whose black-and-white surfaces already gleamed. I could see her shoulder working under her cotton blouse.

"I want to know what you told them," I persisted.

She turned and shook the cloth at me. "I seen you tonight," she said, "flirting with that fellow from the mainland. Cross your legs. Cross them again. You a married woman, getting on for thirty years old. You ought to had enough of that foolishness. In that flimsy skirt."

"I was just talking."

"You ought to be talking to your husband. But here you are now in the middle of the night. Look like you come from a shelter."

After the party, I'd fallen asleep briefly, then gotten up and changed into a T-shirt and jeans. I realized they were the ones I usually wore in the darkroom, and they were stained with chemicals. I touched my hair. Had I remembered to brush it?

I sat down in the wing chair and pushed back into it so Faline would understand I wasn't giving up, that I had no intention of leaving. I looked over at the pile of newspapers. The banner read DEATH OF MAN RULED AN ACCIDENT.

In general, Faline disapproved of storytelling. "Don't waste my time," she would say, when Mary Liz tried to read to her from a paperback. She made an exception only when Patrick and I were hurt or unhappy. Even then her narratives were different, sad and shocking. "One time there was an explosion at a warehouse," she would begin. Or, "One time there was a woman jumped off Pier 22 with a baby on her arm." Patrick and I sat slack-jawed, listening, our own pain forgotten. Later I realized that her stories came from the week's sensational headlines. I was suddenly aware of how close Patrick and I had come to being featured in one of them.

"I can't talk to Michael," I said. "He doesn't talk, he makes speeches. The same ones, over and over, with variations. That's what he's good at."

"Maybe if you would listen he wouldn't have to repeat hisself."

I shook my head. "Faline. There are things I need to know. Things he can't tell me."

She turned back to the stove. "Why you got to go into all this now?" she said. "Life supposed to go forward. People supposed to grow up. Everything all right. Why can't you leave it alone?" She was rubbing hard now.

"Everything isn't all right," I said.

Faline stopped her polishing. She leaned forward on both hands and sighed and her head dropped forward. Somewhere in the house water was running. The sound of it through the walls was like distant rain.

"I was a good mother," I said.

"Well," said Faline, "I know that, baby. I surely do. You don't have to tell me."

I rested my hands on the arms of the chair where the fabric was worn and stringy and the stuffing showed through, the places where she must have rested hers. "That old chair," Faline said. "Same one, all these years. The footstool, though, that's new, Otis got me that. I'm still thinking about putting my feet on it. You want to, go ahead."

I looked down at my bare feet. Probably the soles were dirty. "I better not," I said. We stayed there for a while, neither of us having any idea what to say next. I tried to formulate a sentence, but it was like climbing sand, I kept sinking in and sliding backward. Finally I said, "After Bailey . . . after she . . . I kept thinking about the Island. I don't know why. What I wanted was to remember her, how she looked, the things she said. To keep her memory, at least, safe. But instead I kept thinking about"—I looked around—"all this." I stopped. "Faline, do you think the dead have dreams?"

"If they do, they good ones. There got to be some peace after this life." Faline turned around to look at me. I sensed something different in her manner. "You asking all these questions," she said. "Pull on a string, no telling what going to be on the other end."

"I don't care."

"Easy to say now. You don't know what you going to find." She folded her arms. Again I saw the resemblance, and I wondered where Otis was.

"Otis gone over to Kemah," she said. "See about a boat." She smiled. "You always been easy to read. Not like your mama. She keep herself to herself."

I thought of Eleanor at dinner, her face above a blue-and-white bowl of flowers, the light from the candles shining on her hair. Her posture unyielding. Her eyes half closed, as though she were entirely absorbed by something no one else could see.

Faline stepped over to the kitchen table. I remembered its cool surface, Faline holding a needle to the light. Sleep tugged at me, but I made an effort to rouse myself. "Faline," I said, "do you remember the time you sewed my dress? What you told me?"

I'd torn the waistband and bloodied my arm climbing through the window of an empty house on Avenue K with Patrick. You couldn't call it breaking in when we hadn't broken anything—someone before us had removed most of the glass.

Faline shook her head at my torn dress. "Look like you been to the club with your family at some point. You and Patrick out fooling around, you couldn't go home and change?" She complained, but she didn't ask any questions. "Put your arm where I can see," she said. "At least you had the sense not to bleed on the fabric."

I rested my arm along the enamel tabletop and watched as she washed the dried crust off with a dishcloth. The refrigerator hummed softly, the mixing bowls nested on top of it gave back their own ceramic trill. When she was done, Faline said, "You understand now I got to boil this." When the bandage was in place, she pulled out her work basket and chose a needle. Somewhere outside, a car back-fired. Faline said, "How am I going to sew with you jumping around? Hold still, while I tell you something." She examined the thread, then licked the end. "It so happen, I have the very shade."

She went on talking while she sewed, and her voice soothed me the way it had when Patrick and I were small. Except Faline wasn't recounting events from the paper. She was talking about herself. Probably she thought I was too young to comprehend or recall the details. *This thing sometimes happens. No way to explain it. One love, too young, and you don't get another chance.* It was Otis she'd been talking about. Now they were together. What did that mean for me? The possibilities blazed like fireworks—beautiful, far-off. In no way dangerous.

"You said people don't get a second chance. And I believed you. But you and Otis, you're married now."

Faline took a step back. There was an expression on her face I didn't recognize, a guardedness, and I didn't know what it meant.

"Is that why you here? Baby, tell me that not so."

Before I could answer, the shadows around us deepened, and I realized there was someone in the doorway.

Otis was wearing a dress shirt that covered his tattoos. It must have been two in the morning, but the points of his collar stood out crisply, his belt buckle gleamed. I remembered something else Faline had told me.

"You were in the army, weren't you?" I asked.

"The Marine Corps."

I nodded as if what he'd said explained everything about him. I didn't want to admit the truth—that Otis was someone who understood how things worked, who knew how to fix or find them. Whereas I was someone who broke or lost them.

I had never thought of Faline as graceful, but when she went to him and put her arm around his waist she seemed to glide across the kitchen floor. She fitted herself against his side—she was almost as tall as he was—and he shifted his weight slightly to accommodate her. They looked back at me out of the same dark eyes.

I should have been happy for her. I should have rejoiced to see how the arched doorway with its double outline framed the two of them, making the pose somehow formal and definitive. Instead I closed my eyes.

Faline said, "I suppose you planning to stay there all night."

Chapter 10

BOTH FALINE AND ELEANOR CLAIMED that my past—the fire and its aftermath—had been forgotten. I wondered if what they really meant was that now people remembered things differently. That was the way in Galveston. Real events were absorbed into the Island's narrative and in time became something else. So that life there could go on.

In the days after the fire, Eleanor, my father, and the Galveston chief of police—a nervous, balding man in a suit—all asked me, over and over, to explain what had happened. I told them that Patrick and I had taken a car and driven it to an abandoned house. I said I didn't know how the fire started. When they asked if I knew the girl who had died, I hesitated. Then I said, truthfully, "Not really."

Those are the facts, and they are as meaningless as a row of stones.

When I think of that night, what I recall is the winter fog that wrapped the Island, that surrounded Patrick and me, alone in the car. I remember that we talked about going away together, and that for a fraction of a second, I thought it might be possible. I felt hopeful in a way I never had before, and I didn't want to give up the feeling. If keeping it alive meant stealing a car or burning down a house, what-ever it meant, I would go along.

Not that I ever said so. I never spoke or acted or even made a real choice. I wanted to be with Patrick, that was all, and I trailed after him, doing whatever that required. I never thought to question what he did. As for Patrick, I don't think he made a conscious decision that night either. He just acted, impulsively. We were so young, our lives were not ordered toward any purpose. They were as formless as water.

The adults interrogated us separately. They must have been testing our accounts for inconsistencies. Don't imagine this taking place at the Island's police station. I never saw it. To this day I don't know where it is. We met at Will Carraday's office, a brick building with an impressive white portico. When I wasn't being questioned, I waited outside Will's door. The walls were thick, the doors heavy, so I couldn't hear what was being said. The only sound was the tick and whir of the tall clock in the corner. I remember the sorrowful moon that looked down from above its face, the chained weights hanging side by side, inches apart, in the case below. The clock seemed to have a message for me, if only I could make sense of it.

I went there on three successive days. At first I thought I'd encounter Patrick. Then I realized that our visits had been timed to keep us apart. At home I watched for his signal from my bedroom window. But the light in Stella's bedroom never came on.

What do you call it when you wake up each morning anticipating one eager presence? When you register his smallest gestures, a code only you can decipher? Patrick's role in my life wasn't something I thought about. If we'd been asked about our relationship, I doubt that either of us would have used the word *love*. But I couldn't imagine a world that didn't include him. As I sat waiting in the hall, one ankle wrapped around the leg of the chair, it never occurred to me that I wouldn't see Patrick again.

The newspaper article was brief, no names were mentioned, the heading read simply UNOCCUPIED HOUSE BURNS. It was buried deep within the second section. It must have been Will's influence that kept the story off the front page, that kept our names out of it altogether. I didn't understand then that he must have used it in other ways as well. I was fourteen, and he was still *Mr. Carraday* to me.

It was my mother who drove me to his office every day, who brought me sandwiches and sat with me while I ate. Who talked to Will's lawyer, and also to a heavyset woman with puffy eyes and long artificial nails. The woman carried a square, shiny purse that she held in front of her as though it offered protection. When Eleanor introduced herself, the woman said, "I know who you are." They stood, their gazes locked, the woman clutching her purse. Then Eleanor dropped her hand.

At home, Frankie treated me with new respect. She approached me cautiously, the way you would someone who had survived a difficult illness, someone whose strength you weren't sure of. We didn't talk much, but she didn't question or harass me either.

Frankie and I had always agreed on one thing—that the most desirable feature of the room we shared was the window seat overlooking the back garden. As the older sibling, Frankie had claimed it as her right. After the fire, she took down the clothesline that divided our space and let me sit by the window whenever I wanted. She knew what I was watching for.

When several days had gone by and there was still no sign from Patrick, I crossed the lawn to the Carradays' kitchen.

Faline was working a ball of dough on the marble counter. When I came in, she didn't stop what she was doing or turn to look at me. A fine mist of flour hung in the air around her. She said, "You may as well know. Patrick have gone."

"Where?" In my mind, *gone* meant over the causeway, to the mainland. Maybe as far as Houston. "When will he be back?"

"Gone to Europe. You know, where Miz Rhetta live? His aunt. Patrick gone to school there."

"School?" I said. "But it's almost Christmas. School will be over in . . ." I paused, trying to see the calendar, to remember the dates.

Faline took her time rinsing her hands. Then she shook the drops off and reached for a towel. When she was done, she leaned back against the deep porcelain sink as if to steady herself. "This is something had to happen," she said. "You don't understand now. But you will one day. I'm sorry, baby."

It wasn't what she'd said—I was still struggling to work out what she meant—but the way she spoke, the words she chose, let me know we were talking about something terrible and final. "Don't cry now," Faline said. "You a strong girl. You got to be strong."

A few days later, Will Carraday's plane delivered me to the small, private airport outside Cleveland. There was snow on the ground when the plane landed. I had only the clothes I was wearing—too light for a Midwest winter. My grandmother, in zippered boots, waited at the edge of the tarmac. Her glasses were fogged with the cold. She touched my shoulder tentatively. "Your mother told me you were artistic," she said.

In my pocket I had a shoelace of Patrick's. He had given it to me one day at the beach to tie back my hair, and had walked around the rest of the afternoon with his tennis shoe flopping. Later I wore it around my wrist. Once my grandmother pointed to it. "Would you like me to wash that?" she asked.

I had some photos of him too, but they were blurred. Patrick would never sit still long enough to be photographed. Sometimes during that long winter in Ohio, I would take the snapshots out and look at them.

No one ever asked me if I missed Patrick, but if they had I wouldn't have known what to say. Missing someone sounded like something you could choose to do when you thought of it, when you had the inclination. Something you might talk about with friends. What I felt was more like the persistent, painful awareness of an arm or leg that was gone, the legacy of that kind of radical displacement. It was as though a piece of me had been cut away.

For a time the memories were vivid. Even hidden in the bedroom under the eaves of my grandmother's tidy house with its stone birdbath and chain-link fence, even there I could recall the damp wind, the immensity of sky, the flat, graphite Gulf. I could close my eyes and be on the beach again with Patrick. And for a time, I still believed what Islanders do—that if you look hard enough into the distance, you can see the thing you want most coming toward you.

Chapter 11

THE MORNING AFTER THE PARTY, I found Eleanor in the kitchen arranging her breakfast on a tray. An early riser, she had already been out and was snipping the stems of some yellow lantana. I wondered where she had found them. It was a peculiarity of Eleanor's that she didn't acknowledge ownership of anything that grew, and she had no reservations about raiding other people's flower beds.

"Pretty, don't you think?" she asked. "Harriet Kinkaid grows these. She has quite a successful garden." She folded a napkin and laid it next to her plate. "Harriet, wisely, grows what thrives here. Not everything does. It's a special environment." She glanced over to be sure I'd understood that she wasn't speaking only about flowers. "There's coffee made. And I bought fresh raisin bread."

It annoyed me to hear her hold forth about the Island. She was the Yankee. I had been born there, grown up on Galveston. I had more claim to understanding its peculiar requirements than she did. I didn't want any more of her reminders. "You said Patrick has a place of his own."

She looked up, eyes wide. "Yes," she said.

"Where is it?"

She paused, for a moment, considering. "Clare, it might be best if you and Patrick . . . He isn't the same, you know. He was burned. In the fire. He's badly scarred."

"I don't care."

"I understand. But have you thought about him? Maybe he does."

"I don't believe that. Patrick is probably the least vain person

I've ever met." I spoke with confidence, describing the Patrick I had known, but I couldn't be sure. We had weathered adolescence together—the year Patrick grew three inches and sprouted a tuft of hair on his chin, the summer my small, embarrassing breasts appeared. My feelings for him were not about his looks. But it was possible that Patrick had changed in more important ways.

"Remember, you were fourteen the last time you were together. Fourteen! Hardly more than a child."

"So?"

"Patrick has put a lot of things behind him. He may not want to go back there."

"I don't believe that."

"Did he write to you?"

I felt Eleanor's gaze on me but I looked away, out the window. "Patrick's not a letter writer," I said.

"Did he call?"

In the garden, a mockingbird shot upward, displaying white-tipped wings.

"Clare, I don't say this to hurt you. But those are the facts."

I didn't respond. I didn't know what to think. Patrick had never had to write or call. We were together daily. When I left the Island for my grandmother's house in Ohio, when he was sent to Europe, would he have known how to find me? Would he have known my grandmother's name? It was the 1970s. There was no Internet, no e-mail. I wanted to believe it was distance and circumstance that had kept us apart.

But Eleanor and I both knew that distances could evaporate, circumstances change, with the application of enough money. Carraday money.

Eleanor looked down at the tray in front of her. She made small adjustments to the plate, the flowers, the cup that held her coffee, the pitcher of hot milk. Once again, I felt the pull of her concentration.

Outside the mockingbird chattered an alarm. "I want to know where he lives," I said.

"He's sharing a house with Lowell Morgan out past Jamaica

Beach," Eleanor said. She picked up the tray. "Don't do something you'll regret." She left the kitchen.

I found Lowell Morgan's listing in the slim local directory. When I dialed, the phone rang for a long time. The someone who answered, finally, was a sleepy-sounding man whose voice I didn't recognize. "Are you Lowell Morgan?" I asked. He mumbled something. "Is Lowell there?"

"I don't think so," he said.

I had no idea what to say next. I hung up. Jamaica Beach wasn't far. It would be better, I decided, to drive there.

Outside, the breeze was up, and fast-moving clouds streamed across the sky. It was as if the world had gained speed overnight and was turning faster. The weight of the previous day's heat had lifted a little. The air was fresh, and it gave me a welcome feeling of clarity and purpose.

I took my camera. That was the part of myself I meant to feature when I encountered Patrick—the photographer, the serious professional. I had my story ready. If the whole thing felt a little like a role I was playing, well, when had that not been true? When had I ever truly believed in my own accomplishments? It had happened so suddenly, when I was still so young.

My Leica sat next to me on the front seat of the station wagon. From time to time I reached over and touched its metal skin. The camera was reassuringly solid and familiar, not at all like a prop.

I turned at Seawall Boulevard, where the tourists were already out. Pictures taken when the seawall was new, an engineering wonder, show the owners of carriages and of the first Model Ts dressed for an occasion, the men in suits and ties, the women in full skirts that swirl around their legs like foam. The beach extends behind them for half a mile.

Now the short stretch of sand was so packed and stirred it looked like dirt. In the years since its heroic construction, the seawall had disrupted the equilibrium of the shoreline and destroyed the naturally occurring beach. Foreign sand, darker and coarser than what was lost, had to be hauled in periodically by truck.

There were still a few grand hotels along the seawall with expensive cars conspicuously parked out front. But nearby were apartments whose paint had peeled like blistered skin, restaurants with fake thatch roofs, strip malls, gas stations. This was the least desirable beach, the place where people came who didn't know or couldn't afford better. People who spent the night illegally beside the piers or in one of the cheap motels behind the tattoo parlor.

People who couldn't swim.

Where the seawall ended the Island narrowed so that I could see both shores. Building in that part of the Island had begun modestly with improvisations, trailers raised up on stilts, and there were still a few mom-and-pop grocery stores that sold beer, ice, casting nets, and crabbing supplies. But change was coming—had come. I passed paved drives—Driftwood Court, Osprey Circle—leading to sales offices marked by smiling mermaids or oversize life preservers, the oddly eclectic iconography of beachfront real estate. As I drove, the houses on the Gulf side got noticeably larger. I passed a tall, white-columned colonial and an Italianate castle with a Range Rover parked in front.

On the bay side, toward the mud flats and away from the Gulf, there were fewer new houses. Next to a field of yellow daisies, I found a modest subdivision where pairs of plastic trash cans stood prominently on view. Some of the structures were no more than sheds with outside stairs leading to a second story.

Others were more imaginative, more expressive of their owners' convictions—domes that looked like divers' helmets on legs. Octagons and polyhedrons that must have been daringly futuristic when they were built.

The yards were neatly mowed and full of stuff—propane tanks and fishing gear, boats and boat trailers. Tubs of spackle and oddly shaped pieces of Sheetrock. Dozens of tired-looking houseplants on their own summer vacation. Everywhere, evidence of people dug deep into their own lives.

I parked across the street from Lowell Morgan's house, the one Patrick was sharing. It was unremarkable—white siding with a sagging porch running its length. Several of the stairs were missing. There was no bell, so I knocked on the door. When nothing happened, I knocked again, louder.

Someone called out, "Yeah, yeah, okay." A girl—she looked about twenty—in a Def Leppard T-shirt opened the aluminum storm door. Her bare legs were smooth and tan. "Shoot," she said, "I was asleep. I'm sorry I hollered at you. I thought you were my brother. He's coming to pick me up. Are you a friend of Lowell's? My alternator's shot."

"I'm sorry," I said.

"Come on in. Don't mind me. I'm not pulled together yet. Do you want something? A beer? Is that clock right? It's really ten thirty? Jeez Louise, I'm going to be so late. I got to get to work." She disappeared into the next room.

I called after her, "I'm looking for Patrick Carraday."

A horn blared outside. The girl ran back carrying a pair of red platform sandals. She was wearing a tiny jean skirt. She stopped briefly to tie her T-shirt above the waist. "I haven't seen him for a while." I heard the horn again. She yelled back, "I'm coming! Keep your darn pants on!" In a lower voice she said, "You're welcome to wait. Make yourself at home." She gestured toward the interior like a game-show hostess indicating a prize. The door banged shut behind her.

The room was small and disheveled, the scattered furniture mostly obscured by clothing and towels. An empty pizza box lay open on the floor in front of the TV. The ripe odor of garbage wafted in from the kitchen.

I went the other direction, toward the bedrooms. There were two, side by side, both equally chaotic—beds tousled, floors strewn. I stepped into the first and gingerly picked up a sweatshirt, then a pair of surfer shorts. They might have belonged to anyone. I opened the top drawer of the dresser, but found only some tattered issues of *Road & Track* and several unmatched socks. I understood that it was hopeless. I would learn nothing there, and there was no way to know when Patrick might return.

I felt myself slipping into sadness, and I realized then how much I had invested in our reunion. When I was growing up, Patrick's sudden arrivals had rescued me from my own dark thoughts. Was I counting on him to do that now? Surely, given all that had happened, it was too much to ask of anyone.

I went back down the stairs to the car. I put the key into the ignition, but when I felt the upholstery warm against my back, my arms dropped off the steering wheel. I hadn't slept much the night before, just short periods of unconsciousness bracketed by uneasy dreams.

I woke to find a man leaning in the window. At first I thought it was Patrick, and my heart leaped. But his face was clean-shaven, the skin ruddy and unmarked. There were no scars on his hands or arms. Then I thought it might be Lowell Morgan, until I realized he was too young.

It has been said that any use of the camera is aggressive. Without thinking, I reached down, picked up my Leica, and pointed the lens at him. At the sound of the shutter, he drew back until he stood at least ten feet off, where I could see him clearly. There was nothing threatening about him. I lowered the camera.

"Ma'am," he said, "you think you could move your vehicle? So we can get by?" I looked beyond him to where his wife stood, her hand raised, shielding her eyes. Two small children in bathing suits, a girl and a boy, clung to her thighs. Folded lawn chairs rested against the walls and stairs. A tricycle lay overturned in the grass near a barbecue grill.

I saw that I'd partially blocked what was in fact a sandy driveway. "Of course," I said. I pulled out and watched the car dipping and swaying along the road.

I tried not to think about Bailey, but it was too much for me, the deserted yard with its scattered reminders of family life. I began to cry.

I don't know how long I sat there, but eventually I shook myself and pushed my hair out of my face. I put my hand on my Leica and it steadied me.

The sky had clouded over, conditions were good. I told myself that since I'd driven out, I might at least photograph some of the beach houses. I recalled one that was perfectly round, like a cooking pot, its sheet-metal walls pocked and stained. The front door, eight feet aboveground, was padlocked. An experiment that hadn't quite worked.

The house stood forlornly in a field of tall grass. I got out and walked around it, pressing the shutter now and then, without ever feeling I'd captured anything important.

It was almost too easy. With Bailey in tow, I'd had to photograph in a new way. I had to manage her things—the diaper bag, the one gluey pacifier she couldn't do without—as well as a camera and lenses. I made shorter trips and sometimes took the stroller. And I learned to wait for the moment when I became so much a part of my surroundings—just another young mother with messy hair and food stains on her clothes, riding the subway, or sitting on a bench—that I was forgotten while people's lives unfolded in front of me.

I wondered where the family I'd talked to had gone. Probably to one of the pocket parks, where there would be showers, cold drinks, and other kids to play with. I got back in the car and drove slowly along the beach road. By now they would be staking out their spot together, spreading their towels and angling the umbrella just so. When I came to the first park entrance, I turned in.

The park attendant said, "D.C. plates. You're a long way from home."

"Not really. I'm BOI." I handed him a couple of bills.

"I'm IBC." He meant Islander by choice. "Moved down here awhile back from Omaha."

"How do you like it?" I asked.

"I like it fine. The weather. I like it hot. The water. It was supposed to be a vacation, but I never went back. I like the life. Put this on your windshield." He handed me a numbered square.

I nodded and smiled. The Island was often a point of no return.

The roll of the breakers rose to meet me as I walked down toward the shore, the sound of the Gulf giving up tokens from its store of strange things. The sand was not postcard white but buff-colored, fine and soft as face powder. Everywhere there were children, families. Grandmothers with their hair in rollers sitting next to portable cots. Fathers in baggy shorts chasing kids in the shallows and tossing them in the surf.

My family had never spent much time at the beach. My father was a redhead and burned easily, so he only went there when there was a special bird to see. The Island schools were more likely to take kids on field trips to places where there were plenty of bathrooms and a gift shop full of items that were safe in every sense of the word. Along the shore you never knew what you were going to find.

As if on cue, something white and crumpled revealed itself ahead of me on the sand. Was it a skeleton or a plastic bag? A fish head or a cast-off T-shirt? Or something awful, something I had yet to imagine?

I didn't want to find out. When I stopped and turned back, I saw that the sun was already low in the sky. Near the tide line, a gull was worrying a strand of seaweed, and I wondered if that was what my searching had amounted to. The day that had begun so promisingly was more than half over, and I'd achieved nothing.

I recalled my father then, a notebook in his lap, extending his arm and the palm of his hand, so that his gesture seemed to me less like shielding his face than an attempt to block the light. I could hear him saying, *The beach is for idiots, people who have no way to engage their minds.*

At the park entrance, the attendant was gone. Traffic on the beach road had picked up, people were going the other way now, into town for a drink, for dinner. I pulled out too quickly, spraying sand and just missing a black truck that was speeding past. The driver swerved and hit the horn, hard, as the two dogs in the back skidded and bounced against the side of the truck bed. I heard their toenails scraping metal.

Chapter 12

AT THE HOUSE, ELEANOR WAS WAITING downstairs. She looked up from the mail she was sorting. "Did you visit the archive?" she asked.

"Not yet." I tried to sound carefree, like a vacationer. "I drove around. Looked at things. Took some photos."

"Yes?" She gazed at me inquiringly.

"Out past the seawall." I hadn't planned to tell her, but I found I wanted to. I wanted to make her understand that I could go where I pleased. "I drove out to Jamaica Beach. And beyond."

I'd expected her to protest. Instead she asked, "And what did you find?"

It came to me with renewed force that I'd learned nothing. I shrugged. "I met one of Patrick's friends."

She nodded. "Don't forget," she said, "we have dinner tonight with your sister and Stephen. You'll want to change, I imagine." She set the mail down on the hall table, and I saw that she was wearing a bracelet, a heavy gold cuff that looked as if it might be antique. My father had not approved of expensive jewelry.

I went up to my room and stirred the few clothes I'd tossed into the closet, hoping that something would materialize, but the miscellaneous arms and legs hung limp and disobliging. I sat down heavily on the bed.

Some people, like Frankie and my father, are born knowing things. The rest of us have to discover them for ourselves. For me, growing up, that had meant a series of painful experiments carried out in full view of the Island. Frankie had seen and commented on them all. It was often said that she was like my father. And they were in many ways similar—active, competent, matter-of-fact.

Frankie had done well in school, and she brought home trophies, gold-plated figures on tall mountings that cluttered her bookcase. Their faces were smooth metal with rounded protrusions for noses and hollows where their eyes should have been. I said once, "I think it's creepy that they all look the same." She didn't bother to respond. That summer she had begun wearing sandals with little heels and had perfected a silent gesture of dismissal, a way of flipping her smooth, strawberry blond hair with her hand.

I was intensely curious, but the subjects that drew me were not taught in school, and the questions I wanted to ask were often hard to articulate. How many times had I heard Frankie echo me in her smart-girl, classroom voice for my father's entertainment? It was a regular occurrence at family meals—my father rolling his eyes above the gold rim of his coffee cup while Frankie choked into her wadded-up napkin.

Eleanor never intervened. She was there, and yet removed, her face in profile like the face on a coin, her inner glow dimmed. I wondered suddenly if that was the price of her composure. Had she been obliged to close down some region of herself permanently in order to preserve it? I thought about the effort that must have required.

I hadn't cared that Frankie called me a snoop. It was my way of getting answers without risking ridicule. Now, hearing voices, I walked quietly down the hall to the bedroom we had shared. The window seat was still an ideal vantage point—from it I could see everyone who came and went.

In the garden below, Frankie and her husband, Stephen, sat with Eleanor. From above, I could see down the front of my mother's summer dress, and it dawned on me that this perspective, featuring her breasts, was the one a man—my father or Will Carraday—would have. I could see that Frankie's hair, which she wore short now, was graying at the roots, and the fact that she had lost the natural advantage of her dramatic coloring made her seem unexpectedly vulnerable.

Frankie had never been beautiful exactly, but as a girl she had given off a bright, hard shine that to me perfectly expressed the virtues I lacked. At the same time, she had always been scornful of her good looks, as though any consideration of physical appearance was beneath her. This attitude she shared with my father, along with the freckles she had inherited. Hers were browner and fewer, a spray across her nose and cheeks.

I slid my fingers under the curved brass fittings and opened the window a crack, just enough to be able to hear the conversation going on below.

Stephen was describing a difficult patient. Frankie looked at him with barely concealed impatience, one foot swinging. She turned to Eleanor. "Before she comes down, I want to know. Why is she here?"

"I take it you mean your sister? She has a job to do." Eleanor leaned back slowly and rested her hands on the arms of her chair. She regarded Frankie intently. She seemed to be willing her into repose.

Frankie shook her head. "She's been away a long time. There must be something else."

"If you think so, why don't you ask her?"

Frowning, Frankie began to pleat the edge of her cocktail napkin. "Because she'll just space out and go silent the way she does when she doesn't want to deal with something." She tossed the napkin on the table. "There's a man involved, of course. The one at the party? Oh, I heard. Nothing new there."

"For heaven's sake. Clare is married. She'll be going back to Michael when she's finished with the exhibition."

"Is that what you think?"

Eleanor sat forward. "Frances, listen to me. It's been hard for them, what happened to Bailey. But they'll get on with their life together. They'll make accommodations. People do." She looked off into the darkening garden. "Relationships grow and change. Sometimes they take on forms you don't expect." She rotated the ice in her glass with one finger. Finally she said, "Maybe you two can see each other differently now that you're adults. Anyway, sometimes it's better not to know everything."

I had shared a room with Frankie for twelve years, and I understood that every fiber of her being strained to reject this thought. And yet she sat silent, her head bent.

Frankie had finished high school a year early. In college she majored in biochemistry and did well enough to be accepted into medical school on her first try. She had always seemed determined to live her life as fast as possible. So it was no surprise, really, that she now looked older than her years.

Stephen treated renal dialysis patients. Frankie was a surgeon. They had met when he rented the alley house behind ours for a semester. Frankie had miscarried twice that I knew of. There was a time when I took pleasure in the fact that there was something she wanted that she couldn't have as a matter of course. Now that satisfaction was gone. What I felt was not sympathy exactly, we were too far apart. Frankie had not been kind to me. But she had been capable and resolute, and somehow I had counted on that.

I knew Frankie and Stephen were considering adopting. It was surely a last resort, involving what my father called "mystery DNA." I slid the window closed.

Downstairs, Stephen was in the kitchen refilling drinks. He hugged me and said, "You look well." It was what he always said, and I suppose he meant it, given that he spent most of his time with people in various stages of kidney failure. He was fair, like Frankie, and his coloring also seemed to have faded over time, so that now he looked like an old Polaroid of the boy he had once been. With his mouth closed, he was still handsome. But when he spoke, you saw that his upper lip was a little too short, his front teeth too much in evidence. He wore his pants belted at the waist. It was easy to imagine what he would look like in another ten years.

"Oh, there you are." Frankie was in the doorway. She reached for one of the glasses. "I'll take mine, thanks." She looked at Stephen. "You can give that to Eleanor."

He smiled and went outside as directed, and I wondered whether Frankie knew how little attention he actually paid to her bossing.

She turned and leaned back against the counter. "You haven't changed," she said. She was wearing black pants, a boxy linen shirt, and a few pieces of chunky silver jewelry, a look that characterized her as attractive but not frivolous. She had always worn her clothes as though they were the uniform of whatever group she currently belonged to—popular teenage girls, serious medical students. Now she was a busy professional person, not someone who would spend time choosing clothes.

"Who did you dress up for?" she asked. "Not Stephen, I hope. It's a complete waste of time."

I began to respond, but she held up one hand. "Do you really not understand how you come across?"

I thought then of the one-sided conversations we'd had during our teens. Frankie liked to display her knowledge and I was a ready audience, so she was the one who talked to me about sex. First, the biological facts. Later, the whole taxonomy of high-school dating. I understood that there was a system of clearly defined rules and entitlements, but I could never recall the specifics. *If he does this, you let him do that.* What I remembered was her irritation. *Do you really not understand?*

My only experience with boys had been with Patrick, and the things we did together—exploring vacant houses and setting fires on the beach—I knew enough not to mention. I remember that I asked Frankie once, "How do you know when you're on a date?," a question she found hilarious and duly repeated at the dinner table.

As if she could read my mind, Frankie said, "I was awful to you sometimes." She looked down at the floor. Twilight was seeping into the kitchen. The moving blades of the ceiling fan cast shadows on the high walls and lifted a few fine hairs at the crown of her head. "I wanted his approval."

We both knew she was talking about our father. "Not that it's any excuse. He made it clear which behaviors would be rewarded. I didn't appreciate then what it took to resist him."

I was stunned. "You mean me? But I didn't resist him," I said. "I just—"

"You stood up to him! You did what you wanted. You had no one to speak up for you, and still . . . I just went along and went along until . . . I don't know if I even wanted to go to medical school. Or if I wanted to be a doctor. It's what I am. And it's fine. Mostly I enjoy my practice. Surgery is better than a lot of things. Most of the time, it feels constructive. But it wasn't my choice. It was decided for me. It was as if his way of being was not just the best but the only way, and the finest thing I could hope for was to be part of it."

Frankie paused. Then she said, "You know, I thought about studying music." She looked down at her fingers, spread and flexed them. "That was as far as I got. I never even tried to apply to a conservatory. Because what he told me was, 'It's wonderful to have a musical wife.' Making it clear that if I went on playing, that was what I could expect to be, that lesser thing. Whatever has happened, at least you've made your own choices."

"I think you're giving me too much credit. I did a lot of stupid, dangerous stuff trying to . . . I suppose I was trying to assert myself."

Frankie had always been competitive. Even now she couldn't help saying, "You weren't the only one who did dangerous things. Remember the time I jumped out the window into the tree at the Hildebrandts'?"

I did. When he heard about it, all my father said was, "Frankie would have made a fine boy."

She went on. "I did it because I wanted his endorsement. And he gave it. He gave it! I got congratulated for doing the same things that would have gotten you into trouble. Does that make any sense?" She looked up and her voice was hoarse. "Is that what parents do?"

I saw that there were tears in her eyes. She brushed at them with the backs of her hands. "I should have been on your side. I know that now." Then her tone changed. "Look at you. God, what a getup," she said. "The queen of the Gypsies."

In the past, I would have shot back a comment of my own. But I couldn't do it to this new and unfamiliar Frankie, who not only looked but behaved differently. Then I realized with a rush why she tolerated Eleanor's prodding, why she was willing to say what she never had before. And I knew that Frankie would do anything, make any sacrifice, if she could find and undo the one wrong thing that had made everything else go wrong, the transgression that had left her child-less. I understood that she blamed herself for what had not taken place, just as I blamed myself for what had. At last, we'd found something in common.

"Are you going to join us, you two?" Eleanor called.

We walked out to where four cast-iron chairs stood around a low table. Eleanor was trimming roses, angling the stems, pulling off extra leaves, placing the flowers in a vase. She seemed to know exactly how to position each one, and as we watched an arrangement took shape.

I'd never cared much for roses. They made me think of the kind of movies Aunt Syvvie liked, where the heroine wears too much red lipstick and the sound track is all swelling strings. But these were different—loose, pretty. Fragrant.

A door slammed and I heard muffled shouting. Eleanor sighed. "Trouble in paradise," she said, tilting her head in the direction of the neighbors. "The young parents. I think they're having a hard time adjusting." Stephen's expression didn't alter, he still wore his habitual smile, but his face seemed to stiffen. Frankie began to search for something in her purse. Frankie had endometriosis, that was the reason she and Stephen had trouble conceiving. It must have been disconcerting for her. Frankie's life, her success, had been about having the right answer. Now, as always, she had it, but it did her no good at all.

"We could have put you up," Eleanor went on smoothly. I understood that "we" meant Eleanor and Will. That their relationship was acknowledged and accepted.

"Thanks, but we're fine where we are," Frankie answered.

"Where is that?" I asked.

"We have a condo out past Stewart Beach where we stay when we come down," said Frankie. "Once you get beyond the beach parking lot, it's amazingly peaceful, even this time of year."

"You could have had the cottage to yourselves. That would have been peaceful."

Stephen groaned. "Except for the memories of med school. Calls every fifteen minutes from the ICU staff, just when you think you're going back to sleep."

"That was at the hospital," Frankie pointed out. "Not here."

"You didn't like med school?" I asked.

"Oh well," Stephen said. "You live through it."

Frankie laughed. "I think you've scandalized her." She turned to me. "You know what Stephen said the first time I met him? We were eating lunch in the cafeteria, six or seven of us, all first-years, and he said, 'I think I've made a mistake going into medicine. I had no idea there were so many terrible diseases.'"

"I wasn't the gunner your sister was," Stephen said.

"It was what we were all thinking," Frankie said. "You were the only one who was willing to say it." Stephen ran his hand gently along her forearm.

They might be unhappy about their childlessness, but I didn't sense any uninhabited space between them, no wasteland like the one that had sprung up between Michael and me. I wondered what it felt like to want a child as they did, abstractly, whether their desire might be purer than my hunger for Bailey. Flesh of my flesh.

I thought then that I had no real understanding of Frankie's marriage or my parents' or even my own. What did that mean? That marriage was generally unfathomable? Or that there was a mystery at its core, one that other people shared, that I still knew nothing about?

"So Clare," Stephen asked, "how is the research going?" When I didn't respond, he prompted, "For the exhibition?"

I didn't want to admit that I hadn't begun or describe how I'd spent the day. So it was just as well that Tyler Henry strolled in then from the direction of the alley. He didn't call out, and his khaki pants were the first thing I saw emerging out of the dusk. Stephen jumped up to look for another chair, Frankie straightened and put on a formal countenance, Eleanor waved him over.

Ty sat down next to Eleanor. He indicated the vase. "These are beautiful. You were educating me about growing roses. You said the climate makes it difficult. Who would know?"

"Look." Eleanor picked up a discarded leaf. On its smooth surface was a round, black spot. "This is what happens. It's futile to try and grow roses here."

"But you do."

"I don't actually. Will is the one with the rose garden. He likes to take on the impossible. There." She set the clippers down and relaxed. I saw the others sit back too.

"So Will is a gardener?" Ty asked.

"He *has* a gardener," Frankie corrected him. "Don't imagine Will Carraday doing any actual digging. He just enjoys his flowers. Like God. What's that passage in Genesis? God walking in the garden in the cool of the day?"

"I'm sure he'd be flattered by the comparison," Eleanor said.

Frankie's comment reminded me of my father. He hadn't approved of Will's money or his interests—art, architecture, gardens—either. My father said once, of Will, "I suppose he's some kind of aesthete." I didn't know yet what the word meant, but I sensed that coming from my father, it was a reproach.

Ty said, "I went by the house, and they told me he'd already left. I thought he might be here." He made it sound perfectly natural. Clearly Ty was capable of fitting in. He would do well in Galveston. He laid a manila folder on the table. It was the same color as his khakis, which explained why I hadn't noticed it.

"Will is out of town," Eleanor said. She named the residential facility on the East Coast where Catherine lived. "He has a daughter there. She's disabled. She can't look after herself or communicate. Something went wrong when she was very small. She has to be attended to at all times, or she'll do herself an injury. She doesn't even know him, but he visits every month anyway." I saw her glance in Frankie's direction. Was she thinking there were worse things than being childless?

Frankie said brightly, "He has his own plane, so don't imagine him waiting at the airport, standing in line, dragging a suitcase like the rest of us. His flight never gets canceled." Again it seemed to me that Frankie was voicing my father's opinion. But her words didn't have the weight of his. They seemed to drift away and disappear into the garden.

"Frances." We were adults, but there were limits, still, to what Eleanor would put up with from either of us.

"I didn't know there was a daughter. I've met his son," Ty said. "Patrick." The silence was deafening. No one wanted to be the first to talk about Patrick in my presence, certainly not in front of a guest. Frankie might have said something, but she had been reprimanded. Now she stared up at the lighted windows of the Carraday house, her face a deliberate blank. I waited. "He works at the bank," Ty said.

It was Stephen who spoke first. "Patrick has been in a lot of scrapes." It was like him to cast Patrick's troubles as the shortcomings of a high-spirited boy.

"He works at the bank?" I asked.

"In the trust department."

Frankie couldn't resist. "I'm sure Ty knows the truth. He must! Patrick is a glorified errand boy. He's never held a real job, and I doubt he could. The trust department—that's droll. Word is, he spends more time at Lafitte's. That's where his friends are."

"Frances, was that necessary?" Eleanor turned to Ty. "You'll have to forgive us. We're a little on edge tonight."

Frankie said, "I don't know why we always have to cover for Patrick. To pretend he's still finding himself." She turned to Ty. "Let me tell you a story about him. One night he and this drinking buddy of his, Lowell Morgan, go out together and get wasted. Then they take Lowell's car out to the west end of the Island to see how fast it will go. Lowell's driving, but not fast enough for Patrick, who reaches over and puts his foot on top of Lowell's and pushes down as hard as he can. Lowell's yelling, but Patrick won't quit. They're out where the paved road ends. So Lowell basically has a choice between driving into the marsh or driving onto the beach. He knows Patrick's history, and neither of those options seems like a good one, so he twists the wheel and crashes into the side of a beach house and takes out two of the pilings. When the owner comes out, Patrick reaches into his pocket and hands him seven thousand dollars that he just happens to have on him." Frankie sat back. "Patrick is never going to find himself," she said. "He's a grown man and the only place he's looking is at the bottom of a bottle."

"Listen to you," Faline said. "Drive down from Houston and think you know all about it." She was crossing the lawn, carrying something in a baking dish covered with a towel. She turned to Ty. "You fortunate I happened to be making cobbler, or you wouldn't be getting much of a supper tonight. Little bit of cold meat."

"Will you stay?" Eleanor asked Ty. "I don't know why you'd want to, with all this squabbling. Still, you're welcome to join us. It's nothing elaborate. But really, there is plenty. We're going to eat out here."

Faline said, "He probably going elsewhere, get him some real food." She turned and made for the steps.

I followed Faline into the kitchen. She set the dish down and removed the towel with a flourish. "Too bad your mama never could learn to bake." Faline scorned the kind of meals we had eaten all our lives—roast meat, plain vegetables, fresh fruit. She squinted at the chicken resting modestly on its platter, the salad in its wooden bowl. "You want food to taste good, you got to *do* something to it. Well," she said, "I guess you can manage." She patted my shoulder. "You come by at a decent hour, bring my dish."

I opened one cupboard, then another, and found colorful pottery plates. I counted out knives and forks. I looked out the window and saw that Ty's chair was empty. I wondered if he had gone. But when I turned to look for the napkins, he was standing just behind me. He held out the manila folder. "I wanted to show you this. It's the painting Will mentioned. The one in the Louvre? I thought he'd be interested. I was going to give it to him."

I nodded. It was understandable. Ty, in his new position, wanting to make a good impression. People were always trying to do things for Will. I didn't know how to explain that where Will was concerned there was no opportunity for favors, no interval between the wish and its realization. If Will wanted something done, it happened. If he'd wanted to see the painting, he would have. If he hadn't seen the painting, it was because he didn't care to.

Frankie's sandals clattered on the wood floor. "Are we going to eat anytime soon?" she asked. "Some of us are hungry. You two can carry on later."

Ty took the chicken in one hand, the salad in the other.

"Nobody's carrying on," I said.

"Huh," said Frankie. She reached one hand up toward her shoulder, but the thick, bright hair was gone. The gesture didn't work anymore.

Chapter 13

DINNER ENDED QUIETLY. The next morning I stayed in bed until Eleanor was back in her room with her breakfast tray, then went down to the kitchen. I drank some milk from the waxy beak of a carton in the refrigerator. There was a smiling cow on one side and a blurry photo of a missing child on the other.

I peeled a banana and walked around while I ate, opening and closing cupboards. Frankie would have said *snooping*. There were the plates and dishes I remembered, white with a gold rim, the ice-tea glasses with their delicate curved handles. I don't know what I expected to find, what revelation I hoped for, there was nothing mysterious about any of it. I leaned under the sink to throw away the banana peel, and there in the trash was Ty's manila folder, streaked and smelling of salad dressing but otherwise unharmed.

I heard footsteps upstairs. I took the folder with me and walked outside to where the station wagon was parked down the street.

There was no sidewalk in the sense that most people understand it. Smooth concrete might extend for thirty feet, only to erupt suddenly where old, broken slabs thrust upward like the prows of sinking ships, the spaces between them lively with weeds. There were stretches of homemade pebble aggregate pocked with bits of colored glass. There were places where the sidewalk disappeared, where you made your way through moss and dirt on stepping-stones. It was only after I had lived in other places that I understood how eccentric this mixture of surfaces was and how expressive of the Island's intractability.

Few tourists were out. Mostly I saw people going to work at the same kinds of jobs that exist everywhere. The women had their hair under control—pulled up or back and secured against the wind. The men wore real shoes and carried briefcases.

I thought then of my father and the Island summer, how he disliked and ignored it. As far as possible, he kept to his regular routine, even wearing the same clothes—the long-sleeved dress shirt, the bow tie, the suit jacket (in the summer it was seersucker, in the winter solid dark blue) he carried over one arm. He had nothing but contempt for the tourists with their bursts of uncontrolled behavior, their perplexing inability to swim.

Every year, there was either a drowning or a dramatic rescue. My father was indifferent as to which. "They understand that this is an island, surely. Why do they go into the ocean if they can't swim?" he would say. He ridiculed the pamphlets distributed by the sheriff's department. "Listen to this. This really is what it says: 'Water may contain oxygen, but it's not usable by the human respiratory system.' Do people have to be told that they can't breathe water?"

Drowning was something he explained in detail to us, his daughters. We knew about oxygen starvation and panic. We also knew that many near-drowning victims had been interviewed about their experience. "Do you know what their last thought usually is?" my father would ask. He would pause and scrape the bowl of his pipe with an instrument especially designed for that purpose, giving us plenty of time to consider. "They are ashamed. They are ashamed at having been stupid enough to drown."

THE LIBRARY THAT HOUSED THE PHOTO ARCHIVE was only a few blocks away. Built in the years immediately following the Great Hurricane, it was solid but mournful. The carved stone wreaths above the windows had a memorial air, as though the architects couldn't help thinking about that autumn when cremation fires all along the Island burned so high they were visible from the mainland and the wind carried with it charred bits of bone and singed hair.

I went inside. The once generous rooms had been divided by fiberboard partitions, the original furniture replaced by a few armless chairs that were geometrically shaped to discourage lingering. Everything that was new assaulted the scale and purpose of the original space. It was as though the building had been overrun by a race of smaller, meaner people.

I took the elevator to the third floor, where a glass wall marked off the special collections. Behind the glass, a couple of archivists moved back and forth in silence like fish in a tank. Broad wooden tables awaited anyone interested in viewing the holdings. They were all vacant.

If the man seated at the reception desk saw or heard me, he didn't let on. "Hello," I said. "I'm Clare Porterfield. I'm here to see the photo archive."

He was writing on a yellow legal pad. Looking up, he said, "Oh yes. You're from New York."

"Actually, I'm BOI," I said. "I grew up here. The gallery, Beckmann-Robler, where I show, is in New York."

"Oh," he said, "where you *show*." His tone was carefully calibrated, not quite derisive. His expression didn't change. "Which photos do you want to see?" His twill jacket was not too tight exactly, but it lacked the ease a real flesh-and-blood person would require. He stood then, and I saw that his pants also were tailored as though for a figure that would never run or sprawl or even eat a heavy meal. He made me think of a mannequin in a department-store window, the old-fashioned, unconvincing kind whose fingers were fused together.

He opened a drawer and took out a clipboard with a printed sheet on it. The date, May 25, 1990, was handwritten across the top. "You have to sign in first. Then you have to request them by box number."

I took the clipboard and filled in my name and Eleanor's address and phone number. I lifted the top sheet and looked underneath at the one from the day before. And the day before that. There were no other names. "I'll take boxes one through four," I said.

He shook his head again. Somehow I knew he was enjoying himself. "You can view one box at a time."

I took a deep breath. On the sheet, I wrote "Box 1." I handed him back the clipboard. "So," I said, "what's next?"

He nodded toward the first of the tables, the one nearest his desk. Clearly, he meant to keep an eye on me. Given the absence of other visitors, it wouldn't be difficult. "You are required to wear gloves when you handle the materials," he said. "I'll get them. But first, you'll have to check *that*." He pointed at my Leica. His fingers were white, tapered, perfectly normal.

My hand went instinctively to the camera. "Where?" I asked.

"Downstairs. There are lockers." His face seemed to brighten at the thought of my having to retrace my steps.

It's funny that the same set of traits that makes you a difficult child—a stubborn refusal to cooperate, a failure to grasp the niceties of social exchange—are the ones that enable you to succeed as an adult in a profession, like mine, without many rules. I planted my feet on the gray carpet. "No," I said.

He listed a little, as though he'd stepped on something sharp and sat down in his chair.

"Is there a problem?" A woman strode through the glass door. She turned to me. "Ms. Porterfield?" If she hadn't so clearly been in charge, I would have wondered what she was doing there. No crocheted sweater, no glasses attached by little rubber loops to a chain around her neck. Her short hair was stylishly cut. And her tailored dress would have been just right in a corporate office. She looked at her colleague reproachfully. "We've been asked to extend every courtesy." She turned to me. "You don't need to sign in. Where would you be most comfortable?" I chose one of the middle tables, not too near the reception desk, not so far away that the mannequin would think he'd made an impression.

The librarian's name was Gwen. Thanks to Will, she said, I would have access to all the photo files, as many as I wanted at one time. A place to hold out the pictures I was reviewing. A cataloguer assigned to me for the duration of the project, to fetch and carry, to replace those images I no longer wanted.

It seemed to me that she used Will's name more often than necessary, and that when she did, her face lost some of its professional polish and took on an irritating, dazzled look. As she talked, she stroked the bare, lightly tanned skin of her upper arm.

For each acid-free cardboard box there was an index, but it was of limited use since there was no way to tell whether an image was any good without actually looking at it. I glanced quickly at the contents of one box, then another, and as I did, I felt a ripple of excitement.

The Island's love affair with itself went back well over a century. There were photos of all kinds—portraits, architectural images, interiors, landscapes, street scenes, beach scenes. There were aerial photos and shots taken from the water. There were even a certain number of self-conscious and mostly silly art photographs. And of course there were the images dating from the days and weeks after the Great Hurricane.

I moved through the prints quickly until one caught my eye.

It showed a group of ranch hands leaning against a fence. They were young, still in their late teens, their faces soft. Their clothes had the look of hand-me-downs. Half of them wore not boots but plain lace-up shoes. Two of them were black. Their hats were articles of use, uniformly worn and shapeless. There were no horses in the photo. The horses they rode would have belonged to the family that owned the land. Probably the same family that owned the land today. I thought of my conversation with Ty. What the photo showed was not what you saw in movies.

I worked for about an hour, setting aside half a dozen photos.

Then I came to an image of someone, a boy it seemed, lying on a blanket at the edge of a gravel path. His face was hidden. Only his body in dark clothing was plainly visible. One of the boy's pants legs was rolled up to reveal a slim white calf and the unprotected sole of his bare foot. I looked back at the box for identification. It was labeled, simply, DOMESTIC. I turned the photo over. There was nothing on the back. I looked at it again. Why didn't it show his face?

In a famous photo from the Depression, a child, not much more than a baby, lies on a pair of thin pillows, his face and upper body covered by a flour sack. The child's right foot is wrapped in a bandage. Is he breathing, or not? Asleep, or dead? The image doesn't tell you. It's only when you know that the boy is napping, that the flour sack is there to keep the flies away, that you finally exhale, gratefully. *He's alive.*

What if the facts were different? If you knew that the flour sack was a makeshift shroud? It would be another photo entirely.

I could look again and again at the boy in the grass, and still not know for certain what I was seeing. I put the print aside. I told myself that his pose was just that. A pose. Part of a game.

But my heart was jolting in my chest. I must have moved abruptly. The man at the desk looked up. I stood, jostled my way out of the heavy chair, and made for the door. He got up too. "You're leaving? Are you coming back?"

I nodded. I knew he wanted me to tell him what to do with the piles I'd made, the notes spread across the table.

"When?"

If I'd been able to speak, I would have told him I had no idea.

Outside, I walked without paying much attention to where I was going. What mattered was putting distance between myself and the thing I couldn't bear to see.

I walked quickly, but it was almost noon and the air was heavy, tropical. I could feel the heat of the pavement through my sandals. I began to sweat, and I slowed my pace. *Breathe,* I told myself. With each block the crowd grew, and I realized I was approaching the Strand. I thought with relief that it would be easy to lose myself there.

Once the Strand had been Galveston's business district, the biggest center of banking and finance between San Francisco and New Orleans. Now it was a busy tourist site, and the brick and cast-iron buildings housed restaurants and stores. Streetcars rang their bells as they swung around corners. Open carriages ferried customers to and from the parking lots.

Most of the exteriors remained much as they had been a hundred years ago. The decline in the Island's fortunes had, paradoxically, saved the old buildings. Now the chief thing the Island produced was new versions of its colorful past for the entertainment of summer visitors.

In the places where the high-Victorian architectural detail had been lost, the surfaces had been cleverly painted with faux moldings and cornices. None of the sightseers seemed to notice any difference. Glassy-eyed, they surged along the broad sidewalks or collapsed onto the deep curb where they sat, dazed with humidity and shopping.

The Strand catered to everyone. There were shops selling rare maps and ship models that took years to build. And there were noisy, barnlike spaces that smelled of stale beer and ganja and offered the kind of souvenirs you find only at the beach.

Chief among these were items decorated with shells—now mostly imported from the Philippines and dyed unnatural colors or lacquered to a high, synthetic gloss. As always, I was struck by the terrible ingenuity of these things—the night-lights with their eerie radiance, the planters in bizarre shapes.

There was also that category of objects that surfaces persistently in resort towns everywhere. The T-shirts emblazoned with the same unfunny tag lines that have distinguished them for years. These came in tiny sizes, as well as XXL, and it depressed me to think of children being made to wear them. There were ashtrays that encouraged guests to SMOKE DOPE! and ceramic mugs shaped like breasts with red-tipped nipples you could drink from. I always wondered what the purchasers did with these things when they got home, since I never saw them anywhere else. Probably they disappeared quietly along with the maps and brochures that had seemed so indispensable just days before.

The Strand was a hodgepodge of tastes, everything tossed together, and it occurred to me that the display along the street was like the beach, where the waves deposited, along with tiny, perfect lightning whelks, aluminum cans and used condoms.

I let myself be carried forward by the crowd. The doors of the shops were open, and as I passed by different things spilled out—loud

music, the odor of spicy food. Every so often, I encountered a welcome gust of chilled air. I stopped and fanned myself.

Up the street a little way I saw a familiar head of silvery hair. Today
it was arranged in a long braid that swayed when Harriet Kinkaid
walked. I remembered her friendliness, her laugh. She had encouraged me to visit her. I saw her go into a store and hurried to catch up.

The air inside was thick with the too-sweet smells of potpourri
and candles. At a table, some vacationers were exclaiming over the
merchandise. One of them waved something and called out to her
friend. "It isn't any bigger than my hand," she said.

The woman was holding a shoe, one of a dozen or so that were part
of a display. Most of them were decorative only. But the one she was
holding was an antique, what we would probably call a boot, with a
double row of eyelets and laces up the front. It was made of kidskin,
softened a little with age. The dainty, curved heel was slightly worn. It
was small, but too narrow, surely, for a child.

The shoppers moved on, and I edged closer.

I tried to flex the rigid sole of the boot. I tapped it against the
table. I thought of Stella. Of the sound her feet would have made as
she picked her way across the brick sidewalk to her father's office,
ducking in out of the heat.

She shades her eyes as the young architect, just leaving, steps out
into the sunny street. The light glints off the gold cuff links that were
his father's and reveals the splendid whiteness of his collar and cuffs.
He has two sets, and every night he washes one in a basin in his room
at the boardinghouse on Postoffice Street. It's not quite the thing, the
neighborhood he's living in—there are too many ladies lounging with
their hair down on the front porches in the middle of the day for it to
be quite respectable. But it's only temporary, he's sure of that.

He doesn't really see the young woman as she passes. He has an
impression of fair skin and lavender water, a rustling skirt, a glimpse
of petticoat. His head is still full of the plans he carries rolled under
one arm. This is his biggest job yet, the kind of opportunity that signals the beginning of a career. The client, a man with red jowls and
a watch chain across his vest, envisions a brick-and-limestone for-

tress. He will spend what is necessary to get it, without taking pleasure either in the spending or in the result. But Henry Durand, for all his ambition, has a romantic streak, something he inherited along with the cuff links, and cannot quite suppress, although he knows it is not modern.

The house in his mind's eye is a castle, with turrets and chimneys, a spiraling stair to the second floor. It's only then, as he adds a balcony, that a young woman appears and, bracing her hands, leans over its edge. He stops and turns back toward the office, but she has vanished. There is the closed door, the round, still knocker. Too late, he recalls the finely drawn eyebrows, the upper lip with its sweet curve.

"Ma'am?" The salesclerk was standing beside me. I knew from her tone of voice that it wasn't the first time she'd spoken. "Can I help you?"

She was dressed in the style of the shop—a blouse with a high collar, a long skirt with a ruffled hem—but her hair was cut in a seventies shag. I recalled a flip-book of Bailey's with split pages that let you pair different faces and bodies. I held out the shoe.

"I'm sorry, that's not for sale," she said.

"No. But I was wondering . . . Can you tell me anything about it?"

She tilted her head as if to get a better angle on my question. "What exactly do you want to know?"

"Do you have any idea where it came from? Who owned it?"

"No. But it belonged to a woman. A lady, I mean. It's a lady's shoe." I felt her gaze intensify. "You used to go around with Patrick Carraday," she said. It was a statement, not a question, and her tone suggested that she had won some point. I nodded, trying to imagine her heavier, slimmer, her hair lighter, darker, shorter, longer. "You don't remember me," she said.

What could I say? I didn't recognize her, and I was amazed to find that she had noticed me. Unlike Frankie, who had distinguished herself in various ways, I had never been on a team, or performed in a competition, or even attended a school dance.

I shook my head.

"Well." She folded her hands in front of her and looked down at a tiny diamond and a matching wedding band. "I do. I'm a real people person. Why I'm good at retail. You were always together. You and Patrick. You were just a kid. But still." I wondered how she knew. Could she have been in the crowd the night of the fire?

Now her face was eager. "He might have been a catch. The big house and all. Even if he was a little different. Are you married?"

"Yes," I said, feeling the untruth of it as I spoke.

She looked surprised and a little disappointed. "I wondered, because you aren't wearing a ring. Do you have kids?"

"No."

She went on talking. "It's another world when you're a mom. I have three boys. Travis is my athlete, he's thirteen, playing football, Jason is ten, and Kippy's my baby, my sweetheart." She picked up a paisley shawl and redraped it across the table. "I see him around sometimes," she said. "Patrick Carraday." She paused, gauging my interest.

"You do?"

"He looks different. Well he would after what happened. He works for his dad. If you can call that work. Not like a real job. On your feet eight hours a day." She leaned forward. "You haven't changed much," she said. She registered the camera. "You still take pictures." She brought her face close to mine. "When you left the Island, both of you, the same week, there were a lot of rumors. You know. Not that I ever believed them. They said it was like when Melody Johnson got pregnant and had to go stay with her cousins in Beaumont. I didn't believe it. You were a kid. I mean, you've turned out different, but then, you were just . . . Why would he have wanted to have sex with you? Not that you would have, of course." She paused. The air-conditioning cycled on, and the layers of her hair moved back and forth. "Carla's mom and her boyfriend went someplace up north. Around Dallas. She didn't want to stay on the Island after Carla died. They say she has a nice place now. With a hot tub and everything."

I looked at the high neck of her blouse and felt my own throat close. I recalled stumbling down the hallway of the burning house, gasping for air. I glanced around for Harriet Kinkaid, but there was no sign of her. A customer who had been hovering nearby called out. "Miss, we could use some help here."

I backed away and set the shoe on the table. "I just remembered something," I said. The bells overhead jangled cheerfully as I left.

What was the explanation Eleanor had offered for sending me and Patrick away? *People were upset. Your presence here would have been . . .* Eleanor hadn't finished her sentence, so I did it now for her. *Disruptive.*

But it was clear that everyone remembered what had happened, just as they remembered the cars Patrick had wrecked. That knowledge didn't change anything. Outrage was not sustainable on the Island, it spent itself like a brief squall, and life went on. That was the Galveston way, wasn't it? Survival at any price?

Will had resolved everything. Still, Patrick and I had been sent away. Now more than ever I wondered why.

Chapter 14

ON THE STRAND, THE CROWDS HAD THINNED, the tourists had moved inside for lunch. I realized I was hungry, but I didn't want to sit by myself in one of the busy eateries in full view of anyone else who might recognize me. Where could I go? Not back to the house. I stood for a moment feeling trapped. Then I remembered that a block or so away there had been an old candy factory that also housed an ice-cream parlor.

It was still there, a long, narrow space with exposed brick walls and marble-topped counters. Cashiers in sleeve garters worked the black-and-gold registers. Traditional candies—saltwater taffy, root beer barrels—as well as others available from the supermarket were displayed in glass jars and wooden bins that made even the everyday items seem exotic and desirable.

The place was full of children, running, tagging each other, tangling on the worn wood floor. The clientele was mostly young families, accustomed to the racket. They seemed, if not happy, content at least. Wasn't that what it meant when a couple wore the same shorts and T-shirt? The same rubber sandals? I wondered if they had started out with shared tastes and inclinations. Or had they made, over the years, countless small compromises, so that they no longer experienced them as losses? So that they found their achieved resemblance reassuring.

Toward the back of the space was the factory. A young man in a striped shirt was working the taffy machine. He was so wide-awake, so obviously entertained by what he was doing, that it was clearly a summer job. He stood beside the machine, handing out a long rope of pink taffy, pulling on it and guiding it in front of him in a way that seemed cheerfully, intentionally suggestive.

In front of me, the rope passed through a slicer. Bite-size sections flew out and were spun by the machine into paper twists. The taffy puller looked up and grinned. I took a step backward, but he reached for a wrapped piece and threw it. He expected me to catch it, but it sailed past my shoulder. He winked. I took another step backward, bumped into a chair, and sat down hard. He threw another piece that landed in my lap.

"Clare?" I heard a voice behind me and turned to see Tyler Henry. "I'm sorry," he said, "I didn't mean to startle you."

I smiled at him, relieved. Ty was dressed for work in a tan suit and a tie. His face was open and cheerful. He was not an Islander. He didn't know anything about my past.

"I was on my way back from lunch and I saw you come in," he said. "Can I get you something? Ice cream? Or would you like something more substantial?"

I looked up at the menu board. "Ice cream, please. You choose." The taffy puller kept his head down, focusing on his task. Now that he saw me with a man, he would behave differently. Ty returned with two dishes and handed me one. "Peach," he said. "They say it's homemade."

In my mouth the ice cream melted and separated and I bit into a piece of fruit. Ty pulled up a chair and sat next to me. "Have you seen the movies they show down on the wharf? About Galveston?"

I shook my head.

"There's a silly one about Jean Lafitte. He comes across more like a sleazy maître d' than a real pirate. Assuming there is such a thing."

"You're talking about our founding fathers," I said. "The Island was settled by pirates. By the way, they preferred to be called 'privateers.'"

"And why not? If there's any truth to the film, they were a pretty sophisticated crowd."

"I think Lafitte was, at least commercially. By the time he got here, he'd given up raiding ships. He was more like a broker. Trading con-

traband for legal goods. Laundering money, really. But the important thing is, he was successful. That counts for a lot in Galveston." I
realized how that might sound to Ty and I went on, quickly. "He gave
famous parties, too."

Ty thought for a minute. Then he said, "This place has quite a history. You might be interested in the other movie, the one about the
1900 hurricane. They use a lot of contemporary photos. The voice-
over is mostly from accounts written by people who lived through it.
It's very moving, really. But of course you know all about it. Six thousand dead. A third of the Island gone."

"You grow up with it here, with some version of it anyway."

Ty looked at me inquiringly.

"I think the urge to interpret events like that is irresistible. In
school, we were always encouraged to focus on what came afterward,
on the triumph of the civic will. Galveston carries on! Man overcomes
nature! The idea that after the grade raising, after the seawall was
built, the Island was indestructible. This was at the same time that
they were informing us about evacuation routes." I was talking too
much again. I took another bite.

"So you don't think the Island is safe?"

"No one does, really. The seawall only extends so far. A lot of construction has gone on west of there since Hurricane Carla. That was
almost thirty years ago. Big houses, right on the water."

"Like where I'm staying for now, until I find something in town.
Pretty posh for a beach house. I was expecting old wicker furniture
and bunk beds. I was wondering if they would have a dishwasher!"

"And?"

"They have two. And a refrigerator just for wine. I haven't really
settled in. I feel sort of like a teenager who's been left alone in the
house while the parents are away." Ty paused. "Would you like to see
it? You could come out this weekend. I'll give you the tour. That seems
to be the thing here."

The idea resonated briefly in the air between us. "I'm sorry, I
can't," I said. "There are things I have to do." As I said it, I felt again
the sting of Eleanor's *What did you find?* But Ty knew nothing about

that. He would think I meant the exhibition. I sensed Ty's disappointment, but he went on talking, his manner pleasant, and I felt a rush of goodwill toward him.

"It's not what I expected," he said. "Galveston. I admit that when Will first said Texas, what came to mind was Clint Eastwood. Riding into town, riding out of town. Sagebrush. He straightened me out pretty quickly. I thought it would be hot and, well, closed. A small town on an island."

"Not *an* island. *The* Island."

He smiled, as if he found the distinction amusing.

"The heat you're right about," I said. "It's only May. It's going to get a whole lot hotter. And, in fact, underneath all the commerce and the easy hospitality this place is downright hostile to strangers."

"What do you mean?"

I could probably have produced a colorful story to illustrate my point. There were plenty of tales about mainlanders coming to grief in Galveston. Instead I said, "You know how insistent people are about being BOI?"

Ty nodded.

I hesitated. There were things I couldn't explain to a visitor. Was it foolish of me to try? I looked at Ty's friendly face and knew I had to speak directly. "I'm not sure how to say this, but to Islanders, people from the mainland don't really count. We don't always tell them the truth. And sometimes we treat them badly."

"That sounds like a warning." Ty was still smiling, but I could see that now he was taking me seriously.

I kept my tone light. I could only go so far. "You saw the film," I said. "This is a dangerous place."

AFTER THE GREAT HURRICANE, the Islanders undertook to raise the grade of the entire city, about five hundred blocks. The rescue embraced all construction equally—the iron-front commercial blocks along the Strand, the towered villas, the modest cottages. The most disreputable, the smallest dwellings took on new importance as relics of the storm.

The Islanders leveed off sections of the city and lifted every building on stilts or blocks while dredges pumped fill into the space below. They raised St. Patrick's, the three-thousand-ton Catholic church, using hundreds of jackscrews moving a quarter-inch at a time, without ever interrupting services.

Shoeless children perched grinning on the huge pipes that carried the slurry and cheered when it erupted in an explosion of wet sand.

The grand Broadway houses occupied the highest part of the Island. Some were raised, at enormous expense. But in many cases, their owners chose to fill in part of the lowest floor to gain the required three feet. This left spaces like the Carraday's kitchen, which had originally been the first floor, half underground. Where iron fences survived, they were half buried as well.

Photos taken during the grade raising show houses that seem to float above a swirling sea of fill. Their façades are blank, without expression, like the faces of sleepers.

Neighborhoods and streets disappeared. Gas lines, water pipes, streetcar tracks were torn up and removed. So were trees and lawns and plants. The breeze-borne sounds of passing ships, of bells and shorebirds, full of variety and significance, were replaced by the ceaseless, unmeaning throb of machinery.

In the parts of town where the dredges operated, residents learned to walk to their destinations on narrow planks and trestles high off the ground. The Islanders became accustomed to taking shortcuts through the homes of strangers.

Some of them passed through the Carradays' front hall. If Ward Carraday was not at home, did those unbidden guests stop a moment to look around? Did they see the lilies in the friezes and ceiling medallions, in the golden brown woodwork of the entryway with its grand staircase, on the glazed Italian tiles in the conservatory?

Did they see the portrait over the mantel? Stella with the lilies at her feet?

Chapter 15

THE HOUSE WAS EMPTY WHEN I GOT BACK. I poured myself a glass of iced tea and took it out onto the back porch. The sky was so blue it vibrated along the outline of the roof. The heat was just tolerable in the shade.

This was where Patrick used to appear—on our back steps. It wouldn't be accurate to say he'd waited there for me—he was too full of nervous energy to settle for long. He would arrive, knock or call, walk back and forth a few times, bounce up and down on the balls of his feet, then leave again before I could come out. Often the first thing I saw of him was his retreating back—the dirty yellow soles of his tennis shoes as he jogged off, his shirttail vanishing around a corner.

Once he took me to a shooting range, a long, narrow building that looked from the road like a truck stop, but without windows. Inside, there was a carnival atmosphere. Kids were taking turns popping at moving silhouettes with an air rifle. The real shooting went on behind a soundproof door, where targets of different kinds slid back and forth on metal tracks. One was in the form of a running man, white and featureless, outlined in black, as if a piece had been razored out of the world, leaving behind a blank. Now, when I looked around for Patrick, I saw that fleeing figure everywhere.

I can't remember a time when we didn't know each other. What I do recall vividly is the incident, when we were six and eight, that made us conspirators. Patrick came under suspicion, but in fact, he only watched. I was the one who flushed Mary Liz's platinum-and-diamond horseshoe brooch down the toilet.

I still don't know why. Did I imagine that I would have a chance to snatch it back, once I had impressed Patrick with my audacity? I didn't, of course. It sank straight down in the rush of water and disappeared.

The search went on for days. Faline, her hair drawn back in a knot so tight it narrowed her eyes, made a noisy show of turning the house upside down. She took up the rugs, carried them outside, and beat them, removed the cushions from the larger pieces of furniture and slid her slender fingers down inside their seams. She emptied the vacuum cleaner onto the kitchen floor and picked through the dusty contents—buttons and coins and paper clips, the tiny, desiccated corpse of a baby mouse. She lifted the cast-iron grilles that overlay the heating vents and poked a broom into the grime and darkness below. Patrick and I trailed after her, watching the upheaval, careful to hide our delight. Then one afternoon Mary Liz announced that she was tired of eating sandwiches. "I never wore the damn thing anyway," she said. And as suddenly as it had begun, the excitement subsided.

Asked if we had seen the brooch, we shook our heads. Neither of us ever confessed. So the knowledge of what had happened became a bond between us. Over time there were more incidents.

Why did we do those things? Why did we lie? Was it our response to an adult world that seemed to be full of secrets? Creating secrets of our own?

During the day Patrick would turn up, and no one questioned his presence. At night he'd signal to me and I would slip down to meet him when I saw the light. It seemed right to me that his signal should come from Stella's room. Stella had resisted authority too. So she presided in spirit over our exploits.

Sometimes they had surprising consequences, like the time we wrapped a dead rattlesnake around the steering wheel of the Buick my father had parked in the alley. I had never seen my father agitated or at a loss for words, but he stumbled and half fell in his hurry to get out of the car. He gave a shout—it was surprisingly high-pitched for so big a man—and the door flew open. But it bounced back, and he had to push it away again, his feet scrabbling in the dirt. Finally, he fell onto the ground and sat, head bent, a strange, husky sound coming from his throat. Patrick and I watched in silence from our hiding place among the bed of cannas.

My father was sure we were responsible and wanted to punish us. But I could tell from the way her mouth worked when she heard his account that Eleanor was trying not to smile. "Be reasonable," she said. "It couldn't have hurt anyone. It was dead."

My father's face was red and sweaty over his white shirt collar. "It could have given me a heart attack," he said. "People die of—"

"Of fright?"

He declined to answer. His flushed face made me think about his blood circulating—not the bright oxygenated red that we see but the dark blood that flows toward the heart. A vein pulsed in his forehead, and I wondered if what he'd said was true, that he might have died, we might have killed him. Eleanor went on folding clothes. I think we were eight and ten.

It was only later that our outings involved anything that was, strictly speaking, illegal.

It was easy, there were any number of unoccupied houses to investigate. There was always someone outside the Liquor Mart who was willing to buy us a couple of six-packs or a bottle of tequila while we waited in the parking lot, leaning against the mural. It showed an underwater scene—dolphins, rays, sharks, all looking like inflatable toys—against an implausible turquoise background. "Sure, they're mellow," Patrick said. "They live right around the corner from the liquor store."

It was there that Patrick kissed me for the first time. There was no prelude. We had been talking and my face was turned toward his. He just bent over, as though the possibility had only then occurred to him. I had seen people kiss in movies, kids at the beach, tourists on the Strand. It was not what I expected. His lips were dry at first, tentative, then moist and slightly salty. Except for the trace of something bitter that I knew must be whatever he was drinking, the taste reminded me of when I was small, lying facedown on a towel, licking the salt off my own arm. It had that quality of familiarity, of myself coming back to me.

We called our get-togethers "beach parties." To me they were painful, those gatherings. They confirmed Frankie's judgment that I didn't understand the rules. Only being with Patrick made them bearable.

Some couples made out. Others stood nursing cans of warmish beer or drinking shots, trading insults and cultivating an air of defiance. We passed an occasional joint. Every so often, Patrick would produce some single-malt scotch or vintage cognac. I tried everything just often enough to avoid being noticed.

Occasionally, when fall came and the rest of the crowd lost interest in the beach, Patrick and I would go there alone. We'd take a blanket and stretch out together on the cold sand. There were no lights along the shorefront, no trucks or jeeps with their radios on parked above the waterline. The only sound was the tumbled rush of the surf. Patrick lay on his back, a bottle half buried to his right. I fitted myself against him on the other side, my hip against his, my head on his shoulder. I could feel his rib cage moving. Sometimes he would cover us with his jacket, so that the warmth of his body was enough for both of us. I tried to match my breathing to his.

Patrick would circle my wrist with his fingers, flatten my palm against his, and laugh as if the comparison amused him. He knew my size exactly. Sometimes, when we went out at night, I wore his old clothes, shirts and shorts that were too small for him.

Once when we were under his jacket together, he unzipped his jeans and put my hand inside them. I knew what an erection was, how sex happened, but I remember my surprise at the intense heat of his groin, the unfamiliar combination of soft skin and stiffening tissue. I had no idea what to do with it. I fumbled there for a while, then Patrick said, "Too much Laphroaig, I guess," and rolled over. I knew what he meant, but still it seemed to me that I had failed him. I resolved to listen more closely to Frankie's lectures, so that the next time, I'd be prepared. When no next time came, I took that as definitive evidence of my failure. Sometimes I would see Patrick talking and laughing with other, older girls, and I'd flush, jealous and mortified.

After that, we occasionally did a little touching, but that was all. Patrick said to me once, his hand resting on my bare stomach, "This is as good as sex." I didn't know how to respond. I knew from what Frankie said that sex was what boys wanted. But Patrick spoke with the authority of a two-year age difference.

Patrick had a lopsided smile and a perpetual tennis tan—tawny arms attached to an unexpectedly white torso that made him look more naked when he removed his shirt than the boys who were uniformly brown. He was wiry, like his father, but taller, with a longer reach that helped his game. I knew he was good enough to travel to tennis tournaments in other places. I had heard Mary Liz say, "Some fancy-pants college like his daddy's will want him for the team."

What people said about Patrick was that Mary Liz spoiled him. When he walked out of one of his finals, she shrugged and said he was an athlete. When he lost a game, she said tennis was for sissies. What she didn't see was that she was gradually taking away his options.

It hadn't yet occurred to me that it might also be hard to be Will's son.

Chapter 16

I DECIDED TO GO THAT EVENING and look for Patrick at Lafitte's, the bar Frankie had mentioned, a scruffy place near the bottom of the Strand. I knew it by reputation. Lafitte's had been around for years, changing management occasionally without ever improving. It was not a tourist spot, but it was not a biker bar either. I had been in worse places.

I wondered if I should take my camera. I picked it up and put it down again. I changed into the skirt I'd worn to the party and a pair of dangly earrings I'd discovered at the back of a drawer. I twisted my hair up. I put on lipstick, bracing my arm against my chest to steady my hand. In the end I slipped the Leica into my tapestry bag and slung it over my shoulder.

It was a mistake to look in the mirror before I left. My skin was pale, as always. There were hollows in my cheeks and gray shadows under my eyes. The color on my lips only made the whole effect worse. I rubbed most of it off with my fingers. The house was empty, no one saw me leave.

Lights were just coming on in windows and doorways, and it seemed to me that the street, closed and ordinary a few moments before, now revealed itself, full of interest and variety. Lamps, burning at entrances and above flights of wooden stairs, announced each house the way the riding lights of the ships out in the darkening Gulf established their shadowy presences. *Here we are!* Rooms appeared, bright interiors in what I could see now were dream houses, furnished and ready for occupation, but at this moment, still, unpopulated, silent.

I walked slowly, taking in as much as I could. There was a long-haired cat on a low table, there a pile of books, there a striped armchair and a collection of painted plates against a cherry-colored wall. Looking into those lighted windows, I felt a familiar hunger, one that went back as far as I could remember. A longing to step into one of those waiting spaces, to stroke the cat, to turn the pages of the books, to curl my legs into the chair's broad seat. To enter into that world where each element seemed securely in its place and be at home in it. *Here I am!*

A couple pushing a baby in an umbrella stroller came down one of the side streets and turned in front of me. A small, dust-colored dog on a leash ran along beside them. The dog bounced, the wheels of the stroller went around and around, the baby stuck out her bare feet. The mother laughed and shook back an armful of plastic bangles. My first instinct was to caution them. I knew they were taking it all for granted.

The mother was overweight and plain, making up for it with a perky attitude and colored barrettes that were too young for her. I understood how that could happen, how she could fall in love with her child and want to appropriate for herself some of that sweetness. It was the same feeling that prompted mothers to dress themselves and their daughters alike, something I would never have considered. Still, I'd felt a twinge when Jules gave me his customary, uninhibited once-over, kissed me on both cheeks, and said, "Thank God, you aren't wearing mommy clothes." I'd thought all along that I was an unlikely parent.

I walked faster so I could see the baby better.

She was at least two and getting big for the stroller. She gazed at me, then put her fingers in her mouth and looked away, exposing the soft hollow at the nape of her neck. I remembered running my thumb along that place on Bailey's neck, the springy tendons, the softness of the baby hair. I'd used the stroller only when I had to. I loved the tug of Bailey's arms around my neck, the way her plump, creased legs gripped me. Eleanor, on one of her infrequent visits to Washington, said, "If you don't put that baby down, she'll never learn to walk."

I'd anticipated the frustrations of motherhood, but none of the pleasures. It was new to me, and intoxicating, the satisfaction that came with meeting Bailey's simple needs. I was the overlooked sibling in the fairy tale who finally chooses the right path, discovers the key, unlocks the door to the treasure.

A child is a chance to be someone new and different—the adult reflected in those shining eyes. I might not have been a better person when I was Bailey's mother. I might not have been stronger or more deserving. But I believed that I was.

The couple stopped to look in the window of a gift shop, and I hung back and leaned against a mailbox, pretending to adjust my sandal. I knew I was staring.

The couple went left onto the Strand, away from Lafitte's, and I followed them.

The black cast-iron streetlamps came on. I knew they were electric, but with the elaborate façades of the buildings and the part-brick street with its high curb and steps, the effect was convincing—it really seemed like another time. A horse and carriage went by. On the corner a group of men and women in Victorian dress stood in conversation. Then one of the women laughed and raised her hand and I could see she was holding a cigarette. Actors from the Opera House on a break.

The couple stopped at the Mikasa Outlet and I heard the sound of Bob Marley drifting from one of the surfer stores that stayed open late. Then they stopped again in the middle of the sidewalk. They leaned their heads together, whispered, and nodded. I slowed my pace and looked around for something to occupy my attention, but the windows to my left were all dark. I walked to the nearest one anyway and cupped my hands against the glass, pretending to peer in. It was a gallery, the kind that sells nautical art and beach scenes in rope frames.

When I turned back, the couple was gone.

I looked down the street in front of me. I dropped all caution, scanning anxiously left and right. Then I saw them. They must have crossed quickly—that was what they had been discussing and agreeing on. They were entering a pharmacy.

As soon as the glass door swung shut behind them, I darted over. Inside, under pink fluorescent tubes, a bored teenager was filing her nails at the counter. I pretended to sort through a bin of rubber sandals near the entrance. The father had disappeared down one of the aisles with the dog, but the mother stood at a display of cosmetics. The baby was fussing, and she picked her up, jiggled her, and put her back in the stroller. She tried on a pair of sunglasses, took a brush out of her purse and fluffed her bangs.

The baby twisted in her seat, straining to find her mother. She wailed, and I saw one round arm, then her head appear. Then the stroller tipped, and I rushed forward, feeling already in my own nerves and brain the impact as her small skull collided with the gray-flecked floor. I grabbed the curved handle of the stroller and righted it.

"Hey there. Just what might you be doing?" Up close, the father was older than I'd thought. He was soft around the middle and under his tan there were red veins across his nose and cheeks.

I was still flooded with adrenaline, still breathing hard. I could hear the blood pounding in my ears. "She could have fallen."

His wife joined him. "We saw you following us," she said. She stared at me, her eyes bright. Her plump hands opened and closed. She came a step nearer. "We both saw you," she said. "Didn't we, Robert? We almost called the police. I know about women like you, who want a baby. You'll do anything. It's kidnapping."

"Kidnapping," he said.

"That's crazy!" I gasped. "Why weren't you watching her? She could have hurt herself. She could have been killed."

"You're the one who's crazy, lady." He said it with force, but when I turned to look at him directly, something made him back off. He picked the dog up and held it protectively under one arm. "Look, if you had kids you'd know, they fall all the time. It's no big deal. Cuts and bruises." He shrugged. "They happen." He looked over at his wife as though weighing her willingness to move on. Clearly, he wasn't a fighter.

But the mother was enjoying the drama. "Robert. There was one of them up in Missouri. Kidnapped the mom from in front of the Walmart and cut the baby right out of her." Her skin was smooth, the kind that turns a pale apricot when it tans. She smelled like baby powder. She turned to face me. "Don't deny you were watching her. I saw you. I saw you along the street and after we came in. In the mirror." She preened at her own cleverness.

"Honey," her husband said. "You're okay. You're not pregnant." He touched her gently with his free hand. From the way he did it, I knew he loved her ample shape. "You ought not watch those shows if they upset you."

"Who wouldn't be upset with someone trying to steal their child?" She lifted her chin.

I could tell them what had happened to Bailey and take away their complacency forever. Instead I took a deep breath and said, "Yes, I was watching her. She's a beautiful baby. I'm a photographer." I put on a professional manner, told them my name, and mentioned my gallery.

Maybe it was just relief that I wasn't violent, that I wasn't armed with anything more dangerous than a camera, but when I asked them, they began to group themselves the way people generally do when you offer to take a photo.

It used to surprise me, the way people accommodate a photographer. Is it just that they have been conditioned by years of ceremonial picture taking, on birthdays, at family gatherings, to agree? Or does the picture taking send a signal? When I ask people to pose, am I telling them that they are important, that their lives matter? That they deserve to be remembered?

They would go on with their evening. They would buy postcards and forget to mail them. They would eat fried shrimp and drink beer. They would go back to their rented condo, put the baby to bed, and finish up with a couple of shots of Kahlúa out of glasses they would forget to pack. They would undress with the lights on and have sex in ways they weren't accustomed to and fall asleep suddenly and completely. They would get up the next morning and begin again.

It didn't look hard to do. But that rhythm, the hidden heartbeat of married life, once lost, was impossible to recover.

My hair was coming down. I shook it loose and left it. The couple was at the checkout now, exclaiming over their purchases. I thought of the actors I'd seen earlier and wondered how they did it, every day, over and over. My legs felt weak as I crossed the floor. But I stopped at the door and turned and waved, the way you do from the deck of a departing ship when you are too far away to see the pier. A gesture meant for everyone and no one.

THE OFFICIAL NAME OF THE PLACE was Lafitte's Fort. It was at the bottom of the Strand, where the imposing rows of historic buildings trailed off into humbler, one-story structures housing marginal shops and bars. Most of them opened with fanfare, lasted a year or two, and were then replaced by something so similar no one noticed. That Lafitte's had survived for a generation was a wonder, and for that reason, it had achieved a certain status on the Island.

It had no visible windows, which helped to preserve the inscrutability of the place. The only door opened onto the side street. From the Strand, the weathered exterior with its random repairs seemed to have been boarded up and abandoned.

Every so often, tired shoppers passed me on their way to the parking lot at the end of the block—a sunburned family with too much to carry, a pair of older women in matching pastel Bermudas and sunshades. Every so often the door to Lafitte's flew open emitting a flash of multicolored light and a burst of sound that startled anyone nearby into a trot. Otherwise, the Strand was silent. Emptied of visitors, the place felt oddly purposeless.

It was that moment when the character of any bar changes, when the early patrons leave and the late-night crowd arrives. Some of the first group had probably been there since eleven or so when Lafitte's opened, drinking steadily—Bloody Marys and beer. They were not looking for excitement, just getting through the day. Now they exited, moving cautiously and paddling with their hands as though they were wading through waist-high water, hoping to make it home before passing out in someone else's yard.

I went inside and took a couple of quick steps, then caught my foot on a massive fissure in the concrete floor and stumbled forward. No one paid any attention. I walked to the bar and climbed onto a stool crisscrossed with duct tape.

There was a shuffleboard table at the back and next to it an upholstered bench that looked as if it had been kicked in by someone impatient for a turn. Overhead, sagging loops of exposed wire festooned the ceiling. Damp-stained cardboard boxes labeled COCKTAIL NAPKINS and TOILET PAPER were stacked here and there.

Behind the bar hung a portrait of the pirate. The artist seemed to have struggled, reworking parts of the painting, and Lafitte's features hadn't really come together. One of his eyes regarded me, the other gazed down at a battered TV where a baseball game was in progress. The drone of the crowd was the noise I'd heard from outside. "High and outside," a voice announced. The woman next to me shook her head and muttered.

I lifted my elbows as the skinny bartender wiped the surface of the bar. When he was done, he folded his arms and scratched his biceps. "Well?" he said irritably.

"I'll have a beer."

"I've got Bud Light," he said. "Or . . ." He gestured toward a chalkboard. I wondered if he thought I was a tourist.

"A Shiner Bock," I said and lowered my arms, but the wood was still moist and gritty. I drew back quickly and put my hands in my lap. The bartender grinned, showing stubby grayish teeth. He passed me a chilled glass and a bottle.

I turned back to the room, to the spot I knew Patrick would occupy when he came. I'd picked it out right away. It was impossible to imagine him at the tables with the heavyset men who sat unmoving, wreathed in smoke. Or slumped at the bar with the woman in the flowered muumuu who occasionally raised her head and let fly a stream of commentary aimed at no one in particular. But I could see Patrick at the shuffleboard table, a drink in his hand, shifting from one sneakered foot to the other, bending down to send a puck skimming toward the end of the board. Patrick would do it without effort, without even appearing to think about it, just a lazy back and forth of the arm, and no one would be able to beat him.

I had never told anyone about Patrick and me, because I didn't know what to say. I had no words to describe our relationship. Now that it was too late, I wanted that other life. With Patrick. On the Island. I wanted to disappear into it like a diver going under, arms reaching, no part of me held back.

I dabbed at my face with the hem of my skirt. I took a long swallow of beer without tasting it, and then another. I asked myself why I had left the Island that winter. I could have refused to get on the plane. I could have run away, like Stella. Why had I been so passive? I had again the old feeling that there was something wrong with me. My inability to act was part of it.

The bar had emptied and was filling up again. They shared one trait, these Islanders, you could see it in their eyes. They were idealists whose colorful inner visions had outlasted all the evidence decades of hard living could provide. They were just waiting for things to fall into place.

There was no sign of Patrick. I finished the first beer and ordered another. I scanned the room again. I had the feeling I recognized someone. Why? I looked again, trying to remember where I had been since I arrived.

My eyes settled on a wiry, brown-skinned man perched on the edge of a chair, pretending to read the newspaper spread in front of him. I took inventory—the expensive sunglasses on his head, the T-shirt faded to no particular color. From a distance, he seemed to be in his twenties. You would have to get closer to see the wear in his face, the deep scoring around his eyes. Something set him apart from the other drinkers. An air of purpose, perhaps. A look that had nothing to do with missed opportunities or a future that would never arrive. Then it came to me. When Tyler Henry had asked about illegal traffic, I'd told him, *Galveston is busier, so people are more cautious. But it's a port city.* I wondered what the man with the sunglasses was bringing in.

The light was iffy and I had no flash, but I reached for my camera anyway and eased it out of my bag. I rested it on my lap and felt for the shutter. As I did, two hands caught and held me from behind. They circled my wrists, and a man's chest pressed against me. I swallowed and tried to shout, but most of the sound stayed inside. A batter had walked and the booing from the TV was loud. The woman at the bar looked at me with mild surprise. I tried to push back, but my feet didn't reach the floor and I had no way to brace myself.

I saw my Leica slide between my knees and onto the ground. When I looked up, the man with the sunglasses was gone.

Otis let go of me, then leaned down and picked up my camera. "You best put this away for now. Not everyone like to have their picture taken."

I took it from him and inspected the lens. It seemed okay. I held it away from me and shot a frame or two to make sure the reflex mirror was moving. "This is a Leica," I said. "It's a really good camera."

Otis removed a set of keys from his pocket. "Any damage, he'll get you another."

I knew he was talking about Will. "Did he tell you to follow me?"

He shook his head. "Not him. Faline. She said to watch out for you here. Carry you home if need be."

My head throbbed. I was embarrassed that Faline had so easily been able to predict where I would go. I knew she meant well, that in her own way, she was looking after me. But it was like being small again, all my actions observed and anticipated. Allowed as long as they caused no trouble. I said, "Patrick comes here, doesn't he?"

"Sometimes," Otis said. "But it's different for him."

"Why?"

Otis looked at me the way you do a child who repeats the same annoying question. "Just the way it is. You ready now?"

I walked out with him to the car, one of Will's. The haloed street-lights were painfully bright and my mouth felt sticky. "Do you always do everything Faline tells you to?" I asked.

"It's not like that," Otis said. He opened my door. "You been married. You ought to know." I sank down into the car's dark interior.

I thought about Michael. The constant push and pull of our life together.

"Who was that man?" I asked. "The one who left?"

Otis considered a moment. Then he said, "You want to find Patrick Carraday, you better off going by Saint Vincent's. The Catholic church. On Twenty-first Street. A white building. Saint V de P they call it. You know the one?"

I stared stupidly. What could Patrick be doing at Saint Vincent's?

Otis started the engine. He said, "But I wouldn't take the camera there neither." I felt sick, and the motion of the jeep made it worse. Sour bile rose in my throat. I saw him looking at me.

"It's not what you think," I told him. "Two beers, that's all I had. I didn't even finish the second. It's a headache, that's all."

Otis said nothing.

I closed my eyes and leaned against the back of the seat. I thought about what had just happened. I didn't know the man with the sunglasses. I had never been inside Lafitte's. But I was an Islander, I had all the instincts. "You're not going to tell me what Patrick's doing there, at the Catholic church, are you?" I said.

There was no traffic, and the street was quiet, but Otis kept his face forward, his hands on the wheel, as though the act of driving absorbed him. "No ma'am," he said, "I am not."

Chapter 17

MY HEADACHE LASTED WELL INTO the next day. When finally I went downstairs for some crackers, I passed Eleanor in the hall, and she gave me a knowing look. "There's aspirin in the medicine chest and ice in the freezer," she said.

I poured coffee into a tall cup and took it with me. As I drove to the archive, I thought about what Otis had said. The Carradays weren't Catholic. When they went to services at Christmas and Easter, it was to the Methodist church. I wondered about what had happened at Lafitte's. Did it have something to do with Patrick? Was he involved in something? (I didn't use the word "illegal," even to myself). Or was Otis just doing what Faline wanted, what, it seemed, everyone wanted, keeping Patrick and me apart?

I parked the car in the library lot. Across the street, on either side of the big main door, a pair of lions—their muzzles softened and blunted by weather—gazed out onto the scruffy grass bank. An arch overhead bore a series of names—Virgil, Homer, Shakespeare, Goethe. I wondered how many of them meant anything to those inside, now mostly harried mothers with small children and grizzled homeless men. People who had worn out their welcome in other places but here, at least, could not be turned away.

In the street, a tour bus was passing, a sort of tractor pulling three open cars strung together like an amusement-park ride. There were few children on board. Most of the passengers were adults, but they seemed to have regressed, as people do on vacation. They wore shorts and T-shirts, ball caps, and athletic shoes with bright-colored stripes. They sat with their feet up on the seats in front of them or lolled back, bored and drowsy. An oversize duck head, like a big bath toy, looked back from the roof of the tractor and a loudspeaker somewhere behind its enlarged bill produced a recorded drone. I couldn't make out the words. When it paused, there was scattered laughter.

I was not anxious to go inside. Already my eyes burned in anticipation of the fluorescent light. I tried to muster some enthusiasm for the work at hand, but my thoughts kept returning to the events of the night before.

I wondered if Harriet Kinkaid could tell me anything about Patrick. Clearly she knew the Carradays well. She had invited me to come and see her house—*the witch house*. It wasn't far, just two blocks over, an easy walk down a well-shaded street.

Few trees grow naturally on a barrier island. Those oaks and cypress that survive the weather and wind are hunched and scruffy. In Galveston, the most desirable neighborhoods have always been distinguished by other trees—exotic, imported palms and tall, graceful hardwoods. The spreading canopy above Harriet Kinkaid's roof said that important people had once lived there. Fashionable people.

If you looked closely you could see in each of the front-facing gables a decorative sunflower, the motif recommended by Oscar Wilde during a visit to the Island in its prime. You had to look closely because the structure and all its details were the same soft, weathered gray. None of the surfaces had been painted in years. But the garden, at first glance a riot of color and unruly greenery, showed signs of tidying. And I saw that a board in the porch had been replaced recently.

I had not expected to find the front door open. A couple of cardboard cartons waited outside on the porch. I had reached the steps when Harriet Kinkaid emerged. Her hair was up, in a crown of neat braids. "There, now," she said, "I was hoping you'd come by. You can help me with these." She indicated the boxes. "You may have to make two trips, they're pretty heavy." She added something to one of the boxes, making it heavier. "In my day I could have managed them easily, but I'm so much bigger than you." She straightened briefly to her full height, as if thinking about her younger self had given her new energy, and set off down the walk. Her car, an ancient Peugeot with bulging headlights and a grille like a crazy smile, was parked at the curb.

I picked up the first of the boxes. It had no lid and I could see on top several framed photographs. Halfway to the street, the cutout handles began to dig into my fingers. I hurried the last few steps and deposited the box on the ground with a bump. The contents shifted, and I wondered if I had broken something. Harriet didn't seem concerned. She leaned against the car. "I'll just catch my breath." Patting the hood, she said, "Have no fear, it's nicely warmed up. We've already been for a run, out past the Coast Guard station. I'm keeping track of a black skimmer nest on the beach. Such fascinating birds, with that remarkable lower bill, like the edge of a knife. They skim it along the surface of the water and snap up anything edible."

" 'The lower mandible is elongated and flexible,' " I said.

Harriet clapped. "Bravo. Of course. Your father." She looked at me closely. "I'll say this for him, Anson Porterfield understood habitat. I want to make sure no one disturbs it. The nest. At least for now. It will all be gone by this time next year. You can put that there." She gestured—a sort of backward wave—but kept the other hand on the car, and I realized she needed it for support. Walking from the house had tired her.

"We're almost ready," she said, smiling encouragement, and I went back for the second box.

Seated behind the wheel, she looked stronger and more purposeful. As we drove, I saw that most of the houses in the neighborhood had been lavishly restored. I wondered what their owners thought about Harriet's property. You couldn't say that it was run-down, but it certainly was different.

I realized I was still thinking about her earlier remark. "What did you mean, it will all be gone?"

"The beach will be. The beach as we know it. There will still be water and sand, of course. But fewer birds. More cars. And many more tourists. They're going to build a high-rise. And what they call a 'beach village.'"

I pictured that part of the Island, where there were no houses or boardwalks, just the road that ran past the ferry landing, through clumps of tough-looking bushes that gave way gradually to tall spikes of cordgrass. Families went there at dusk to seine for crabs and sand trout. The land sloped off so gradually that waders a hundred yards out stood only waist-deep, the water flat and still around them. In the distance you could see the skeletal forms of derricks.

I was not surprised to learn that it would be developed. That was what happened in Galveston. Who would want to save that low, mixed, unimpressive landscape? I realized sadly that it was the thing I would have wanted to keep most.

"It's selfish of me, I know, but I'm grateful I won't be here to see it," Harriet said.

"You're leaving the Island?"

She smiled. "I am." She indicated the boxes. "But first I'm giving away the family history." I thought I must have misheard, but Harriet looked at me and said, "You'll see. Turn right at the next corner."

The shop was called Sally's Stitch in Time, and I understood immediately why it appealed to Harriet—it had the unrestrained abundance of a half-wild garden. I stared at the bewildering array of time-worn belongings—furniture, old kitchen appliances, tools, piles of linens, clothing, boxes of buttons, rows of medicine bottles and cosmetic jars, military medals, pistols, swords. On one side of the room, two fully dressed figures—a World War I doughboy and a WAC wearing a mohair tie—stood together uneasily, like different generations at a family reunion. Although it was midsummer, strings of tinsel were draped here and there.

Harriet settled into a dark red chair while a woman with penciled-on eyebrows exclaimed over the contents of the first box. Although she was breathing hard again, there were spots of color in Harriet's cheeks. She was enjoying herself.

A long table to one side was given over to photographs, and I went to look through them. There were images of all kinds—group photos, shots of men in stiff collars behind large desks, wedding portraits of couples in formal clothes. *We were prosperous. We were in love.*

On the counter by the cash register, Harriet's photos stood a little awkwardly, latecomers to a party that was already under way. I saw that they were about to join the others on the table, and I realized that someone might indeed buy them.

"You understand now," Harriet said, smiling. "I wonder if someday, someone will point at me and say, 'This is a picture of my grandmother, when she was seventeen. When she visited San Francisco. You can see the cable car in the background.' I'll have another whole life. Yes, that's me," she said, her voice full of satisfaction.

I could see why. In the photo Harriet stood at the top of a hill, sky and distant water visible behind her. The wind lifted her long hair and waved it like a banner.

"It won't be true," I protested.

"Oh my dear," Harriet sighed. "Come here." She patted the broad arm of the chair. "Does it matter? Think of the portraits you have at home. They aren't your family. What about them?"

"The Hayeses. Well, they go with the house," I said, not mentioning my early confusion about their identity.

Harriet tilted her head. "Possibly. In any case, my house is going to be sold. So what to do with these? People like to say you can't choose your relatives. But who knows?"

"What about the portrait of Stella?"

"Ah," said Harriet. "That's another thing entirely. I saw you looking at it during the party the other night."

Once again the strangeness of the relief struck me—the winsome, childlike face above a body that was plainly adult. The womanly breasts and thighs revealed in a way that contrasted sharply with the photo of Stella below—her formal dress with its stiff bodice and yards of heavy fabric.

Sally came back carrying two small landscapes. "You're sure about these?" she asked.

"Oh yes," Harriet said happily.

"But there must be someone—" I said.

"No." Harriet spoke firmly. "There isn't. And I prefer this. My dear." She touched my cheek, and her hand felt as cool and dry as paper.

Sally wrote some figures on the back of an envelope. "I'll have to speak to my partner before we can make an offer," she said.

"Oh, an offer," Harriet said dismissively. "I don't want an offer. You can have them."

The woman looked doubtful. She pursed her lips. "But the frames alone—"

"I'm not senile," Harriet responded, "and there's no one to object. Give me a receipt, if you must." She sat back in the chair. "Clare," she said. "Will you come back with me? You've been very patient."

At the far end of the room, Sally was talking to another woman in a suit. She waved the envelope. The other woman pursed her lips. They were disagreeing in a way that was clearly familiar to both of them, comfortable and without any real risk. I realized that they were a couple. Sally returned carrying a slip of yellow paper. "This is highly unusual," she said, frowning.

"Good," said Harriet. She reached for my shoulder as she stood, and the pressure of her weight reminded me suddenly what it felt like to carry a child, how even a small body could anchor you, make you feel that you were exactly where you ought to be.

"You know," said Harriet, "I've been looking forward to this little jaunt. And now it's over. So quickly. Well, that's the way, isn't it?"

THERE WAS A BANK OF HIBISCUS and a railing on either side of Harriet's front steps, but she linked her arm in mine and went straight up the middle. "We'll go out to the veranda," she said. "Unless it's too hot for you? I've never minded the heat and now, well." She pushed the front door open. Inside I paused, waiting for my eyes to adjust. The staircase with its big, turned baluster came into focus, then Harriet standing against it, resting, a shape only at first, but looking different somehow. I blinked, confused. Her hair was gone.

She laughed, the wonderful rippling laugh I remembered from

the Carradays' party, and pointed to the hall table. Next to a vase of gerbera daisies stood a row of heads, each wearing a wig. They were all the same silvery white, but each was done in a different style—the crown of braids, the figure eight I remembered from our first meeting at the Carradays'. Harriet's real hair, what remained of it, was soft and downy, like the feathers of a baby chick. It stood out around her head, a fluffy aura. I remembered the papery feel of her hand. "Pure vanity," she said. "It doesn't leave you just because you get old. Or sick. Come."

I followed her to the back porch. She walked more slowly now, pausing occasionally to steady herself with a hand on a bookcase, a doorframe. Outside were a pair of fan-backed wicker chairs that creaked pleasantly when she settled into one of them. "Now this is nice," said Harriet. "A young visitor. I don't mean to sound ageist, but a lot of older people are just not very exciting. Sit down and tell me what you're thinking."

I didn't know what to say. "What I'm thinking right now?"

"No, I can make a pretty good guess at that. I mean in general. What occupies your thoughts? What occurs to you when you wake up in the morning? What do you dream about?"

There are places on the Gulf side of the Island, parts of the stone piers, where water shoots up unexpectedly through the openings in the rocks. You can be standing there with dry feet and never see it coming. I was completely unprepared for her question and I sat down suddenly. Then I bent forward and covered my face with my hands. Harriet seemed unperturbed. When I looked up, she removed a Kleenex from her sleeve. "Here," she said. "I haven't used this. Well, only to clean my glasses. I heard what happened to your little girl. It's a terrible thing to lose a child." She reached over and touched my knee. "I'm so sorry." After a while, she said, "There's ice tea in the refrigerator. Why don't you go and get us some?"

In her kitchen I wiped my eyes and blew my nose. I was surprised to find that my headache was gone.

The room was orderly in the fashion of a person who rarely cooks—seed catalogues and woven baskets stacked on top of the stove, the porcelain sink dry. But there was little clutter and I found the glasses easily.

"Ah," said Harriet when I held one toward her. "Perfect." For a while we sat together quietly. Harriet's head was turned, she was looking out into the garden, and I had a chance to study her, the soft folds of translucent skin along her jaw, the ear, like candle wax. I let my gaze follow hers. There too, despite an air of randomness, the beds were trim, weeded, and watered. I saw pink-and-yellow lantanas, zinnias, marigolds. More gerbera daisies. "It's a frightful mess," she said. "I plant in hope of butterflies, and I do get a few, though not so many as I used to. Also lots of floppy brown moths."

She sipped her tea. "Will gives a good party," she said. "I always try to go. You must have been looking for Patrick? Well, no mystery there. You two were inseparable." She paused and her face grew thoughtful. "You were good for him. People think it's a blessing to be born into that kind of money. I don't know why. His drinking isn't any better."

I said nothing. I understood how Patrick seemed to other people. And yet, however hard I tried, I could never see him the way they did.

"I was good for him?"

"Your persistence."

"You can say that now because of the way things have turned out."

She regarded me almost fiercely. "Don't be silly. If you're going to take the blame for what happens in your life, you must learn to take the credit too. All success entails some element of chance. You were very young, I understand that. Which may have made it seem chancier still. But if you were a man, you wouldn't hesitate to claim it."

"Oh, I claim it. For the record, anyway."

"You're just not sure you deserve it? My dear, who does? The fact is, you have always been . . ." She thought for a minute. "Focused." She smiled at her own small joke. "Patrick, on the other hand . . ." She sighed. "A person needs to have something to do that matters. And I don't mean sitting around his daddy's office."

"Is that all he's doing?"

She looked at me sharply, then shifted in her chair and reached into a pocket. "I'm going to smoke now, I hope you don't mind." She pulled out what looked like a little cigar and lit it with a kitchen match that she struck against the wall. There was a pattern of scratches there as if someone had begun to write a message but had never gotten past the first stroke.

Harriet shook out the match. She gazed at me for a moment. Then she said, "You must wonder about this house, why I don't paint it. I know your parents were diligent about that. In this climate it's an endless burden. Eventually the responsibility fell to me. I didn't want it. So I don't do it. I've replaced some rotten wood over the years, but that's all." She exhaled and watched the smoke rise.

"Why didn't you leave? Sell the house? If you didn't want to . . ." I stopped myself. I had been about to say "keep it up," but that wasn't right. The house was kept up.

"I did leave. I was gone, on and off, for years. I rented the house, and it gave me a nice little income. I went to Mexico City and Taxco and San Miguel, and of course money goes farther there. And then I lived in Taos for several years. But I think I always knew I'd come back eventually. It draws you, doesn't it?" She paused. "And in your case, there's Patrick. It's hard to leave things unfinished."

She leaned over and extinguished her cigarette and pushed it through a crack in the porch. "Fear not, nothing down there except dirt. And a lot of those—cigarette butts. I hide them because I'm not supposed to smoke." She pointed to a striped cushion. "If you wouldn't mind? I can't always get comfortable." I positioned the cushion behind her and she sat back. "Better," she said. "Now." She took several deep breaths and gazed off into the garden, until I began to wonder if she had forgotten me.

When she looked back, all the color was gone from her face. "I'm sorry. These days it doesn't take much to wear me out. Give me just a sec." She closed her eyes, and I saw that her lids were crisscrossed with tiny purple lines.

In the garden, the sunlight turned the dancing bodies of passing insects from brown to gold. Harriet Kinkaid's chest rose and fell, and the hot wind moved the plants and eddied across the porch. It was as if the house and the garden breathed with her. After a few minutes she roused herself. "We can talk a little now. And perhaps you'll come again. I'm not the most scintillating company, I know. But I'm willing to tell you what I can. If that's a bribe, so be it." She smiled.

"About Patrick. You said things were left unfinished."

"You must have sensed that? I don't mean that they didn't take care of the situation. After the fire. Everyone was . . . compensated. The girl had only her mother, who worked at one of the hotels. She moved away. The people who owned the house never came here. And they had insurance."

"You know this?" I asked. "For a fact?"

Harriet waved my question away. "I know how things happen in Galveston. And so do you." She paused, then went on. "But I don't mean all that. I'm talking about you and Patrick."

"I've tried to find him," I said. "To talk to him. But he didn't come to the party. And when I drove out to his house, the one on the beach, he was gone." I didn't feel it was necessary to mention Lafitte's or what had happened there. "Eleanor said he looks different. That he was burned."

"That's true."

I waited for Harriet to say more, but she was either tired or reluctant. Finally I asked, "Do you think he doesn't want to see me?"

Harriet seemed to settle more deeply into her chair. "I think it's complicated," she said. "He is shy about appearing publicly—that may be why he skipped the party. And why he so seldom appears at the bank. I'm sure he knows you're here, though."

I didn't say anything. We both understood how information percolated through the Island. Harriet said, "We'll talk again." Her eyelids fluttered. "Don't worry about the door, I never lock it." She lay back against the striped cushion, lines of effort still visible around her mouth and eyes. Her closed face held the promise of more. Slowly, I rose and left her sleeping.

Chapter 18

I'D BEEN PREPARED TO DISREGARD Eleanor's comments concerning Patrick. *He's put a lot of things behind him. He may not want to go back there.* But Harriet was different. I had no reason not to believe her. I had to consider the possibility that Patrick knew I was on the Island but didn't want to see me. *It's complicated,* Harriet had said. Did he think of me now as one more awkward social situation to be avoided? Did he imagine me turning away from his burned face?

Back at the archive, I noted with satisfaction that my notes and the piles of photos I had left the day before were undisturbed. A new box sat next to them. Across the way, the door of Gwen's office was open. My feet made no sound on the carpeted floor as I approached.

I had expected a more impressive space. There was just room for a scarred desk and a small bookcase. A single window with a cracked pane overlooked the side street. Gwen was leaning back in her chair, her bare feet propped against the edge of her desk. She was gazing at the wall to her right, and she had an absent, dreamy look on her face. Her narrow skirt had inched up toward her hips. Taped to the wall was an image clipped from a newspaper. A man bent over a ceremonial shovel smiled into the camera. It was Will Carraday.

I had just time to raise my Leica and press the shutter before she reacted, sitting up abruptly and tugging on her hem. She reached out a foot and wriggled it into one of her shoes, but the other had traveled under the desk and she had to bend over to retrieve it. She stood up, flushed and breathless. "I hope you don't think that I . . . that I was . . ." she began. Then she must have decided it was wiser not to say exactly what it was she hadn't been doing.

"How are you?" I asked. The silence between us grew, and I saw that a discussion was unavoidable. "It's a good shot," I said. "Nice light. Interesting composition." She looked over at the wall. "You wouldn't let him see it?" Her discomfort at the thought was palpable.

"It's not for the exhibition," I said. I paused, then I added, "He's a sophisticated man."

I could see the idea registering. If she objected to the photo, refused to let me use it, and I told Will, what would he think of her? That she was naïve, provincial? Her features took on a clenched look at odds with her usual poise.

"If I do show it," I said, "sometime in the future, here's what will happen. There will probably be a title. But it won't identify you. And the people who see it will be interested in photography, not library science." I smiled in a way I hoped was reassuring.

"Well." She took a jacket off a coatrack, put it on, and straightened the lapels. "Since you tell me it's a good picture." She gathered some things from the desk and checked her watch. "I have a meeting downstairs," she said.

I wondered how long she had been in Galveston. Where she had come from and what she had left behind. Clearly she was good at moving on. I thought then that Gwen was probably the sort of person Michael needed, someone who could part with pain or anxiety as easily as she took off her shoes. Already she had let go of the awkward present and was anticipating a time when she might want to claim the photo. Of course she didn't care about her office. It was only temporary. For now, what mattered was Will's good opinion. And therefore mine.

I remembered how she had gazed at his picture, the way she'd lifted her chin toward him, her lips and thighs parted. I had never intended to show Will any of that.

I went back to my table. Next to the photos was Ty's folder. I'd forgotten all about it. When I opened it, what struck me first was the color. There was so much that was already familiar from the relief portrait of Stella—the figure of the girl, slim but rounded, the cling-ing folds of her dress, the hip-shot pose. But the effect was different. Everything that was cool in the ersatz bronze of the relief was warm in the painting—the girl's red lips, the blushing skin of her neck and breasts, and above the bodice of her dress, just visible, the rosy arc of one nipple. The image was plainly erotic. I noticed that, in the paint-ing, the pitcher was broken.

I thought of Ty offering it to me, then of someone else—Eleanor perhaps—finding it and throwing it away. I thought of the young architect, Henry Durand, offering it to Stella's father. I felt uneasy, as if the body being passed around were my own. Why had Ward Car-raday chosen to portray his daughter in that way? Of course, the relief was less overtly sexual than the painting. I wondered if Stella had ever seen the original.

I went back to examining and sorting.

It must have been around four when I felt something like a change in the atmosphere. There was a murmur of voices, and the glass door opened. It was Will. As usual, there were several people following him, but he smiled and held up one hand in what was clearly a gesture of polite dismissal, and they fell back.

He crossed the room, his step springy, his face full of the convic-tion that he was welcome wherever he was. I don't know what he saw in mine, but it wasn't what he'd hoped for. He stopped and put his hands in back of him. "I'm sorry," he said, "I didn't intend to inter-rupt you, but I couldn't help myself." He looked down at the images I'd been considering.

"This box is mostly shots of the municipal water board. And so on. Not very exciting," I said. His face fell ever so slightly, and to my surprise I found myself wanting to encourage him. "There is this, though." I pulled a print out of a pile I had made earlier.

The photo showed the approach to a trade show in some kind of public space. At the curtained entrance was the marble bust of a woman in fluttering drapery, her hair piled on her head, her sightless eyes as smooth and white as two hard-cooked eggs. A banner above identified her as "The Spirit of Progress." The print was grainy, but

I had recognized the piece immediately as the sculpture in our front hall at home, the bust that was supposed to be a portrait of Lavinia Giraud. I pushed the photo toward Will.

He sat down, leaned forward, and placed both hands on the table, as if he meant to give all his energy to the act of observation. After a moment, he threw his head back and laughed. "Well I'll be darned."

"Did you know?" I asked.

"I hadn't a clue."

"My father wouldn't have thought it was funny. He was very serious about our house and its history." As I said it, I understood how silly it sounded, how unimportant the Hayes-Giraud house and its associations must seem to Will.

He seemed not to notice. "Really?" he said. "I try not to take any of that too seriously."

"My father did."

Will said gently, "You know, family history's full of twists and turns. With these old houses, it isn't always easy to tell where things came from."

I said, "My father didn't believe the stories or listen to hearsay. He always wanted proof." That was how he had represented himself to us—as the provider of facts. *Believe what you want*, he would say when we resisted the gift he offered, the bitter, improving truth. *They are ashamed at having been stupid enough to drown.* Now it appeared that he had engaged in willful self-deception. The bust wasn't a portrait. It had nothing to do with our house or its past.

Will was looking at me expectantly. "I said, I wonder if you'd like to come and have a drink with us?"

"Are you asking for a progress report? Because I'm not prepared to give one."

Will smiled. "No, nothing like that. Actually, I have some photos at home I'd like you to see. Most of them from the last century. Family photos. In Stella's room. I'd like you to be the first."

I felt my cheeks flush. His offer was generous, and I had been rude. But Will seemed prepared to ignore it. "I saw your car in the lot. You can follow me. Or I can give you a lift. If you'd like?"

I nodded.

"You'll ride with me? Good. Someone can come back later for the station wagon. Now. I'll go around the corner to the museum. You can meet me when you're ready." And Will left, fading away gradually behind the glass door. Something about the sight of him disappearing made my breath come quicker.

My concentration was gone, but I made myself sit for fifteen minutes, shuffling prints, leafing through the notes I'd taken, before I began to gather my things. Then, with all the dignity I could muster, I went after him.

The museum consisted of objects that had somehow become the property of the library—ships' compasses, family Bibles with brass clasps, Mardi Gras masks. Its content was not so different from what Sally had accumulated at her shop, except that the individual items were more effectively lit and laid out next to little texts that explained their importance. I had a photo in mind: the mannequin from the desk, standing next to one of the displays, looking as if he had stepped out of a case.

Will was regarding an old ledger, its pages covered in black, spidery script. The card next to it identified it as Ward Carraday's. "Shall we go?" Will asked. It wasn't really a question, more a polite way of letting me know what he wanted to do.

We rode down in the elevator. "You look like a teenager," he said, nodding at the old windbreaker I'd found in a closet and was wearing in the air-conditioning. It was much too big. I knew what he meant—a girl wearing her boyfriend's jacket as a way of advertising their relationship. But I hadn't had a boyfriend, I'd had Patrick, which was different. Will had seen us together often enough, before we were sent away. Thinking about it brought back my feelings of resentment. "That was a compliment," Will said. "You're glaring at me." I pushed my hands deeper into the pockets.

Outside was the convertible, the two-seater I had seen in the garage, parked in a loading zone. A meter maid was at work down the street, but there was nothing on the windshield.

The air was still and heavy, full of the charged awareness that precedes a storm. I looked at Will and knew what he was feeling—the curious mixture of fear and longing that is the legacy of the Great Hurricane. If you're an Islander, you carry the thought of it with you, like the invisible layer of salt that collects on the skin.

"I can put the top up," Will said. "Or we can try and beat the rain. What do you think?"

He opened my door, effectively answering his own question. As he drove, he continued the conversation, with only sporadic help from me. But Will seemed not to notice when our dialogue faltered, and that gave me confidence. His attention felt like a fixed thing, as solid as a well-built wall.

He pulled the car into the garage. We walked toward the house, then he said, "Wait. I have something to show you first." He quickened his step and went into the rose garden.

I followed him to where he was standing. The flowers, growing in clusters, were full and soft. He slid his fingers under a blossom and turned its face toward me. I remembered my father saying *some kind of aesthete*. A few drops fell, but Will paid no attention.

The sky grew gray and a light came on next door. Eleanor would be alone in the house. I wondered if she knew we were together. Will reached out and touched another rose. Was that how he looked at her, touched her face? The thought was both irresistible and painful.

There was a whoosh of wind and all the flowers stood up straight, then bent low and swayed. Then the first rush of real rain came, and with it the smell of baked clay off the hot ground, so strong it seemed to color the air. For a moment, we stood still. There were drops in his hair and on his eyelashes too. The shoulders of his shirt began to darken. When he gave a shout and ran for the house, I was right behind him.

I followed Will up the broad stairs to Stella's room. I had been there before, of course, with Patrick, but those had been brief visits, flying raids. Now I would have time to investigate at my leisure. It felt strange to be encouraged to go through someone else's belongings, something I had been told all my life not to do. "The photos are mostly in scrapbooks," Will said. "And there are some old letters and postcards. I don't know if those will interest you." Down the hall I heard Mary Liz clear her throat laboriously.

I looked around, trying to see past what I recognized. The wall-paper was cream-colored with a pattern of stylized lilies. But the furniture was all ponderous Eastlake mahogany—a half tester bed with brass bars that would have supported mosquito netting in the days before air-conditioning, a bureau whose marble top had yellowed like old soap. The ensemble seemed to belong more to the master suite than to a young girl's room. I wondered if it had been recycled when the house was built—another one of Ward Carraday's odd economies.

Will opened a drawer and left it so that the contents were partially visible. Then he turned a key in the wardrobe. "I hope you will come and go as you please." He paused and smiled almost shyly. "The way you used to."

I thought of the trouble Patrick and I had caused together in and around the house and wondered how much Will knew about it. He had never quizzed us or threatened punishment, but one day he called us both into the kitchen and said gravely, *You are not to make work for Faline.* Did that mean he knew we had put the remains of our uneaten sandwiches down the laundry chute? Dripped honey between the keys of the piano? I felt suddenly ashamed. I turned away so he couldn't see my face and walked toward the window. The shower was already over, chasms of sunlight slanted down through the clouds.

Will said, "I never minded, you know."

I stood looking out at the lawn. The house was so large and thickly constructed it seemed to swallow sound. As the silence settled around me, I felt Will's gaze on my back. I knew he was waiting for me to speak. But it was too late for childish confessions, and I didn't know what else to say. I closed my eyes and leaned my forehead against the glass, needing to feel its hard smoothness.

"Well, I'll leave you to it," he said. "Faline is here during the day, of course, but I'm going to give you a set of keys so you can stop by whenever. In the evenings, if you want. Mary Liz is usually upstairs.

She enjoys company, if you'd like to say hello." His damp shirt gave off a starchy smell. I heard the sound of the keys on the bureau top, then his footsteps going away down the hall.

I opened my eyes. I was used to looking out my own window toward the Carradays', to seeing the big house looming over the alley. Now I understood that the view looking back was different—it took in three properties. The Carradays' second story was substantially higher, too, so that everything below seemed smaller.

I pulled out the first drawer of the bureau. As Will had said, there were a number of albums. One, covered in faded silk, had a title, *My Trip to Paris.* Inside were souvenir postcards depicting tourist sites— the Arc de Triomphe, the Eiffel Tower. I removed it and set it aside.

Next was a notebook of drawings, mostly in pencil. Careful studies of flowers, a crab, a broken sand dollar. I riffled the pages. I noticed that toward the back of the album, everything became smaller. The last few pages were so densely covered they were almost black.

Underneath the notebook was a hardcover volume bound in cracked leather and embossed, and on top of it a kid glove, stained with age. I picked up the glove and smoothed it against my palm. It seemed so little, I wondered if it had shrunk. I thought again of the shoe I had seen in the shop on the Strand. I knew that we were all of us healthier and larger than the Islanders of a hundred years ago. Our feet and hands were bigger. The idea should have been encouraging, but I found myself thinking unaccountably of the way farm animals, steers and hogs, are raised to set records for size.

Down the hall a door opened, and I heard Mary Liz's voice: ". . . bother to talk to me about it. You'll do what you want anyhow. Jesus Christ. A grown woman, and I'm never alone in my own house. There's always someone. You, Faline, Otis, Patrick. You think I don't hear him sneaking around?" The door closed again.

The glove had left a partial outline on the book's faded binding. No one had thought to disturb these things for years. The book's title was *A History of Galveston.* Holding it carefully in both hands, I settled into a nearby armchair.

It wasn't really a history but a collection of biographies. Most of the entries were accompanied by an oval studio portrait. In the index I looked up "Carraday" and found the gold-bordered text.

> *Ward Carraday began his enterprise in a humble manner. For many years he operated a dry goods establishment. He remained a bachelor, living frugally in quarters situated above his business until the age of forty, when he wed Adelaide Stussy, a schoolteacher twenty-four years his junior.*
>
> *Over time and as his means permitted, he expanded his holdings. At his death, he possessed a residence of rare comforts, among them a French chandelier and the first piano west of the San Pedro River.*
>
> *It was his habit to turn his head when speaking to give his right eye the advantage, because his left orb had from birth a tendency to wander. Perhaps for this reason, he was not inclined to the pleasures of society, but kept to his home and family.*

There was no photo of Will's grandfather.

I heard the sound of conversation, then a pause, and Will approaching. Was he going downstairs? Away? Would he pass by without saying anything? He put his head in the door. "I promised you a drink. Would you like to join us for a few minutes? Only if you want to, of course."

I closed the book and followed him. In the hallway, the walls were lined with more photos. I realized that there was nothing in the house—no painting, no photograph—that wasn't in some way related to the family. Nothing that might be, for a child growing up there, a window into any other world.

Mary Liz was smoking a cigarette in a long, black holder. "Come in, come in," she said waving it so that a thin contrail of smoke drifted above her. She was on a chaise, her wasted legs, as always, covered. "Sit, will you, I dislike people looking down at me." She gestured toward a sofa filled with pillows. "I understand you're interested in old things. Damned if I am." She laughed harshly. "Never expected I'd be one myself. Animal has an accident like mine, you put it down."

Faline came in carrying a tray with a chilled bottle, a variety of glasses, and a bowl of ice. "Nobody around here feels sorry for you. Not one bit." She set the things out. "Now, you got everything you want? You think I might go and see to my husband?"

"Don't let her fool you," Mary Liz said. "She doesn't have to be here, fetching and carrying. She could have made something of herself. She had three semesters at the College of the Mainland." Mary Liz looked at Faline appraisingly. "Now it's too late. She's getting to be an old woman. Cords in her neck." She reached for the loose skin under her own chin and laughed again, a raucous sound that shook her chest and shoulders and then became a cough.

"All right," Faline said, "I'm leaving now. You going to have to survive without me until tomorrow."

"We'll be fine," Will said. "Thank you."

I moved a few of the pillows, trying to make room for myself on the edge of the sofa.

"So here you are," said Mary Liz. "Without the camera, for once. And here I am, the captive audience. Well, are you going to pour her a drink or not? And me, while you're at it." She raised her glass toward Will and rattled the ice. Her thin, iron-colored hair stood up from her head, as though it had been freshly coiffed. "You're not a sorority girl, are you," she said.

I was momentarily confused.

Mary Liz inhaled deeply and a tube of ash fell onto her lap and scattered. She brushed it onto the floor, and repeated her comment, slowly, as though it were the language I hadn't understood. "You don't have to say so, I can tell. I was the same way. I hated those sorority girls with their charm bracelets."

Will opened a cabinet. "The selection up here is limited, I'm afraid," he said. "Is white wine all right? It's that or bourbon, and you don't strike me as a bourbon drinker."

"That's his way of saying he thinks you're more sophisticated than I am."

Will handed me a glass of wine.

"I was reading about Ward Carraday," I said.

"Jesus. Ugly bastard."

"My grandfather." It seemed to me that Will's manner changed then and became more formal, more like the way he had been with his guests. "You must have found the book with the biographies," he said. "I haven't seen it in years. The family had an opportunity to participate, which they refused. Then, when it was published, they didn't like the result. There never was a picture. My grandfather always said he didn't want to be photographed. Well, you can understand why. The eye. It gave him a strange look. Angry."

"It was more than a look," said Mary Liz. Her gaze rested on me as she swallowed and gave a sigh of satisfaction. "They called him the Old Goat. He liked them young. Christ. I don't know who was worse— Ward and his teenage bride or Franklin with his face like a bankruptcy lawyer. You've heard the story about the horse?"

Will looked hard at Mary Liz.

"I think she ought to hear it," she said. She put her glass down with emphasis. "I think she ought to know something about the Carraday family. I think it's appropriate. Don't you?" She was talking to Will, but her eyes never left mine. She seemed to want to hold me there, the way a predator fixes its quarry. "Ward Carraday was trying to unload a wagon, wanted to bring it right up to the door. Horse wouldn't back to suit him. He lost his temper. Got down, tore a board off the back. A board with nails in it. He beat the horse to death in the street. Left it lying there until someone complained." She smiled, her lips narrow, vivid. "They were tough old boys in those days, and even they couldn't stomach it."

I glanced at Will. "It may have happened," he said. "Or something like it may have happened. Time goes by, and those old stories take on a life of their own."

Mary Liz drew on her cigarette, exhaled at the ceiling. "It was your daddy, Franklin, told me," she said. "He saw it happen."

"He was a child."

"Nice thing for a child to see."

I felt myself slipping off the edge of the sofa. I glanced at my wine.

The room was warm, already the glass was misted over. I reached for it and felt the moisture run under my fingers. I hoped I wouldn't drop it.

Mary Liz removed her cigarette from its holder, stubbed it out, and returned the empty holder to her mouth. "Will doesn't really like to talk about his folks," she said. "Does that surprise you? You've seen him give the tour. The truth is, he'd like to believe he just sprang up out of nowhere. But he doesn't mind hearing other people's stories. They all do that here, repeat other people's. You know the Moodys?"

I nodded. Mary Liz went on. "You know William Moody formed the Cotton Exchange way back when? He had an interesting system. A farmer would bring in his crop, Moody's cotton hands would weigh it and take ten pounds off each bale as an allowance for water. After the cotton had sat around on the dock for a few weeks getting heavier in the humidity, the state inspector, who was in Moody's pocket, would weigh it again. His figure was the price the buyer would pay. Moody kept the difference. Will doesn't mind talking about that." She sucked on the empty holder, and it made a whistling noise.

"M'Liz," Will said, and his voice held a clear note of warning.

"You're the one wants her to see all that old stuff. You think it will stop there? You do, you're a goddam fool."

"The exhibition is about the photos. That's all. Clare's a professional. She knows that. She's not going to go digging up old gossip. And as far as Colonel Moody is concerned, in fairness, it was a muckraking reporter who made those accusations, and he had his own agenda."

Mary Liz turned to me. "Don't you just love the way he talks? 'In fairness. An agenda.' I think that was what made me fall in love with him, when I was young and foolish, the way he talks. It wasn't something you heard a lot in Bend, Oklahoma. We all have our own *agendas*, Will. You do. She does. Oh yes, she does. She's after something, I just don't know what it is yet. Maybe she doesn't either."

I was tired of the two of them talking as if I weren't there. "Why do I have to be after anything?" I asked.

"Because it's how you are. How you've always been. I've watched you your whole life, you and Patrick both. I probably know as much about you as you do. Maybe more. Maybe a lot more." She tilted her head and looked at Will thoughtfully.

"What do you know about me?"

"I know that even when you were a little-bitty girl you were into everything. And that you are persistent as hell."

I wanted to ask about Patrick. But I hesitated. Harriet had been kind. I couldn't count on Mary Liz for that. Would she confirm, scornfully, that Patrick didn't want to see me? I didn't think I could bear it. Instead, I changed the subject. "Tell me about Stella," I said. "What happened to her? Did she leave the Island? Or did she drown in the house, the way people say?"

Mary Liz laughed once, a sound like a dog barking, then stopped suddenly. "Good for you, get to the point. We can do with a little more of that around here. You want me to tell her?" she asked. "Or will you?"

Will's head was turned toward me, but his gaze passed me by. When he spoke, his tone was carefully neutral, but his jaw was set. It made him look, for a moment, a little like his father. "There's a stone in the old city cemetery. Stella's buried there. With her mother and father." He turned away and busied himself with the drinks tray.

But Mary Liz was right. It would take more than a little coolness to deflect me. "So the part about Stella's hair getting tangled in the chandelier?"

"There was a woman found like that," Mary Liz said.

"It wasn't Stella," Will said. Then he stopped.

Suddenly I felt an unexpected urge to take Mary Liz's side. Why didn't Will want to know more, or discuss what he did know? Why had he never examined Stella's belongings himself? "Why didn't you ever look through her photos?" I asked. "Why did you wait so long?"

Will sat down. He crossed one leg, then uncrossed it. Then he said, "I told you, I think, that I wanted you to be the first. Because of your interest in photography. Your career. And this seemed like the right moment. But I guess you could also say I was just lazy."

It's commonly said that Galveston's climate, the heat and humidity that produce luminous pastel skies, drains people of energy, making it easy for the Colonel Moodys of the world to have their way. The Islanders claim this laziness, boast about it even. Who, after all, would want to be a hard-bitten, grasping Moody? Doing nothing was laudable, if you believed that was the only choice. Was that what Will believed? His face was impassive, except for the muscle working in his jaw.

I stood up and looked for a place to put my glass. It was still half full. Will reached over and took it from me, but his eyes didn't meet mine.

I remembered then how I had felt growing up, that there was a conversation going on around me that I didn't understand, that passed me by and never acknowledged my presence. It came flooding back, the sense of exclusion, the obscure feeling of shame that accompanied it.

"I think I'll get back to the photos now," I said.

In Stella's room, I grasped the chair I had been sitting in and shoved it clumsily toward the window. It was heavy and required several attempts. When I was done, sweat was starting along my hairline. But I experienced a satisfaction out of all proportion to the task. I stacked the two photo albums on a small table nearby.

It seemed that no one wanted to think about Stella except me. I knew what it meant to be ignored. Was that one of the reasons I felt drawn to her? Because her family had chosen to forget her? Because her life had been turned into a series of quaint vignettes for tourists to enjoy?

I at least didn't have to settle for that version of Stella's story. The evidence was in front of me, if I could only understand it.

We imagine people in the past as different from ourselves. We see their clothing—all those layers—and confuse it with the bodies underneath. We see how upright they are in their formal photographs, forgetting that the women wore corsets, that men and women both were strapped to a wooden backboard for support. We picture them as simpler beings.

But people don't change in any essential way. Time passes, conventions are thrown aside, clothing is discarded—how did they endure it in the heat? Underneath, things are not so different. Sweat. Nerves. Desire. All the feverish complexity of emotion.

I thought about Stella's father, Ward Carraday, gone all day at his office on the Strand. In the evening, unwrapping a cigar at the Artillery Club, trading anecdotes, drinking a slow glass of whiskey. Then one more.

It's astonishing how he can make it last. Stella's mother, ill or unhappy—it amounts to the same thing—lies stretched across a chaise in a room where the blinds are drawn. From time to time, she measures out a spoonful of liquid from a brown medicine bottle. She calls in a tired voice for ice to refresh the compress on her forehead, ice that has to be chipped from a block in the kitchen and carried up three floors, quickly, before it melts. She calls for her daughter, but Stella pretends at first not to hear. But her brother is a child. Only Stella can prepare the ice and fix the compress exactly the way her mother wants it done.

Stella is seventeen, restless, preoccupied. Without noticing, she strips the leaves from the potted ferns, pulls the ribbons off her best hat. She never reads anymore, not even the issues of *The Ladies' World* that slide from her mother's bed onto the floor. She is impatient. She wants to begin the only narrative that matters, the story of her real life. Soon she will shed the house and its inhabitants—these people she hardly knows—like a husk. She feels it. Every day she dresses her hair differently. She polishes her nails with a silver buffer until they shine. She tucks a lily into the waistband of her dress. She feels sorry for her mother, whose gown is soiled and whose fingers tremble, but she is tired of running up and down stairs fetching ice.

Leaving her father's office, she sees the young architect, who fails to tip his hat. She is old enough to understand what has made him forget himself. From the corner of her eye, she watches him pause and look back.

Chapter 19

THAT EVENING, ELEANOR CALLED ME into the room that had been my father's study. "It's for you. Michael." She stood cradling the phone against her neck and shoulder as if it were a pet animal or a small child, although I had never seen her hold either. Something about her pose struck me. I steadied the Leica and shot from my hip. The shutter clicked.

Eleanor said, "I can't believe you haven't phoned. You owe him that much." She took her hand from the receiver and spoke into it. "She's right here." She replaced her hand. "Just try," she said. "Make an effort." She gave me a look and left the room.

The study was still very much my father's. Sitting there among his things—the walls of books, the Audubon prints, the gold fountain pen on the desk—confronted with their persistent reality, it was hard to believe I'd ever had another life. This space was what endured—the stripes of light, the complex old-house smell.

Michael said, "Hello? Clare? This is the third time I've called."

Of course. He had been keeping track, carrying the information around with him, hefting it the way he did the handful of change in his pocket, trying to determine its worth. His voice was clear and full of energy. I could almost see it zinging through the wires, shooting out the receiver. *This is important,* it said, *pay attention.* Juries always paid attention to Michael.

There was a pause, and I could feel him adjusting his manner, taking it down a notch from what he would have offered a client or a colleague. Measuring out exactly the level of response our relationship required. "I called to see how you are," he said.

"I'm fine."

I thought of my father then, and how he had objected to any other reply. *It's a formal exchange, for God's sake. A social gesture, not an invitation to rehearse their symptoms. Do they expect me to give medical advice on the street?* In the end, he had stopped asking people how they were. Instead he went directly to the weather talk that was always acceptable on the Island.

I tried to listen to Michael, who was describing a trial that involved a hit-and-run. *I owed him that much.* It was one of many debts I had incurred—a small one, but still, another mark on an invisible scorecard. Had there been a time when our marriage wasn't an exercise in assessment? I remembered Michael's proposal. What he'd said was, "I love you enough to marry you." I didn't know how much that was, but I was equally sure that Michael did, exactly. At the time, it had reassured me.

I spoke into the phone. "Do you miss me?" I asked.

There was a pause. Then Michael said, "Of course. Well, there's a lot going on. So the car made it okay?"

"Yes. Otis cleaned it up."

"Otis?"

"He works for Will. Will Carraday."

"You found places to stay on the way down?"

"Yes." I knew Michael meant overnight, that he was thinking of motels, bed-and-breakfasts along the route he had drawn. He would not want to hear that I'd left the highway, that I'd slept by the side of the road and in parking lots. He still talked about safety and risk as if they were things we could control. When what had happened to Bailey made it clear that no one was safe.

"And the exhibition?" Michael asked. "How is it coming?"

"I just started." I looked around the room. I couldn't explain the feelings it aroused, anxiety and something else, pressing. The need to hide, to disappear. "I was tired," I said. "I got here and went to bed and slept a long time. Then I went to a party." I thought of the photos I'd set aside at the archive. I hadn't made much progress. Part of me didn't seem to care. I recognized the feeling, the irresistible slide into indolence that was part of Island life.

I could hear Michael breathing. Was he laboring as hard as I was to keep things going? I pushed on. "The party was for Will's birthday. You would have enjoyed it." I recalled Will with his guests, imagined Michael at the door. I thought how easily Will would have managed him.

There were noises on the other end of the line. "Call me next weekend," Michael said. "I've got to go."

Then I heard another voice. "Hi hon." It was a female voice, a little sugary, familiar, though not immediately recognizable. There were muffled sounds, then silence.

"Is that Denise?" I asked.

"Denise who?"

I couldn't remember his assistant's last name, and it made me feel as though I were somehow at fault. Was this what he did to witnesses? No wonder he was so successful. Already, he was turning the situation into a test of my interest and competence.

"It's Maureen. One of the second-year associates. We're going over some paperwork."

"It doesn't matter," I said, and found that I meant it.

Michael began to speak, and I listened until I understood that he wasn't talking to me. I waited for a minute. Then I asked myself what I was waiting for. Deliberately, I hung up.

I picked up the gold pen that had been my father's. I could easily imagine what had gone into choosing it. He would have tried and rejected dozens before selecting this one, the pen with just the right weight and balance, just the right flexion in the delicate nib, so that its use was a unique source of pleasure. But as I held it in my hand, I could get no sense of this. It was like trying on someone else's shoe. I think he would have liked that—the fact that no one else could experience or enjoy this thing that was his in precisely the same way.

I tried the point against the desk pad, tentatively at first, then with more force. Nothing happened. It seemed to be dry. I shook it hard, and when I tried again a sudden stream of ink flowed out. I wiped my fingers on the blotter, leaving long smudges. I licked my fingers and wiped them again. The smudges spread. The blotter was ruined. Before I left the study, I worked it out of the leather frame, folded it several times, and buried it at the bottom of the wastebasket.

BEFORE I MET MICHAEL, I'D THOUGHT, naïvely, that a good witness was someone who told the truth. Now I knew that it was more complicated than that—that evidence had to be presented in a form that was appealing to the jury. A good witness was likable. A good witness was someone who would see life like a game board, laid out in vivid primary colors with clear dividing lines and straightforward routes. Who rarely hesitated or expressed uncertainty. I thought about that a lot in the months after I lost Bailey. When I was certain of nothing.

Eleanor took care of the funeral. She found the cemetery where we buried Bailey on a small hill. I remember how cold it was, the closed buds of the dogwoods shaking, the cloth enclosure surrounding the grave flapping in the wind. None of it felt real to me, certainly not the letter my father sent explaining his absence. He spoke of his role, his students, his responsibilities.

It was the thing Michael fixed on, the thing that kept him going. *That son of a bitch,* he said. He tore the letter to pieces and threw them in the fireplace. Then he put his fist through the screen door. A few days later I found him sobbing in the bathroom, and I understood that already he had accomplished something I hadn't even begun.

What Eleanor said was *I think you need a rest.* She chose the place and I went willingly. I didn't care where I was. Or that I would be observed. As an Islander, I was used to being under observation. And to defending myself against it.

The hospital resembled a country hotel. The buildings were aged brick or white clapboard with long verandas, the staff dressed in casual clothes. There were picnic suppers outside, a badminton net,

lawn bowling. Only the heavy doors, locked at night, and the bathroom mirrors, made of polished metal instead of glass and fixed permanently to the wall, revealed the true nature of the place. It must
have been incredibly expensive.

Most of the time, I dozed. I knew there were other patients who
wanted to act out, to run away. There were times when the idea hung
in the air, like a low-pressure system, making the staff anxious. I
had no desire to do anything. I felt as heavy as I had when I was nine
months pregnant. I wanted to lie down and let it crush me, the gro-
tesque weight that no one else could see.

During the time set aside for exercise, I settled myself on one of
the outdoor chairs with my feet up like a passenger on a turn-of-the-
century ocean liner. But nothing moved, every day the lawn rolled
down in the same still, green waves toward a wall of trees. I stayed
just where I was, drifting in and out of consciousness.

From time to time I wondered whether I would ever take another
photograph. But I wondered in a remote way, as though the question
had to do with someone else.

I knew a photojournalist who suffered some nerve damage in his
right hand after an illness. Matt had learned to shoot with his left
hand, using a special, left-handed camera, and he took photographs
and sold them as he had done previously. But they were not, he said,
the same photos he would have taken before.

He had been the least constrained of men. I remembered him, at
a political fund-raiser, jumping on a dainty, brocade-covered stool
to get the shot he wanted, impervious to the glare of his hostess or
the twittering of the houseboy, who seized the stool and carried it off,
the impress of Matt's boot still clearly visible.

Now, he said, self-consciousness presided over everything he
did. He was thinking of going to work for his brother's construction
firm. "No such thing as a left-handed hammer," he said.

I wondered if now I would have to think about what I was doing
every time I raised the camera, consider every possible consequence.
And if I did, would I be able to go on taking photos?

After three weeks, I went home to Michael. We were carrying groceries in from the car when I felt rain on my hands and hair, and I longed suddenly for the sky to open and wash away everything around us—the winter-brown lawn, the house, its windows vacant in the late-afternoon light, the miscellaneous objects we carried and would carry again and again, clutched to us as though they mattered. I let go of my sack. It hit the pavement with a soft scrunching sound. Cans rolled along the driveway.

"I can't do this," I said.

"Come inside," said Michael, as if I hadn't spoken.

We moved to an apartment. Away from the yard, the tree, the swing. And things were different but not better. The boxes remained unpacked, their open flaps waving. Dishes accumulated in the sink. At first Michael was patient, then he was annoyed. He had done what he could, hadn't he? Now it was up to me. *To make an effort.* So that we could go back to our old life.

The kind of effort he and Eleanor expected was beyond me. The one thing I did do during that time was a series of photographs of him—Michael in the narrow kitchen drinking coffee, steam rising from his cup; Michael sleeping on the floor in front of the TV while the colorful bodies of a cartoon family hover brightly above him. The images are tranquil, domestic. The kind of work I had always been afraid of doing. They are among the most popular of my photographs, and I understand why. Anyone looking at them would be reassured. Anyone looking at them would think, *It's all right,* no matter what had happened the day or the night before.

Chapter 20

THE POPULATION OF GALVESTON is almost sixty thousand. Enough, a visitor might think, to provide the kind of anonymity most city people take for granted. But the odds of encountering someone you would prefer not to meet are greater than the numbers alone suggest. Life on the Island requires a high degree of social vigilance.

I meant to avoid any further conversations with Ty, and so far, I had succeeded.

He'd called me, and Eleanor had dutifully relayed his messages. There was nothing in them to suggest more than friendly interest, and no reason not to respond. If I'd been less preoccupied with my own concerns, I would have. But I didn't want to hear myself talking like a tour guide. And the thought of answering Ty's questions, of trying to explain the Island and its ways to him, was overwhelming.

Since the day he bought me ice cream, I had seen him only once. Or, to be accurate, he had seen me, since I watched for him in the places along the Strand where he was likely to be. Twice I had spotted and avoided him, stepping back into a shaded doorway and turning to walk suddenly the other way. Once, he had waved at me from across Twenty-fourth Street, but I pointed to my watch, pantomimed an appointment I didn't have, and hurried on.

I felt foolish doing these things and also vaguely resentful. The need to be on the watch for Ty was an unwelcome distraction from the very different need—one I was prepared to indulge—to watch for Patrick.

Harriet was right, Patrick must know I was on the Island. I'd resolved not to call Lowell Morgan's beach house or go back there again. I would take a less direct approach.

I drove by Saint Vincent de Paul. Once I even pulled into the mostly empty parking lot and observed the parishioners coming and going. They paid no attention to me. Either they were absorbed in what they were doing or they chose not to acknowledge my presence. They were casually dressed, and at least half of them seemed to be Hispanic. According to a sign, mass was offered daily at 7:30 AM in English and Spanish. Too early for Patrick.

I looked often for the light in Stella's room.

That was the first part of my plan.

The second part was to question everyone. Faline, Frankie, Harriet Kinkaid. To learn something.

What, exactly, I didn't know. But my thoughts went often to the days after the fire. I replayed each scene, reviewing the cast of characters, struggling to recall all that had happened. I felt certain that there was more to discover, more to be learned from that experience, if only I could bring it back.

I carried the keys Will had given me in my bag, but I had yet to use them. I preferred to find my way into the Carraday house as I always had, through the open back door. Faline tolerated my presence as long as I didn't touch anything in the kitchen or interrupt her progress. I perched at one of the marble counters, as if I had just happened to stop by. That was how we had always been most comfortable.

The subject matter of our exchanges had evolved a little. She was willing to address a wider range of issues, but the tenor was the same. There was no sign of the emotion—apprehension? pity?—I had glimpsed the night of the party. I understood that it was something I was not supposed to have seen. Light escaping from underneath a closed door. Now Faline's manner was, I thought, intentionally opaque. Her hooded eyes revealed nothing. But I remembered how they had widened. *Is that why you here? Baby, tell me that not so.*

I kept hoping the door would open just a little. I remembered, too, what Mary Liz had said about never being alone. About Patrick sneak-

ing around. If I lingered before going upstairs, there was the possibility I might run into him.

"I seen in the paper some Shriners come down from Houston,"
Faline said. "Put up in a bed-and-breakfast. Went out and had theirselves a good time. Some kind of function. Then they went for a swim,
left their clothes on the beach."

"That wasn't in the paper," I said.

Faline shrugged. "They got out, everything gone except their hats.
Tall, you know, with the tassel." She twirled her finger and I nodded. "Took them a while to get back without being seen. Stooping
behind cars. Ducking down in back of trash cans. Must have been
a sight." She giggled, then covered her mouth with her hand. When
she'd regained her composure, she said, "They got back to the house,
the lights still on. A group of ladies occupying the front porch." She
paused and began taking things out of the refrigerator.

"Go on," I said.

"Seems they was obliged to wait across the street, behind the construction. A pile of lumber. Mosquitoes bit them all over so bad they
left the next day. Went back to the big city." Faline was not BOI, but the
Islanders' peculiar sense of superiority was a natural fit. "Serve them
right anyway," she said darkly, "grown men running around nekkid."

"What else could they do? They had to go home."

"Home?" Faline frowned. "They should have *stayed* home in the
first place." The idea of tourism—travel for its own sake—offended
her.

"It's a good story."

"Otis told me."

"Oh. Well, then."

"Tell you what I seen with my own eyes," Faline said. "A woman
comes out of one of those three-story houses on Sealy Street, maybe
the one with the bay window. Had on a print dress and a real pretty
hat, straw with a big brim. She comes down the front walk, taking
little steps, nice as pie, right up to the curb. And what do you suppose
she does when she gets there? Leans over and spits in the gutter."

Faline banged the pans she was rinsing for emphasis. "Just because someone look a certain way, don't mean they won't surprise you. You can't say what a person thinking. Or what they might do."

"You're not telling me anything I don't know," I said.

"Yes, I am," she said. "I truly am. Only you not listening."

She tucked a dishtowel into the waist of her skirt. "For instance, you see her upstairs, with her legs, you think that's how it's always been. But I got a perspective you don't. I started here when I was twenty-two years old and she wasn't much more. Times was different then. What was expected. How a girl, a woman, had to be. I never met anyone—man or woman—like her before, carried on exactly as she pleased. Watching her in those days was something, let me tell you. He followed her around like a puppy dog."

"Will?" I hadn't talked to him since I'd left Mary Liz's room. There had been a perceptible coolness between us. I was surprised at how much I missed our exchanges.

"He had to chase her all over the state of Oklahoma to get her to marry him."

This was interesting information, new to me, and I wondered what else I might elicit. Faline put a pot of water on the big enamel stove. There was a hiss and a series of clicks as she turned on the gas and adjusted the flame.

"Did she drink then?" I asked.

"Drink to excess, you mean? Yes, she did. She did everything to excess and back then drinking was just one thing. Now she got to fill up her days somehow." Faline unwrapped a brisket, laid it on the counter, and turned it over several times. "What they want for this at the grocery is a sin," she said. She put the meat in the sink and turned on the water.

"What was wrong with Catherine?" I asked. "I mean, what exactly?"

Faline shook her head. "Might could have been a fever." She moved the meat to the counter and patted it dry.

Catherine had not been allowed into the kitchen, or any other room where food was laid out, because she would gorge herself until she vomited. Outside, unattended, she would stuff her mouth with twigs or dirt, or with poisonous oleander blossoms.

"How old was she?"

"Little. A baby."

How many fevers had Bailey had, I thought, with no lasting harm? How many children had played for years on backyard swings just like ours and grown up and lived their lives? How could the consequences of the same unexceptional experience be so different?

Faline was lining a baking pan with foil. I watched her elbows moving back and forth, the muscles working in her arms.

"Patrick was sweet with Catherine," I said.

"Patrick have a good heart," Faline said. Then she stopped abruptly. I knew she was on alert. There was a wire basket of green apples on the counter to my left. I reached out for one. Quick as a snake she turned and grabbed the basket. "What happen to your manners? You don't know to ask before you take something?"

"May I have an apple?" I knew it was a game, still it irritated me.

"If looks could kill, I guess I wouldn't be long for this earth. Take it on upstairs, now. I got work to do."

On the landing I stopped and listened. Light poured in through the stained glass and made patterns on the wainscoting and the red runner. I could hear Faline moving around. The only other sound was the sigh of the air-conditioning.

In Stella's room, I stood next to the table, leafing idly through an album stuffed with loose photos. I bit into the apple, enjoying the way the skin popped against my teeth, savoring the tart sweetness. I wondered if Stella had known that sensation. She would have been expected to eat an apple off a plate, to cut it first into pieces with a fruit knife.

I thought about Stella's dress, the layers of concealing fabric she would have worn, even in the heat, the boned corset that would have left ridges on her skin. Her clothes, her eating habits, her behavior. So many constraints. *What was expected. How a girl, a woman, had to be.* And yet, there was the evidence of the relief that revealed her body, that showed something completely different. Evidence of what, exactly?

Among the photos was an image of a woman standing in front of the Carraday house. There was no sidewalk of any kind, but sidewalks had never been a priority on the Island. The figure in the foreground stood on an expanse of bare, sandy earth. There were no trees in the photo, no grass either. I turned the picture over. On the back, in pencil, were the initials S.C. Could it be a photo of Stella?

It was nothing like the formal portrait on the living-room mantel, the one Will had shown his guests. There Stella posed gracefully in an upholstered chair. Her silk gown with its train probably cost more than the photographer earned in a year. One small, white hand cupped the curve of her cheek.

The woman in front of the Carraday house wore a shapeless cotton dress. She stood stiffly, her hands hidden in her skirt. Her hair seemed not to have been combed, and she squinted, chin tucked, in the harsh light. Her face was blotched, windburned. Everything about her spoke of discomfort, as though she had submitted, only, to be photographed. She seemed much older.

Or was it just the images? One made by a professional under ideal conditions, the other snapped casually, perhaps under protest?

I looked again at the photo, at the Carraday house. There was the imposing façade, a little lighter in color, the brick still fresh, still impressively new. There were the tall windows, the three-foot black cast-iron fence, like our own, but more elaborate. The gate where tourists gathered.

The gate. The three-foot fence. All at once I understood what it meant. When Stella was growing up in the house, the fence had been six feet tall, the same height as the gate. I looked again, this time at the windows on the lowest level of the house. They were cut in half at the ground, elongated ovals that had been half buried. The absence of trees or grass, the absence of any walkway confirmed it. The photo had been taken just after the grade raising. After the Great Hurricane.

Stella had survived.

If it was Stella. I sat down. I looked at the photo, front and back.

This wasn't like the image from the trade show. I couldn't be sure. Were the initials really Stella's or someone else's? Had someone added them later, making a guess at the woman's identity? Did the letters signify something else entirely?

I was tempted to talk to Will, to share my thoughts. I recalled the way he had laughed about the bust that was supposed to be Lavinia Giraud. For just a moment, I let myself imagine his excitement and approval. Then I remembered his face when I inquired about Stella. What Mary Liz had said. *Will doesn't like to talk about his folks.* I recalled, too, our family dinners. Frankie and my father laughing. I didn't want to be wrong. I sat turning the photo over and over in my hands.

If Stella had not died during the hurricane, where had she been during the storm? Had she left the Island and then returned? I looked again at the face in the photo. If she survived, what had happened to her? What else had she endured? Probably Will knew, though he wouldn't discuss it. And Mary Liz.

I believed Faline knew too. If she did, it might be something she'd be willing to tell me.

When I went downstairs, she was outside on the broad veranda, gazing toward the street. Faline's back was ramrod straight, she gripped a broom, upright, the way a lookout might hold a rifle. There was sure to be a group of tourists just outside the gate. As long as they stayed where they were, there was nothing she could do about them. But their presence had always provoked her. How often had I heard her complain? *They got nothing better to do than stand around staring in other folks' yards?*

I went to the big front door and opened it. I waved at the tourists, who drew back. They seemed surprised that as onlookers, they were visible too. "They're just curious," I said to Faline. "They've heard about Stella, what happened to her."

Faline stabbed her broom into a corner of the veranda. "They fools if they believe those stories." She raised her voice and said again, "Fools."

I sensed an opportunity. "So it isn't true? About Henry Durand? And Stella running away?"

"They ran away all right."

"But she didn't drown," I said.

Faline smiled. "No such thing." Clearly she enjoyed knowing what the despised tourists didn't. "They ran away, her and the young man, Henry. Crossed the causeway before the storm hit. Afterward, no one knew was she dead or alive. Then they thought they found her. The girl with her hair caught." Faline lifted the doormat, exposing a rectangle of sandy dirt. She shook the mat, and hung it over the stone balustrade. "They found another one too. Some of her fingers gone. Cut off. Somebody wanted her jewelry."

Reflexively, I made fists. But my need to learn more was urgent. "What really happened?"

Faline shrugged, as if the answer was obvious. "Her daddy went after her. Brought her home." She leaned the broom against the wall. There were begonias in pots grouped on the veranda. She bent and examined the first.

"Then what?"

"Then nothing."

"Nothing? She never got married?" Faline pulled off one dead leaf, then another. I knew she enjoyed making me wait. When she was satisfied, she straightened.

"She had offers. One from the doctor owned your house there. His wife had passed. They had to let him through when the street was tore up and all the digging going on. But her daddy said no."

So Phillip Giraud had met Stella during the grade raising. The marriage would have been a step down for her. Was that why Ward Carraday objected? Because a man who was merely respectable wasn't good enough for his daughter? Or did he think she was too young? It seemed unlikely, given the age of his own bride.

"Why did he say no?"

"Why? He didn't like him. He didn't like any of them came courting. Planned to keep her for hisself."

"You mean . . ." I didn't know how to express what I was thinking, not to Faline.

She turned and said, "You seen the picture. In the drawing room.

Is that the way a man look at his child?" She gazed around, satisfied. "I'm done here now. What about you? I thought you supposed to be working upstairs."

I went back through the house toward the garden, thinking about what Faline had said. I wasn't the only one who thought the relief portrait was peculiar. I'd begun to wonder if it was only because I'd seen the painted original that Ty had found. And having seen it, could no longer separate the two.

I thought again of the photo, Stella's worn dress and sad, chapped face. This much was certain—Stella had survived the storm. And her life afterward had not been easy.

I asked myself, how does a man look at his child? I remembered the arguments Michael and I had had about Bailey. I remembered too that when he wasn't busy working he would willingly watch her, play with her. At those times another Michael, open and undefended, was briefly visible. Whatever happened between us, I had never doubted that he loved her.

I thought too about my father, about his fondness for facts and data, his scrupulous attention to historical detail. I remembered him speaking about the bust in the hall, the way his tented fingertips touched and touched again. I recalled all this, and it seemed to me that the same man who had identified thousands of birds, who could distinguish minute differences in their appearance, had hardly seen me at all.

Chapter 21

WHENEVER I TRIED TO CALL UP AN IMAGE of my father's face, what I saw instead were the freckles that overlapped his lips and swarmed into his ears, the pale eyes, the tufts of graying red that were his eyebrows. I waited, thinking these distinctive traits would come together for me the way the characteristics of birds—bill shape, leg color, feathers—must have done for him. Like all serious birders, he had kept a life list. He could classify a hawk, silhouetted against the sky, without the help of binoculars.

When I was five or six, the idea had come to me that identifying birds was an important activity, like the practice of medicine, but, since birds were everywhere, one I could take part in. I began paying attention, and soon I could identify a few common species. I tried out my new knowledge on Faline. "Look, there's a dove."

"Sure is. Looks like dinner has come right to us. Bring me down a gun out of the upstairs hallway."

"Faline!"

She shrugged. "People got to eat."

I was in the back garden when a gull settled on the cottage roof. Flushed with excitement, I ran to tell my father, stumbling, going down on one bare knee in my hurry. I pointed. "A seagull!"

Without raising his eyes from the newspaper he was reading he said, "There's no such thing as a seagull."

I stood again and turned to look. There it was, perched on the gable, still as a carving. It had a white breast, a black bead of an eye, and a red mark on its beak. I squinted, turned away, looked back. The gull was still there.

"I see it."

"There is no such thing," he said.

I know now what he meant. "Seagull" is a catchall term not used by people who study birds. There are laughing gulls, Bonaparte's gulls, ring-billed and herring gulls. More rarely, there are Franklin's, lesser black-backed, and glaucous gulls. But there are no "seagulls." In fact, many species of gull nest inland. But as a child I didn't understand. All I knew was what was in front of me, the evidence of my senses, and this he had dismissed.

It felt like the time I ran into the swinging cafeteria door at school just as the janitor with his trolley started to back through from the other side. It was like lying flat on the streaky green linoleum in the hallway, stunned and gasping, watching the plaster walls move in and out.

Except that I was still in my own backyard, and the green around me was grass. The breeze riffled the edges of my father's newspaper. His head was still buried. I looked down at my plaid shirt, my shorts, at my knee streaked with dirt and blood. He didn't seem to see that either.

Years later, I went to the library and checked out a color volume on birds. I studied the plates. There were dozens of species, and the distinctions between them were so minor that it turned out to be more difficult than I had expected to tell *hyperboreus* from *delawarensis*.

As I turned the glossy pages of the book I realized that my father must have possessed a formidable talent for visual distinction. Without conscious thought, he registered primary and secondary feathers, coverts, scapulars, folded and in flight. *The rump is white with faded gray-brown bars*, I read. The rump? *The head is moderately sloped, the brow heavy. The iris is pale yellow, the orb-ring yellow to pale pink.* I wondered what had gone through his mind as he made his notes, added to his list. Had he ever looked at a gull and thought to himself, *The breast is delicately marbled?*

At that time, I wanted to believe it. I wanted to find something sympathetic in his determined observation and cataloguing.

In the end, I had to accept the truth. What my father and I saw when we looked at the world was different. He perceived and registered details better than I ever could. But once he had seen and logged a bird, it no longer mattered to him. So he missed the astonishment of the familiar, of the ordinary thing perceived suddenly in a new way. He saw and recorded the features, the type, but missed entirely the flight, the song.

GROWING UP, I HAD ENVIED FRANKIE. It didn't occur to me then that the role of favorite might have its own drawbacks. Since our conversation in the kitchen, I viewed her differently. I believed too that there was more to be learned from her.

I called Frankie and told her I wanted to talk. From the silence on her end of the line I knew she was surprised, but she agreed to meet on Friday for a late lunch. When I hung up, my hand was damp, but I felt exhilarated, as if I'd achieved something important.

I met her in the lobby of the condominium where she and Stephen stayed when they were on the Island. It was new construction, but the decor had been carefully chosen to suggest the laid-back raffishness of the old shore—wicker furniture with canvas cushions and inexpensive green plants. Everything was expendable. But the building itself was solid concrete raised up on massive legs. In a storm, the glass walls would blow out and the ocean would pour through and carry everything away. Afterward, someone would hose the floor and sweep up the debris.

The condominium units were all thirty feet above ground. I knew it must make Frankie feel safe. I don't know why it had the opposite effect on me. I stood looking out at the deck, at the pool rimmed with trailing bougainvillea and the sky beyond. It was overcast, the sun visible only as a bright disk, a white spot like the blind eye of an old dog.

I felt Frankie's hand on my arm and started. "Oh, you're here," I said.

It was her chance to make a routine cutting remark, but she let it pass. She had on tan linen pants and a black shirt with the same pieces of silver jewelry she had worn before. Maybe it wasn't fair to call it a uniform. She looked like what she was—a competent, educated woman whose vanity was not about her looks.

"I was thinking how different this is," I said.

"From the house? Yes, it is." Frankie gazed toward the pool and nodded her approval. "Imagine, before this place went up, there was nothing here except sand and bugs. No history! The condo is just a space that contains the things we need. Beds. Chairs. A refrigerator. It's nice but anonymous. I love that about it. It doesn't make any demands. In fact," she looked at me slyly, "we rent it out when we're not using it."

I turned to look at her and Frankie laughed. "You should see your face. Oh, I understand, it didn't come naturally to me either. Just buying the condo was a production. The two of them wanted us to do over an old house. Research it, of course, find out exactly how the front door looked in 1885, go into debt to some contractor, then live for years with the work itself. Nails on the floor, sawdust in everything. But we have hard jobs! We don't want to come home to more work. I like being free of all that effort. I don't want to live what feels like someone else's life. The life of a person I never knew who died a hundred years ago."

Frankie's features were lit with conviction, and for a moment I could see again some of her old brightness. For the first time, I understood that she too had struggled with our parents, that things had not been as easy for her as I had assumed. I was impressed that she had cast off entirely our father's legacy—the sense of indebtedness to the past that he expressed to us as self-denial. How had she done it?

She went on: "If Eleanor wants to worry about whether she's got the right . . ."

"Carriage block," I said.

"Precisely. If Eleanor wants to deal with all that, let her."

"Let them, you mean. Eleanor and Will."

Frankie looked at me. "Eleanor and Will," she said. "Yes." She gestured toward the double doors that separated the lobby from the landscape outside. "You said lunch? I'm hungry."

We walked out to the raised parking area where flags snapped in the wind. It occurred to me that you could drive up to the building, occupy your rooms, swim in the pool, sit on the deck, and never set foot on the sand or in the water. So that the beach was only a distant, cheerful panorama signifying vacation, with no more reality than a postcard photographer's painted backdrop with its cartoon palm.

I wondered if future generations of visitors, who settled for the view through the big windows or from their balconies, who never floated in the warm ocean or felt the sand against their skin, would behave better. If the seedier bars would lose some of their business and the police would get fewer disturbance calls. I wondered too if these same visitors would see their experience as different from what could be had in any other modest resort. Would they care about the Island at all? About what happened to it?

Frankie regarded the jeep. "That's Will's car, isn't it?"

"Yes."

"You're driving his car?"

"For now. Otis is working on mine." It had been three days since I'd seen Will, three days since the last time he'd stopped by Stella's room to talk to me, but I was driving his car. I found I needed that connection.

I started the engine and nosed down the ramp to the beach road. When I shifted into second, the jeep balked and shuddered. Frankie said, "God, you're a terrible driver," but she smiled.

It was the kind of thing she'd always said, but it felt different. So did Frankie's questions. I didn't resent them as I once would have. Reluctantly, I thought back to what Eleanor had said. *Maybe you two can see each other differently now that you're adults.*

The restaurant was on the first floor of a converted warehouse near the factory district. Crystal lights hung from black crisscrossed tie beams. The floor was concrete, the chairs leather and comfortable. "This is interesting," I said.

"We like it," said Frankie. "No macrame. No gulls. No concessions to tourism. It's too far away for the docs and the med students. And the food is really good. The owner is from someplace up north and thinks he's died and gone to heaven. He's survived his first winter, so maybe he'll make a go of it."

We talked that way for a while, sharing information. A waiter came and took our drink orders. No one listening would have found our conversation noteworthy. No one watching would have known what it meant for the two of us to sit together peaceably over a meal. I noticed that the line of gray along Frankie's part was gone, and that the color of her hair was more subdued now that she had to choose it. Those reddish glints had always seemed to me evidence of a kind of energy I would never possess. Now I found I missed them.

Frankie laid down her menu. "What about you and Michael?"

I was ready for this question, and prepared to answer. Still, my first reaction was to tell her it was none of her business. I took a deep breath. Then I said, "I think it would have been over for us sooner, but there was Bailey. Something would happen, and we'd fight, but then we'd keep going. For her."

It seemed to me that Bailey's death marked the end of that process, not the beginning. For a long time, there had been nothing to suggest we wouldn't stick it out like so many couples. If Michael had not always been faithful, I had not always been kind, and as long as there was Bailey to consider, we were both prepared to try.

"What are you going to do now?"

"I don't know. But I'm not going back to him."

"Mother's telling everyone you are. That you'll be done with your research in a few weeks and you'll be leaving. Christ! It makes me crazy the way everyone attends to her. She is not the center of the universe." She raised the oversize menu and disappeared behind it. When she set it down again, she said, "I used to think it was just a habit we'd all gotten into. But I've seen her do it to other people.

Including Stephen." I could hear the disappointment in her voice. So Frankie had imagined that Stephen would win that battle for her. I hadn't thought of her as someone who needed help.

"I used to blame Michael for what went wrong with us," I said. "I don't anymore."

The restaurant was filling up. Two men sat at the table next to us. A family of four settled with more drama near the door. There were two daughters, the elder girl about fifteen, in a short skirt and tube top. When she crossed the room, one of the men at the table next to us watched her over his tortoiseshell half-glasses. Up close, I could see that she was more like thirteen. She wore sticky lip gloss that matched her top. I watched the man's eyes tracking her.

"Don't you think the relief portrait of Stella is strange?" I asked.

Frankie looked perplexed. "Of Stella Carraday? Are you talking about the one over their mantel? I thought that was supposed to be a copy of something in a museum."

"It is, but it's Stella, too. And there are goat legs on either side of the fireplace."

"I don't know. You said you wanted to talk about Daddy. What does any of this have to do with him?"

"Nothing, I guess."

Frankie pointed at the menu. "The shrimp salad is good."

The waiter returned and we ordered. After he left, I spoke first. "What Eleanor's saying doesn't surprise me. She's always liked Michael."

"What she likes about Michael is that he keeps you at a distance. No, wait. I know how that sounded. What I mean is this—she's thinking of herself. Of what she wants. Not what's best for you or for him."

"Maybe that's her secret," I said. It was true that Eleanor never doubted her own desires. If she wanted something, she took it. While other people were pulled in different directions by inclinations at odds with their sense of what was right, Eleanor's feelings and convictions were all lined up like metal filings in the presence of a magnet.

Our food arrived with a little flurry. When the waiter was gone, Frankie said, "She doesn't want you here. You must know that."

I thought back to the night of the party. Eleanor's strange remarks. "She said she wants me to be happy."

"I'm sure she does. As long as it doesn't mean giving up anything she wants."

"She was the one who called me about the exhibition."

Frankie stirred her tea with an impatient up-and-down motion that made the ice cubes dance. "It was Will's idea," she said. "He made the whole thing happen. Funded it, I assume. Got the library involved. Mother would never have called you if he hadn't pressed her."

I experienced then a moment of clarity—like what happens when you paint the walls or replace the carpet, and the space you have known, the room and its familiar contents, rise up fresh and vividly detailed around you. My thoughts arranged themselves in a new and compelling order. All along, it had been Will who had moved things forward. Will who had prompted the official invitation. Will who had led me to Stella's room.

"Are you sure?"

"Would I say so if I weren't?"

We sat quietly for a while. Then finally she spoke.

"I heard about what happened at the party."

I sighed. "If you're talking about Tyler Henry, I'm sure it's all over the Island by now. But I promise you, there is nothing to talk about."

Frankie speared a cherry tomato neatly with her fork. "You do understand how it is here? There are only two sides, the Island side and everything else. We're not from Galveston anymore. We're fair game." She paused. "You said there was something you wanted to show me?"

I reached into my bag and pulled out the plaid camp shirt. "Do you remember this?"

Frankie looked puzzled. "It's old, isn't it?"

"I found it in Eleanor's closet."

"You haven't changed, have you?" she said. "Still snooping in other people's things. I don't remember it. Why? Should I?"

"No, it's nothing exceptional." I looked down at the limp handful of faded cloth. "I don't think she chose this shirt in particular. I wore it a lot, that's all. But she has some old clothes of ours mixed in with hers. Do you know why she kept them?"

"I have no idea." The delicate lines between Frankie's brows deepened, and I sensed her impatience. "Was this what you wanted to talk about?" We had come a long way, but I could see that I was asking too much. I put the shirt back in my bag.

"Did either of them—our parents—ever discuss the fire? Did they ever say anything about it? About why Patrick and I were sent away?"

Frankie shook her head. "I don't remember anything. But there's no mystery there. If you're Will Carraday, the easiest way to deal with any problem is to make it go away. Literally. Why not? Think of Catherine." When Frankie put it like that, the logic seemed irresistible. There was no reason to look for anything more.

"There's something else," I said. "I found a photo at the archive. Of the bust in our front hall."

"You mean Lavinia?"

"It's supposed to be Lavinia, but it's not really. It was part of a trade show. It has nothing to do with the house."

Frankie sat back. "You're kidding."

"I can show you," I said.

"No, I believe you." I could see she was thinking hard. Finally she said, "All right. We have plenty of time. I want to eat, and then I want to tell *you* something."

"You don't have to—"

"I know." Frankie cut the tails off two shrimp, then pointed with her knife at my plate.

I pushed the food around, watching her as she ate, efficiently, like a person who had limited time for meals. Inevitably, one of the few bites I took fell apart and salad dressing dribbled onto my chin. I reached for my napkin, and Frankie's mouth twisted.

"You've always done that," she said. "What I've never understood is how you can look beautiful with food on your face. Faline used to say, 'A girl pretty enough it don't matter how she do.'"

"She did?" I was amazed. Then I realized it was just the sort of thing Faline might have said to put Frankie in her place. I knew she meant well, but I wondered if, growing up, we might have gotten along better if we had been encouraged, even a little.

Frankie nodded, her mouth full. She rested her forearms on the table. "You haven't eaten much."

I started to respond, but she shook her head. "You need to hear this. When I was getting ready to apply to med school, I asked Daddy to contact some of his former colleagues at the hospital where he did his residency. I thought I might like New York. Talk about different! But he refused. He gave me a speech about striking out on my own. At first I believed it. Then I began to have doubts. Remember, he was the one promoting medicine as a profession."

She picked up her glass and drank as if it were an assignment she'd been given. When she set it down again, she said, "Doctors have mentors. It's a big part of why they choose one specialty or another—because the chief of surgery is a genius, because the pediatric oncologist is a saint. So who were they? His mentors? He wouldn't say. It didn't make sense. I went to Eleanor. I said I knew something had happened. Now it makes me laugh to think I didn't know. I asked her to tell me."

"What did she say?"

"She didn't. Not the first time or the second. You know how she is. She looks at you, but she's seeing something else."

I nodded.

"She actually backed away. But I followed her through the house. She kept talking about plants and the natural order. I remember she asked me if I knew what a sport was. A mutation." Frankie snorted. "She was hinting at something. I've always hated the way she makes you feel less than subtle because you want a straight answer. So finally she went to the kitchen sink and turned on the water so she couldn't hear and stood there with her back to me. She thought we were done. But I picked up the garden shears and held them between her shoulder blades. Don't look at me like that. I wasn't going to do anything. I just wanted her to understand that I was serious." Frankie closed her eyes and shook her head, as though refusing something.

"What did she do?"

"She smiled. Not a social smile, *Hello, how lovely to see you, can I get you a drink?* The private one she does when she's looking in the mirror. Then she told me. 'Since you're so determined to know,' she said."

Frankie folded her hands in front of her. "Daddy had a young patient. She told her parents that he hurt her. The hospital kept it quiet, but he was asked to resign. He was lucky to get the appointment here. Someone did him a favor. Someone with local connections." She looked down at her lap. Frankie had followed him into the profession. His shame was her shame, and she felt the weight of it.

"She stayed with him. She never told anyone," I said.

"Don't imagine she sacrificed herself. It wasn't like that. Mother has always been clear about what she wanted." Frankie glanced at her watch. "I have to take a call at three." She reached for her purse and made as if to stand. Then, instead, she leaned forward, her voice straining with the effort she was making. "Didn't you ever wonder why our parents had separate bedrooms? She told Daddy that if he wanted her to stay with him it would have to be on her terms. Do you understand? This thing with Will Carraday isn't new. It's been going on for a long time."

I know Frankie expected me to react. But the memory came back suddenly. A morning in the garden in back of our house. I was emerging on my hands and knees from under the porch when my father, who was passing by, swung his leg into me. His heavy brown shoe caught me just below the ribs. He said nothing, just kept on toward the alley. He must not have noticed Eleanor, who had been working, half hidden, among the plants. She straightened slowly. "I saw that," she said.

"Well, damn it." My father flushed. Half circles of sweat showed under the arms of his white shirt. He clutched the handle of his briefcase. "What is she doing under there?"

There was a long pause. I saw Eleanor fix him with a look so cold it burned. I didn't understand it, but I had a sense then of her power, I felt that she could make him stay there, bear that contemptuous gaze, for as long as she wanted.

Frankie pushed back her chair. "I'm glad you called," she said. "I'm glad we talked. Stephen and I will be down for a couple of weeks in July. If you want, we can get together."

I looked at my sister, so known to me in so many ways, and wondered who she really was. "I'd like that," I said.

Chapter 22

MY FATHER KEPT HIS BIRDING BINOCULARS in the alley house. Once I grew too big to fit under the porch, it became my principal refuge. Since the med students were always at the hospital, and my father rarely visited it except on weekends, the alley house was surprisingly safe.

So was the clump of cannas nearby. No one tended or cut them back. In Galveston, cannas were poor folks' flowers—cheap, easy to find, rhizomes that grew and naturalized in any kind of soil. The clump was bigger each year.

In the days when Catherine still lived at home, I often visited the alley in order to listen for her. Catherine didn't speak. She made guttural breathy sounds, long fluting calls, and when she was frustrated, grinding shouts of rage. These sounds both frightened and fascinated me because I knew they came straight from inside her. They were not complicated by thought or constrained by any standard of behavior. It seemed to me that, for all her limitations, Catherine was able to express herself in a way I was not.

I should have realized that the routes we took—mine, Patrick's, my father's—would converge in the alley eventually.

One evening, a group of boys, four of them, turned down the sandy path. Hearing voices, I stepped in among the tall red-orange blooms.

"Tony's got to piss," said one of the boys.

"So let him." There was shuffling, and I heard the unmistakable sound of a stream hitting the packed earth.

"That's pathetic," said a voice. "I bet I can hit that trash can."

I parted the leaves just enough to see them standing together. One was zipping up, two of them had their flies open and were holding themselves in readiness. I had never seen a naked boy who wasn't still a baby, and I was curious about their bodies in the detached way of a child who is generally inquisitive. I remember examining their penises, the tender, proprietary way they held them, and thinking for some reason about the newborn mice I had seen once at school.

At that moment, Catherine blundered through the hedge. Somehow she had eluded Faline and found her way to one of the places where Patrick and I had created an opening. She had to press herself against the thick, springy branches to squeeze through, but she seemed not to notice that they had scratched her bare arms and legs.

In the fading light, her size and broad fleshy face made her appear older than she was. The boys were ready to run, and if she had kept moving they might never have realized their mistake. But finding herself in a strange place, she stopped and stood still, giving them time to examine her. As usual, she breathed loudly through her open mouth. Her tongue protruded slightly. A stocky boy with black hair that stood up stiffly said, "Look at her. She's not normal." He stared at Catherine, considering. "Maybe we can do something with her."

"Like what?" asked a skinny boy with a pronounced Adam's apple.

The bigger boy took a step closer. He smiled, showing a gap between his front teeth. "Give her an Indian sunburn," he said. Then he reached out, put both hands on Catherine's arm, and twisted. When she didn't react, he did it again, longer and harder. This time she let out a wail.

"She's a retard," said the skinny boy in disgust.

A third boy who had been standing quietly said, "Don't mess with her." He was clearly younger than the others. His shirttail hung down over his shorts and his ears stuck out like handles from under a baseball cap.

"Why not?" the black-haired boy responded. He made fists, and the muscles in his arms jumped. "She don't know the difference."

"She's crying."

"That's not crying. Haven't you ever heard a pig squeal? My grandfather kills pigs." He reached for Catherine again, but this time he took hold of the hem of her cotton dress and lifted it. "Let's see what she looks like with her clothes off," he said. "I bet she looks like a pig. I bet she's got a little curly tail."

He couldn't know that Catherine hated being dressed or undressed. Naked, she was unself-conscious, and she seemed to forget her clothes once they were on, provided they fit loosely and didn't chafe. But she fought any kind of change. So her wardrobe was limited to the essentials. Details of any kind—buttons, pockets, a sash—she would tug on until they came off, leaving torn places. So Catherine wore plain shift dresses that zipped in the back where she couldn't reach and fell straight from the shoulder.

I had seen how Faline managed her, heard her crooning and kneading Catherine's scalp through her short hair so that she grunted with pleasure, before swiftly sliding the dress up and over her head in one practiced motion. But Catherine still experienced the process as a kind of violation.

When the black-haired boy yanked at her dress, Catherine, surprised, reacted with all her strength, swinging both arms wildly. One of them struck him in the face.

He sat down abruptly, stiff-legged, and the others laughed.

"What the hell, Tony. Knocked down by a girl," said the skinny boy.

"Shut up, asshole," said the black-haired boy. Scrambling to a crouch he lunged at Catherine. But she was solid, her feet planted stubbornly. She might not understand exactly what was happening, but her body knew how to resist. She took a step, but remained standing, and reaching down she seized hold of his hair. I don't know if she meant to do more than steady herself, but it must have seemed to him that she was fighting back. He began to pummel her soft midsection. When she sank to her knees, the skinny boy joined him.

I watched her go down. Part of me wanted to cry out, to stop them. But I was too used to listening, to keeping quiet. I stayed hidden among the tall leaves.

The sound of their fists made me think of Faline, the way she worked a ball of dough, turning and smacking it. From the end of the alley I heard other sounds, the swish of a car passing, a woman's voice calling a child to supper, the sounds of everyday life, somehow full of sadness.

The black-haired boy, Tony, paused and looked back at the others. "What are you, afraid?" They shook their heads, but stayed where they were.

Catherine was on the ground with two of them on top of her, her dress hiked up around her waist. She made swimming motions with her thick arms and legs. She must have bitten her lip when she fell—when she raised her head I could see, along with smudges and the streaks left by tears, blood running down her chin. I closed my eyes.

Time passed, then one of the boys cried out, and I heard a new voice, one I recognized as Patrick's, but raw, full of some new emotion. I peered out and saw him swinging, hitting, and kicking at them both at once. When the skinny boy stood, Patrick pushed him backward against the trash can that rattled as it fell over. I smelled coffee grounds and decaying food. Tony seized Patrick's leg and pulled him down and they rolled together into the loose garbage.

Neither of them noticed the lights of the Buick entering the alley or saw my father unfold himself from behind the wheel. There was no urgency in his manner as he approached. The beams of the head-lights lit the ground in front of the car and the bodies of the boys. My father took hold of Patrick's collar and pulled him up. He gazed at the boy on the ground, then prodded him with his foot. "You," he said, "go home."

The boy staggered to his feet. My father regarded Patrick at arm's length. "I know what I'd do with you if you were mine," he said. He paused, his face unreadable.

The world was now the bright space in front of the car. Everything else was dark. I felt my heart strain in my chest and something hot and wet running down the inside of my leg. I closed my eyes. When I opened them, my father had turned back to the car. Catherine was gone.

I stayed where I was until everyone had left, then I took off my underpants and threw them into the trash can that was lying on its side. I pushed some of the trash in, too. Later, when Patrick showed me the dead snake and told me what he proposed to do with it, I understood.

When I recall what happened that night, what comes back to me first is my own shameful inability to act. To move or call for help, to do anything for Catherine as she lay in the dirt. Then, as I peered out from the cannas, Patrick's face. As familiar to me as my own, but unexpectedly joyful, the face of someone willingly risking everything.

Chapter 23

JUNE CAME TO THE ISLAND and the crape myrtles bloomed—first the pale pinks and lavenders, then the stronger shades, magentas and dusty reds, as if the color were intensifying with the heat. Watermelon trucks, their tailgates down, appeared along side streets and on vacant lots, each with a wedge cut open for display, ripe flesh stuck with a knife.

Sunrise took place slowly through a pearly mist, disappointing visitors familiar with the tropics, who had to settle for a pale line along the horizon. At daybreak the sand was brown on the beach and brown in the water where the surf pushed it back and forth. The Gulf was dull as asphalt. But by nine the same landscape was all vibrating brightness—sand that glittered, water that was full of light, sky so profoundly blue it hurt your eyes. Shadows so black that everything within them was lost to sight.

At the hardware store that sold plywood and generators and, for the fancier houses, metal storm shutters, the sign went up: HURRICANE SEASON IS HERE.

Four more days passed before Will stopped by Stella's room again, time enough for me to gauge precisely the effect of his absence—the depth of the silence, broken only by an occasional cough, the weight of the air in Stella's room that, without the energy of Will's presence to stir it up, pressed on every surface. Occasionally I heard his footsteps, heard him speak to Mary Liz as he closed her door. That was all.

I would not have gone down the hall to him—I had that much

pride—but when he put his head in and suggested a fishing trip, I agreed immediately. "I used to see you on your way to the bait shop," he said. It was not the moment for me to explain what had really drawn me there. "It's too hot to go fishing during the day," he continued. "But we can do some flounder gigging. The bay will be pleasant at night." He smiled at me and I felt as though something larger had been resolved. Will went back to his study whistling.

That evening we drove out to the shore. Will talked and laughed and listened, his head tilted. The strong beam of his attention had turned my way again. When we stopped for the light at Sixty-first Street, he looked me up and down, his gaze full of approval. I sat back and stretched my legs.

The sun was setting as we pulled up to a wooden shed near the causeway. I had thought that there would be only the two of us, but as always where Will was concerned there was a crowd. Four or five men, one already in the boat, the others milling around. There was no one I recognized. Suddenly it occurred to me. "Is my mother coming?" I asked.

Will looked surprised. "Eleanor gets terrible motion sickness." He paused. "You didn't know?" His tone was mild. Still, the question stung.

"I guess there's a lot I don't know," I said, but he had already turned back to the group. Several of them seemed to have been waiting for his arrival. They greeted him the way you would a public figure, without expecting a real conversation. They spoke his name, shook his hand, then headed for their trucks. I'd heard that Will sometimes forgave loans when Islanders were in need. I wondered if any of these men had benefited from his largesse.

Will gestured toward a big, bearded man in baggy shorts. "Clare, this is Captain Red Kellums. If there are flounder anywhere in the bay, he'll find them."

Kellums was too shy to shake hands. He ducked his head. "Ma'am." To Will he said, "Tide's in our favor. On its way in. But the wind's blowing pretty good. So it won't be as clear as it's been. I thought we could take a look along some of the shell reefs."

"Red not only knows every inch of the bay, he knows everyone who's fished it for the last twenty years."

I looked at Kellums. "You must have gotten an early start."

"Had my first commercial boat before I was fifteen."

"Red ran quite a successful shrimp operation." Of course Will knew all about Kellums and remembered his accomplishments. Will always knew who had received an award or a promotion, whose son or daughter had graduated from high school or college. But a good sales-man could have done that. What I was just beginning to understand was that Will could make you forget things too—like your shyness—the same way he seemed to forget Catherine's difficult and limited existence, Mary Liz's complaints, Patrick's troubles. Somehow Will was able to put it all aside, like a book he was reading, picking it up again only when he chose to.

Encouraged, Kellums spoke up. "At one time I had four boats working for me."

"Tell Clare about Shotgun," Will prompted.

"Shotgun. Well, he must have been fifty when I hired him, and he looked twenty years older. But he did know how to fish for shrimp."

I knew I was expected to ask. "Why was he called Shotgun?"

"He'd been in a fight. Some old boy blasted him in the midsection at close range and he lost a lot of his intestines. Had to wear a bag." Kellums grinned. "It didn't slow him down none, though. He'd go out drinking, and when they wouldn't serve him another round, he'd take that bag off and slap it on the bar."

"Where was this?" I asked.

"Out by the Texas City dike. Nowhere you'd go."

I looked at Will, wondering if he'd heard anything about my visit to Lafitte's. He pointed to my sandals. "Do those have rubber soles?"

I shook my head.

Kellums said, "She can sit on one of the coolers."

"Clare's done plenty of fishing. I'm sure she'll be fine." I opened my mouth to speak, then stopped. Will offered me his hand as I climbed aboard.

It was not what I had expected—a blunt-nosed boat, flat and shallow as an oven pan, about twenty feet long, surrounded by a high metal railing. At the bow, where a bank of lights hung, a man stood with his back to me. Something about him was familiar. As we moved away from the dock, the man turned and came toward us, and I saw that it was Tyler Henry.

"You already know each other, I think," Will said. The boat shifted as the wake from a passing cruiser struck the side. Ty reached out and would have caught my arm, but I took hold of the rail.

"Weekend warriors," said Kellums. "Anyone want a soda? Beer?" I shook my head. Kellums called to Will, "I've got a couple of spots in mind. Past the airport runway is a good lee shore." Will nodded and we went fast for a while, bouncing over the chop and, now and then, sliding up and down the wake of a passing boat.

Across the bay, vivid streaks of light began to spill out along the horizon. Ty said, "It's pleasant this time of day, isn't it?" When I didn't respond, he shoved his hands in his pockets and rotated his shoulders. He looked uncomfortable. "I hope you don't think I . . ." he began, but trailed off midsentence.

I felt sorry for him. I understood that he couldn't turn down an invitation from Will. Will had hired him, brought him to the Island. Ty couldn't know how complicated things really were.

"You're saying this wasn't your idea."

He looked relieved. "God, no. I don't know one end of a flounder from the other." He paused, then said, "I didn't know you'd be here."

From the stern Will called out, his voice raised above the sound of the motor.

"Ty! What do you think? The heat's not too bad, once the sun goes down."

"No, it's fine," he called back. He lowered his voice and said to me, "I phoned. I wanted to thank you."

I looked at him, surprised.

"What you said about the Island. That it might be hostile to strangers. It made me think. Made me look at some things differently."

I flushed, remembering what I'd said. *People from the mainland don't really count. Sometimes we treat them badly.* I could have returned his call.

I felt a curious urge, one I remembered from childhood, when I had said or done a wrong thing, to do another, as if to demonstrate conclusively my wrongness. "Of course it cuts both ways," I said. "Visitors have been coming here for generations, behaving badly, then going home to their friends and their reputations, telling themselves, 'It doesn't matter. No one will know. It's only a vacation.'"

Ty's reaction was not what I expected. He nodded. "That's it. That's the problem. I'm not here on vacation. I came here to work. To live, for a while anyway. But I haven't been acting that way. I haven't been paying attention. Not the way I should have. It didn't seem necessary. I know how that sounds, but I wasn't even aware that my attitude had changed. My perspective. Everything was moving along so smoothly. What you said was a wake-up call." Ty gazed at me steadily. "Just because a place feels relaxed and friendly doesn't mean . . ."

I thought of the tourists in their childish vacation clothes. Officially, a resort town like Galveston was all about play. And yet it wasn't. I remembered what had happened at Lafitte's, Otis's obscure warnings. "It doesn't mean you should let your guard down," I said.

"Exactly."

The land lay behind us, low and featureless. It was the time of day when, gazing out from a brightly lit window, you believe night has fallen. But as you watch, the yellow and green lights of ships, the red lights of drilling rigs, gradually take on color, and the sky and water become truly black. And you realize you have no measure of darkness.

Will made his way to the bow, bent, and picked up a long-handled fork. "Ever used one of these?" he asked. He held it out for us to inspect. Each of its three prongs was threaded like a screw.

Kellums cut the engine and raised it out of the water. He turned on the fan that was mounted above it and picked up another fork. "We're coming up on a likely spot. The flounder will be laying on the bottom. You want to gig him right behind the eyes. You know what a flounder looks like? Flat, with both eyes on one side?" He was about to pass a fork to Ty, but I stepped forward and took it. It was lighter than I'd expected. I would have to push hard with it to stick a fish. "You get one, the threads will keep him on the gig. You want to turn around and put him in the box, here. Keep your gig north and south and no one will get hurt."

Brightness burst around us as the boat's lights came on. I could see that we were alongside a rib of what looked like rock that extended across the middle of the bay for several hundred feet. The shallow water around the boat was alive with darting bait fish. The fan roared in my ears.

"What are those?" Ty asked.

"Mullet," I said.

Kellums leaned over. "And needle-nose gar. And over there's a crab."

"And that?"

It was a curved shape, heavily encrusted. Kellums grinned. "An old tire."

Will said, "We might see a ray."

"If we get lucky." Kellums was peering over the side of the boat. I looked too and saw nothing but sand and water. All at once he plunged his gig down. When he raised it, there was a flat, spotted fish flailing on the end. He turned and lowered it into the box and withdrew the gig through a slot. "Your turn," he said. From the box came a hollow slapping sound.

"I don't see anything."

"That's because the wind's up. On a still night the water's clearer. Plus, flounders are tricky. They dig in. But we'll find you one." The boat proceeded slowly along the edge of the shell reef, the fan moving us forward. Will and Kellums pushed off, using the gigs as poles. After a few minutes, Kellums beckoned me forward and pointed.

In the glow of the lights, I saw a motionless, fish-shaped outline. Then the smallest shiver along its edge. Without taking the gig from me, Kellums maneuvered it into position.

"Now," he said, and I pushed down hard. The fish jerked and fought, the water exploded into a chaos of swirling sand, and I leaned on the gig. "Whoa, easy there," said Kellums. "You're good. You got yourself a flattie." He guided the flounder, flapping, its underside gleaming white, into the box and passed the gig to Ty. "Don't hesitate," he said. "That's the key. Now you see him, now you don't." The sounds from the box were muffled. There was bright-red blood on its metal rim. Ty stepped forward.

Kellums spotted another flounder and Ty went for it and missed. Then Kellums took the gig and added another fish to the box. Ty didn't seem to care whether he caught anything or not. It seemed to me that his mind was elsewhere.

There were lights moving in the tall grass along the shore. Kellums saw me looking, and before I could ask, he said, "People gigging on foot. Wading. With lanterns."

"You can do that?"

"Sure. It's peaceful. You don't have the engine, the fan. Just the water, the night birds, and so on." Then Kellums seemed to remember himself, his professional role. "It's not too efficient though."

Ty said, "I thought they might be . . ."

Will finished his sentence. "Wreckers? Smugglers?" His manner was upbeat, the way Islanders always sounded when they discussed Galveston's lively past.

"No need to do that at night," said Kellums. "Take a fellow like Shotgun. Lives off the grid, doesn't own a photo ID. It's a cash business, fishing. He doesn't pay taxes. Maybe he brings in something else too. Who's going to know?"

Will said, "But you pay taxes, Red."

"Sure do," said Kellums, and winked. He turned off the fan.

I sensed Ty's uneasy presence next to me, and I turned. The moon was a pale shape over his shoulder. Ty was gazing fixedly at Will.

Will smiled and beckoned and I went to him, leaving Ty alone in the bow.

The boat lay beside a grass island that rose about eighteen inches above the water. Land, of a sort. Land that could come and go in a season. Will reached for me. He held his finger to his lips and pointed to the water, and I saw the rays—one, two, then three of them—glide silently past, their fins rippling, their slender, spiny tails trailing. Will put his arm around my shoulder and pulled me close, letting me know that this sight was a private pleasure, a gift for me only.

IF ELEANOR FELT LEFT OUT, she didn't show it. When Will dropped me off, around midnight, she was on her way upstairs. She smiled over her shoulder, showing me one high cheekbone and the upturned corner of her mouth. "Someone named Jules called," she said. Her voice was warm, her step full of energy. She kept climbing. "He'd like to talk to you about a show. I told him you'd get back to him. I was sure you'd want to. He said you have his number."

I followed her up, wondering if I really should call. I wished there were a way to know what Jules wanted without talking to him about it. Our conversations generated their own set of pressures.

My head was full of what I'd seen on and in the water. I could still feel Will's arm around me, his breath in my hair. The boat moving gently back and forth beneath us, so that we rocked together.

I made a brief, halfhearted attempt to tidy my room, then I undressed and got into bed. But my body wasn't ready to sleep. I felt warm, as if I'd gotten too much sun, a sensation that somehow wasn't unpleasant. I would willingly have given myself over to it. If only I could forget Ty gazing at Will, the look on his face. I threw off the sheet and lay on my back, breathing hard. I heard Eleanor's door open and close. Then her step on the stairs.

After a while I fell asleep briefly, dreamed of falling, and woke again, my mouth furred with thirst. I stumbled to the bathroom, leaned down, and drank from the faucet. The water came out with a rush, warm at first, tasting of the Island. The brackish smell of marsh, of the tidal night, seemed to rise from the drain. With it came images—low trees blasted by the wind. In them ancient nests, carpeted with bird felt.

I discovered that I was hungry, so I went downstairs, through the empty kitchen to the pantry. I rummaged among the boxes and bags, and came away with a handful of crackers. The overhead light was painfully bright, and I switched it off. There was no sign of Eleanor. I wondered what exactly Jules had said to her. What had made her so happy.

Phosphorescence from the streetlamps outside fell in watery sheets through the tall windows. In the half-light, the ordinary spaces were changed, full of some unexpressed meaning. I felt again the need to search for something, I didn't know what.

At first it was enough to move through the half-familiar rooms, to touch the light-drenched, mysterious furniture. To shift and examine the everyday objects, hoping that they might speak to me. But not for long. Soon I was opening everything I could.

In my father's study, the books still slept heavily on their shelves, but there was nothing in the desk or in the mahogany file cabinet. I went to the front hall closet. There were both men's and women's clothes hanging there. Were some of them Will's? I turned the pockets inside out, but found nothing.

I went back to the kitchen and pulled open the cupboards and drawers, making the glasses ring and the silverware chatter. Carefully, I removed the tray from the silverware drawer. Underneath was a handful of papers—an invitation from the local garden club, a flyer for a museum in New York, a train schedule. Everything that had a date seemed to be several years old. Then I found a folded sheet, heavy and cream-colored.

I held it to the window. There was just one line written in ink. *My heart is in your hands.* A man's writing, even and bold.

Of course Will would have thought of Eleanor's hands. They were what I thought of too when I summoned her image—Eleanor's hands in the garden, in the house, shaping and arranging, at the piano, drawing the music out.

There was no envelope. Had the note come recently? Had she put it away quickly when I arrived so that I wouldn't see it? I held the paper up to the light and saw that it had yellowed along one edge. *This thing with Will Carraday has been going on for a long time.* Could Eleanor have forgotten it? Was it possible to feel yourself so loved that you could discard the evidence as easily as you might an old train schedule? Or was it a talisman, one she had kept hidden in plain sight, concealed by the stuff around it? Did she take it out and examine it from time to time?

Briefly, I considered leaving it on the kitchen table to show that I had been there and had seen it. Then I put it back.

I saw Eleanor at the piano, playing from memory on into the night, long after we had gone upstairs, Will's words supplying the lyric for her private music. Eleanor, hearing my father at the front door, scraping his feet on the mat. Slipping her lover's note back into the drawer. Taking it out again from time to time when she was alone and had finished folding our laundry, arranging flowers for the table, preparing our meals.

But any vision of her I could construct was immediately overlaid with borrowed perspectives. My father's view of her—a kind of infuriated hunger. And Will's—something his almost courtly treatment of Eleanor only hinted at, something well beyond the companionable, midlife relationship I had imagined.

I still knew so little about her then.

I think now that desire runs like a thread through the fabric of our experience, holding our lives together. And when that thread unravels, everything gathered around it comes apart.

Chapter 24

WITH SUMMER IN FULL SWAY—the beach parking lots oily and rutted, the seawall a noisy riot of color—I was grateful to have a daily task that set me apart from the tourists. On my way to the library, I found myself exchanging meaningful glances with other Islanders—the forty-something waitress at the café where I sometimes ate lunch, the owner of the corner store where I bought film. *Mainlanders,* we said to each other wordlessly. *None of this matters.*

At the archive, the pile of photos had grown, I'd made progress. I knew what I wanted, I had discovered a frame of reference, like the white lines in the viewfinder of my Leica.

There were many images from the turn of the century, but as I examined them, what I thought about was Stella, her life on the Island. How little of it was truly private. The kind of informal scrutiny I had grown up with hardly counted compared to what she must have experienced. Her appearances in public would have been a topic in the local press, her destinations, her wardrobe discussed. She would not have been able to leave the house alone. She might have seen from her window the streets of the city, full of interest and possibility, and, in the distance, the hazy strip of bay. But those views were entirely notional. She could no more enter into them than she could step into one of the painted landscapes on the walls.

I wondered how she and Henry Durand had been able to plan and carry out their escape. If someone who shared their secret had helped.

More often, I thought about Will and the marvel of his interest in me. It was an observable fact—since the boat trip, I had been singled out. And gradually, being with him, experiencing the sense of well-being that accompanied his undivided attention, had become not just something I enjoyed when it happened but something I looked forward to, even counted on. The likelihood of a visit from him shed a kind of light over even the longest and dullest afternoon and some-how made it possible.

At the archive, I had moved my chair, so that without turning my head, I could see the elevator and know who came and went. On those days when I visited Stella's room, I sat facing the door. I found myself listening for Will's characteristic footsteps on the stairs and in the hall, the sound of his whistling. I pretended to be absorbed by the spread of photos, the album in my lap. I didn't want to appear to be waiting for him. Not until I felt the air vibrate with his presence did I look up and meet his gaze.

He brought me things—a piece of fruit, a small vase of roses. "These won't take up much room," he said as he helped me clear a place for the flowers on the table. Then he brought me a pair of earrings.

He was smiling, holding out both closed fists. "Pick a hand," he said. I don't know what I expected, but it wasn't what I saw when he opened his fingers.

They were gold, antique, with curved ear loops like fish hooks. On each was an irregularly shaped pearl and a small diamond. I was stunned.

"They work like this," Will said. He opened one of the lever backs. "Would you like to try them? I've seen you in earrings, and I thought you might like these." His manner suggested that this was no differ-ent than any of his other small gifts.

I took one of the earrings from him, found the piercing in my left ear, and slid it in.

Will sat back, his pleasure evident. "What do you think?" he asked. "Take a look." He indicated the mirror over Stella's dresser. I stood and stepped in front of it. When I moved my head, the diamond caught the light and the pearl trembled.

"Were they hers?"

"I can't be sure. But I like to think so."

It never occurred to me to refuse. To disappoint him.

Often Will would sit and talk for a while about the heat or a possible water shortage. The planned Fourth of July celebration that would snarl traffic off the causeway and increase the need for beach patrols. The usual Island themes. The conversation I had heard for years growing up came back to me easily. The difference was that now those commonplaces were charged with significance.

Eventually Will would go down the hall to Mary Liz. Then to his study. I had not been invited there since the night of the party, but that didn't prevent me from investigating.

The room had belonged to Will's father and grandfather before him, but the things in it were his. I saw everywhere evidence of those pursuits—art, architecture, gardens—that my father had mocked. There were books, many of them old, some probably rare, in Italian as well as English, with marginal notes in brownish ink. There were portfolios of engravings tied with soft, worn strings. On one of them rested a silver magnifying glass. There was just enough disarray to suggest comfort and the absence of any desire to impress.

There were photos too among the books, including one of Catherine as a baby, before the illness that had changed her forever, and I realized that this other Catherine, whose small, perfect features were all pleasing promise, was as much lost to Will as if she had died.

Looking around, I found myself imagining a different life for him, away from the Island. As an architect or a scholar. A professor, at the center of a crowd of admiring students. Any one of them seemed possible.

His sister lived in Paris. Will could live anywhere. I thought about Mary Liz and Eleanor and the odd back-and-forth arrangement between the two houses. Surely he must dislike it. Yet it seemed fixed, permanent, as though Mary Liz's inability to move had somehow translated into a more general paralysis.

My inspection done, I went back to Stella's room. I picked up the little notebook of drawings. It was pocket-size, and I imagined Stella carrying it with her into the garden, to the shore, when she was able to go there. As I turned the pages I noticed that the subject matter changed. Plants and shells gave way to designs featuring them. There were pages of decorative motifs, of carvings and borders. Were these somehow part of the lovers' conversation? I flipped to the last few pages. The lilies were the ones in the bedroom wallpaper. With every page, they became smaller. On the last page, the pressure of the pencil had left furrows in the paper.

I opened the travel album and idly turned the stiff, oversize black pages with my left hand. There was Notre Dame, there a bridge over the Seine with a boat approaching. I flipped through quickly, looking for something interesting or personal, but it was all the same. I didn't notice that the weight of the album had shifted until it fell off the table.

Quickly I bent over. I saw immediately that the damage was serious. The back of the album had separated from the spine. I felt something close to panic. How would I explain to Will what I'd done? What would he think? That I'd been careless with material that wasn't mine? It wasn't until I touched the pages, tried to close the album again, that I understood what had happened. The back had broken free, revealing a sort of pocket whose contents had spilled out.

I had seen my share of explicit period photos, plenty that were purely salacious, so I wasn't unprepared in that way. At home I had a print from the twenties that Jules had given me when he learned I was pregnant, with a card that read: *Remember who you really are.* It showed a woman wearing nothing but a tiny apron and a pair of red high heels dusting a bookcase. Soft porn, kitschy. When Bailey saw it, her only interest was in the feather duster, a wholly unfamiliar object.

This was different. It was a picture of a child. A girl—she looked about eight—sitting on a man's lap. He was dressed in a heavy suit of the kind wealthy men wore a hundred years ago, even in the hottest months. He wore a stand collar and a cravat with a stickpin. A watch chain hung in an arc across his waistcoat. He gazed at the camera out of one good eye. The child sat on his knee in the pose sacred to family photographers everywhere. She was naked.

I sat down slowly on the floor. I felt dizzy, and I rested my head between my knees and closed my eyes. I was unpleasantly aware of the taste of my own mouth. Gingerly, I began to reassemble the album and its contents. I tried to think of Stella idealized and classically draped in the relief over the Carradays' fireplace, Stella wrapped in layers of gathered and pleated fabric in the photo on the mantel. Instead I saw Stella slender and naked, her childish nipples like pips above her gently curving belly, her ankles delicately crossed.

I covered my eyes with my hand. But there was no unseeing it. What did the photo mean? Was there an explanation that would somehow make it right? An explanation that had been lost? *The baby is sleeping, the cloth keeps the flies away.* I wanted to believe it. I did not want to have discovered what Will would cringe to see. I didn't want to be the one to show it to him.

I looked again at the photo. I had to look, even though I hated what I saw. I wished I hadn't been the one to find it. It was none of my business. Wasn't that what I had always been told? Hadn't I been ordered to keep out of other people's things, other people's lives? If I stared too long at someone, Eleanor would put her hands on either side of my head and forcibly turn it away.

I don't know how long I stayed there. My head ached. The light, even through the lace curtain, was painfully bright. The window hung over me, enormous, surrounded by a fuzzy halo.

I thought then that perhaps I could reassemble the album and put it where it would never be seen. Keep the knowledge of it to myself. The possibility made itself felt with special strength there, in the house whose past I knew so well, where generations passed and nothing changed. Certainly there was no reason to act right away. The bed was nearby and I pushed the album under it.

But I thought about Stella's real life, in the Carraday house. With her mother, the invalid, lying in a darkened room.

She'd been just sixteen when Ward Carraday married her. Now she is older, and there are brown spots on the back of her hands. Her bedroom smells of medicine, there are piles of discarded clothes, unopened letters. Ward Carraday stays away.

Stella visits him at his office and lunches with him in the dining room at the Tremont Hotel. They have done this since she was a child. It is one of his few indulgences—their time together. Stella is the only person in the world who has never been shocked by his appearance. Ward Carraday rests his ringed hand on hers and thinks that this is his real fortune, this young woman who belongs to him alone. Her even features, her large eyes set perfectly beneath black arching brows. The skin that is without any kind of blemish.

When she begs to come more often to his place of business, he doesn't know it is because she hopes to encounter the young architect with the curly hair and white cuffs. That they have already had several quick talks in the passageway outside his door. Ward Carraday doesn't know that Stella finds his hand heavy and hot, that his knuckles make her think of barnacles. He doesn't notice when she pulls away from him and hides her hand under the tablecloth where she wipes it over and over on her skirt.

Ward Carraday has ordered lilies, her favorites, for the table, but someone has misunderstood. The vase holds the wrong kind— stargazers, they are called, vulgar spotted flowers. With a backward gesture he dismisses them. When a fresh arrangement appears— white, luminous—and Stella smiles, he feels that her happiness is worth any trouble.

After lunch she will break off a stem and tuck it in the waist-band of her dress. As they pass out under the porte cochere, Henry Durand, who has been waiting near the cab rank, balancing on one foot, rubbing the tops of his boots against the back of his trouser legs to remove the inevitable sandy dust, will step up to greet them, mark the flower, and begin his elaborate, largely silent courtship. Lilies along the walls, carved into the woodwork. Lilies crushed beneath Stella's feet.

Chapter 25

I STOOD UP AND WENT TO THE DOOR. I could hear Faline in the kitchen downstairs. I imagined Will arriving home, greeting me, seeing my face, and knowing right away that something was wrong. There wasn't much time. I gathered my things and left the Carraday house.

When Eleanor saw me coming across the lawn, she waved and called out. If she sensed the turmoil in my mind, she didn't let on. Her creamy linen dress set off the color of her arms—not tan, nothing as obvious as that, or pale like mine, but the golden buff color of Island sand on a clear day.

"Did you call your friend?" she asked. She was wearing the gold cuff bracelet I'd seen before, and as she spoke, she turned it around and around her wrist.

"What friend?"

"The one who wanted to know about the show?" I realized she meant Jules, and it occurred to me that I had never thought of him as a friend. We had a history together, he knew things about me no one else did, but his manner had always been, in its peculiar way, entirely professional.

"You mean Jules."

"I suppose." She looked at me brightly, eyebrows raised in a show of animation, like a grown-up offering a small child a treat, something sweet and sticky that she wouldn't want for herself. "I think he mentioned a gallery. The Corcoran? Something like that."

Jules must have been serious. "He called again?"

"I left you a note."

I hurried upstairs and found it under some clothes I had taken off and thrown on a chair. When I returned his call, Jules confirmed what Eleanor had told me. His manner was casual at first. "Of course they love your work, they would have offered it to you eventually. But they've had a cancellation, they need something right away." He paused, then gave up all pretense. "It's an amazing opportunity."

It was.

"When?" I asked.

"September."

"That soon?"

"Don't worry," he said. "There's no rush. You can finish what you're doing there. It's all about quality."

I hung up the phone. I felt oddly flat. I thought about what Harriet Kinkaid had said. Was it that I'd imagined this moment too many times, so that it now seemed unreal? Was part of me afraid to take what I had worked for, what I wanted? Or was it Eleanor's reaction?

I went slowly up the stairs and lay down on the big, white bed. I stayed there listening to the murmur of a dove on the windowsill. I wondered what it felt like to fly into a pane of glass. When the dove flew away, I turned my face into the pillow.

One thing was perfectly clear. Frankie was right, Eleanor wanted me gone. I could see that the idea delighted her. I saw her again, fresh and happy in her linen dress, beckoning to me as I came in the door, and it seemed to me then that she had always done that—called me to her only to send me away. I thought of her in the garden, the kitchen, at the piano. When had she ever wanted me near her?

I replayed my conversation with Jules. It had lasted a few minutes. But its implications were seismic. Not that Eleanor would care, as long as whatever I was doing took me away from Galveston. I asked myself if it was time to go.

Then I thought of Patrick. Patrick would care, even if he had no idea what it meant. How could I leave Galveston without seeing him? Growing up, I had trusted him completely. One day, soon, he would materialize on the back steps. A pebble would hit my window, and

I'd look down to find him there. It was what he had always done. I heard Eleanor walk toward the bedroom I had shared with Frankie and thought of my younger self there, watching for Patrick's signal.

It was dark outside when I got up and retrieved the plaid shirt from the wooden stand in the bathroom where I had hidden it behind a stack of embroidered hand towels. I couldn't explain the feeling it aroused—a persistent aching sadness that belonged only to me. I spread the shirt out on the bed, willing myself to receive the revelation that would make its meaning clear. I paced back and forth until the space became unbearable, then I went out into the hall.

Fog had blown in with the night air. In our old bedroom, there were no lamps, just the single bulb dangling overhead. The corded spreads, the utilitarian furniture—two unmatched dressers and a desk—would not have been out of place at a summer camp. The worn rag rug muffled sound, so that you could walk quietly to and from the window seat. The room was nothing like Bailey's with its animal cutouts and bright comforter.

I sat on the bed that had been mine and bounced once or twice like a visitor to a motel, testing the springs. I went to the dresser and opened the top drawer. It was empty, except for a faded sheet of wrapping paper that served as a liner. I leaned over and inhaled its smell— aged wood and damp and loneliness. For a moment I thought I heard the susurrus of air moving in and out of another body. I turned, but there was only the humid dark, and the branches of the crape myrtle moving against the window. Outside, the rasping cry of an owl.

I walked to the window and looked out toward the Carradays'. There was no light there. I turned back toward my bed.

I remembered then that someone used to come into our room at night. Someone who stood near me. That I listened for the sound of his breathing, like a hand rubbing against cloth. I slept fitfully— I would doze, then wake suddenly, my senses straining in the dark. Sleep and wake again, alert. When I heard it, when I knew he was there, I went rigid. My shoulder grew stiff with the effort of keeping still. I tried to imagine myself in another place. I tried to imagine myself invisible. I tried not to think. I'd heard Faline say, *Thinking about it brings it to you.*

Sometimes, in the moonlight, I could see Frankie, through my eyelashes, in the bed next to mine. She lay sprawled, her mouth open, her long legs tangled in the bedclothes. She didn't move. But I had, obscurely, the feeling that my sister, sleeping there, defended me in a way she would not have done consciously during the day.

I went back to Eleanor's room. I had never come to her for help, never believed that I deserved it. I leaned against her door, listening, but there was no sound. Was she there? I knocked, softly at first. Then louder. I banged the flat of my hand against the wood until my palm stung. I made a fist and beat on the door. I called her name. There was no response. There never had been. Eleanor's room was empty.

THE NEXT DAY I WENT TO THE ARCHIVE as usual, but I was distracted, I hardly saw the photographs I handled. I was aware of other things—the drone of the air-conditioning, smudges on the glass partition. As I sat at the broad table, pictures of the Island spread before me, I thought of Eleanor and Will, thoughts that generated their own heat, so that even in that chilly space, my skin burned.

In the afternoon I gave up and walked the few blocks to Harriet Kinkaid's house. I might not be able to talk to her about Eleanor, I didn't know her well enough for that, but I could tell her about the photo I'd found of Stella with her father. I hadn't discussed it with anyone else. I still held out hope that there might be an explanation. Harriet would know.

Her Peugeot was in the driveway and I rang the bell. I heard it chime, once, twice, but no one came to the door. I tried the handle—hadn't Harriet said she always left it open? But the door was locked.

"No here," a voice said.

I turned to find a man with a bamboo rake in one hand standing at the corner of the house.

"I'm looking for Harriet Kinkaid."

"Miz Kinkaid no here." He was short, with a heavy dark mustache and a shock of startlingly white hair.

"Do you know where she is?"

Something about his manner suggested that he did, but he remained silent.

"When will she be back?" I asked. I didn't really want to hear his answer. I was afraid I knew what it would be.

"No here," he said again. If he understood my question, he wasn't going to respond. Probably he had learned that there was nothing to be gained by delivering bad news. We stood eyeing each other for a moment. Then I turned away.

I walked toward the library, but I knew there was no point in returning to the archive. Will was at his office, and I didn't want to run into Eleanor.

On the streets, visitors to the Island chatted and laughed. The air was gauzy, full of salt. It blurred the edges of the houses and softened the colors of everything, so that the view was pretty, tranquil, like a postcard. But the haze was corrosive, eating through paint and wood. The damage was imperceptible—no one would notice until suddenly something gave way. That knowledge, and the willingness to accept it, was also part of being an Islander.

I looked back toward Harriet Kinkaid's house and saw her yardman still standing there. I wondered who else might be observing me and why.

I remembered then a place I could go that might offer up information, one that had the added advantage of being unoccupied, so I could search at leisure without being seen. The alley house. It was the one place I had yet to investigate. Some reluctance I couldn't account for had kept me from it.

Chapter 26

GROWING UP, I HAD NO WAY OF KNOWING how different Galveston was from most other places. I had nothing to compare it to. I had never spent a night off the Island until the winter Will's plane took me to my grandmother in Ohio.

In my grandmother's neighborhood, each lot was visibly rectangular, a box of air, divided from its neighbors by the power lines above, the chain-link fence below. The lawns were edged, the shrubs squared off or rounded into balls. Everything constructed, everything that grew expressed the taut geometry of the place. Because it was pervasive, I thought that it must be the result of some local force, the same one that prompted my grandmother's interest in quilting. I believed that I felt it working on me, gradually winding up my muscles and tendons, so that every day it was harder to move.

Galveston had always defied that kind of organization. An early plan of the proposed city shows a framework of blocks superimposed on an irregular, tapering sandbar, like the imprint of a waffle iron on batter. The whole thing has an air of unreality. On the bay side, the grid pattern overlaps the coastline and the blocks sit, all or partway, in the water. Bayous meander across the avenues to the south.

Did the surveyor understand instinctively that in Galveston the natural tendency of things is toward disorder? Sidewalks heave and melt, houses lean, shutters and verandas sag. Vines race up fences and smother telephone poles. Order gives way first in the side streets, the alleys, the areas not on public view.

When my parents moved in behind the Carradays, families still lived in the alley houses. Some of the occupants ran small businesses, unsanctioned by the city, like the woman who sold stuffed crabs from her kitchen window to a line of waiting customers at lunchtime.

The alley house that became ours belonged then to a man I knew only as Greek Pete, who carried a string of worry beads that made a constant, soft clicking sound. Greek Pete kept his door open, and a steady stream of children came and went, clutching the trinkets he gave away—little toys he hadn't sold to tourists. I remembered standing just inside the threshold, unsure of my welcome despite the music from the radio, the general atmosphere of festivity. I hung back, fists in the pockets of my shorts, enjoying the whir of the oscillating fan. He had to come to me, his big fingers closed around a marble, a whistle. Once Greek Pete lifted my chin and looked at me. "So beautiful and so sad," he said and pressed something into my palm.

When my parents bought the alley house, the fence between our properties came down. That fall, Eleanor planted the bougainvillea that covered the walls, completing the transformation. Soon it seemed, from the outside anyway, that the alley house had always been ours. Nothing was done to the interior. We rented the space occasionally to medical students like Stephen who wanted a cheap, temporary place near the hospital.

At the far end were a galley kitchen and a small bathroom. Mildew stippled the bottom of the plastic shower curtain and there was a circle of rust around the drain like a sore mouth. The bedroom was opposite, its floor covered with moldy carpet squares. The remainder of the house was haphazardly furnished, and mostly given over to my father's birding equipment—the Zeiss binoculars, the reflecting telescope and tripod, the stacks of notebooks and guides. Hats for the sun and jackets for cooler weather hung from a rail by the door. I recalled the faintly resinous odor of my father's rain gear, the oversize sawtooth treads of his rubber boots.

My father made no effort to oblige our student renters. He believed they were lucky to have found lodging with a doctor. Their few belongings either stayed in the bedroom or got lost among his.

I liked the dilapidated comfort of the alley house—the mushroomy odor of the place and the steady drip of the shower.

I remembered all this, and the recollection seemed straightforward enough. And yet, standing outside the door, I hesitated to go in. The alley itself appeared smaller, as childhood places do to an adult eye, and less colorful. By daylight, the clump of cannas was limp and ragged. No one lived in any of the alley houses now. There was no smell of browning crabs, no music, nothing to interrupt my reverie. I found the key under a flowerpot by the door.

As I stood turning it in my hand, I heard far-off thunder. Heat lightning flashed behind the roofs and chimneys, and I smelled the possibility of rain. A few drops fell and I told myself to do what anyone would with rain coming. Go inside. I unlocked the door and stepped over the threshold.

It had been a guesthouse for years, I knew that. Still, I was unprepared for the extent of the change. The coat rail was gone, the creamy walls freshly painted, the old carpet replaced by sisal matting. Two director's chairs flanked a wooden chest with brass fittings. Even the light seemed different, more diffuse, as though passing through the crisp blinds had strained it of all intensity. The past was gone—ours, Greek Pete's, the unknown years before that, all had disappeared completely.

I walked through to the back, but it was the same—clean, unobjectionable. Airless, like a photo in a catalogue. The appliances were new, the bed piled with pillows. I went into the bathroom. With a feeling of foreboding I couldn't explain, I turned the water on and off. I looked in the medicine cabinet and flushed the toilet. Nothing happened. I stared at the shower wall, closed my eyes, opened them again.

I began to feel oddly detached from the things around me. It was a sensation I remembered from childhood, from our family dinners, from my early years in school, when I felt a part of myself withdraw and leave the dining room, the classroom, while another part stayed behind, slouched at the table, at my desk, preparing to drop a plate or snap a ruler. Now I watched as that wayward self got up and began to move around the small rooms, pulling out drawers, flinging open cupboards one after another. My hands trembled. The air-conditioning was turned off and the house was warm and stuffy. Sweat prickled along my hairline and ran under my arms. Finally, everything in the kitchen that could be opened stood gaping except the refrigerator. It gave way with a heavy sucking sound. There was nothing inside but bare metal shelves and the smell of synthetic cold.

There was more I had to do. I went into the bedroom and got down on my hands and knees and raised the fitted bedspread, twisting to look up at the lacework of springs. I felt behind the pillows and under the mattress. I pulled everything off the bed—the sheets, the pillows, right down to the mattress with its shiny brocade cover. The urge to do these things was both irresistible and awful. I realized that my eyes stung and my mouth tasted as though I had swallowed blood.

I went to the wooden chest and lifted its lid. It was empty. There was nothing remarkable in that, the house had been cleared and readied for the next set of guests, but somehow this last vacancy, the sum of all the others, was too much to bear.

My legs gave way and I sank to the floor. What had my life amounted to, after all? Thirty years, a failed marriage, a dead child. What remained? Only photos and what I could remember. Not long ago, I had thought that the pain of recollection was unbearable. Now I understood that it was worse to forget, that the price for forgetting was this gnawing emptiness.

There was a sort of conversation going on in my head. *I'd like to see her with her hair combed. Then tell her yourself. Look what she's done. So? Where is she? Taking pictures, probably. Doing nothing.* I turned to the window and saw that the sky had darkened. The rain that had been announcing itself all day had arrived. I went to the open door and stood on the threshold.

The wind when it came was like a huge sigh. Then for a moment the silence was absolute. The trees stood motionless, waiting. As if from far off I heard a bicycle bell, footsteps running on the sidewalk.

Then a wedge of sound split the space between the houses, a noise so loud it shook the building and rattled the windows. The sky lit up yellow behind the roofline of the Carraday house, and the real rain came all at once, hard and drenching.

I turned back and closed the door. The interior of the alley house was dark now. Flashes of light like tracers came and went, as if the lightning had followed me inside. My face and hair were wet, I wiped my eyes and blinked, trying to find the outlines of the furniture, but I couldn't make the room come into focus.

The smell of aged wood and salt—a kind of decay peculiar to the Island—rose from the wet timbers. In the half-light, I saw it all the way it had been—the old chair, the clothes hanging on the wall.

I remembered an evening in the fall, a sudden shower, pushing my way into the alley house. I was six years old. I remembered my knees shaking, my arms and legs dimpled with cold. My hair and clothes soaked.

The room was dark. I collapsed into the big chair. Only when it was too late did I realize I was sitting on some papers. I stood up and looked at them. I switched on the light and confirmed—they were long, ruled pages covered with what had been lines of fine writing, done in ink. My father's notes, written with his beautiful gold pen. Crushed now, and blurred—as I watched, the words and numbers ran together into black, unreadable smudges. I tried to blot the first page with the tail of my plaid camp shirt. That seemed to help a little, so I took off the shirt and tried again. I was standing, wiping the pages, when he opened the door.

As he came closer, I saw the vein pulsing in his forehead. "Do you know what you've done?" he asked. "You've destroyed weeks of valuable data." I tried to explain that I hadn't meant to. That I'd only meant to sit in the chair. He thought for a moment, and I had time to hope that I might be told to go away. Then he said, "You want to sit. Fine," and pushed me back onto the chair. Wiry fibers stood up from its upholstered surface.

I began to cry. "Stop that," he said. My nose was running, tears and mucus ran together into my mouth and I tried to wipe my face with my shirt. He said, "Put your hands in your lap. Look at me. You'll sit there until I tell you to move." He went over to the table and busied himself with something.

I don't know how long I stayed in the room with him. I had been given a watch on a plastic strap, but I had lost it. That failure came back to me then with added force. Every so often my father would look up from his reading, his features calm, unreadable. Once he said, "Cross your ankles." A faint smile played around his mouth. After a while, he went to the kitchen and fixed himself something to eat. My legs and shoulders ached. I remember feeling ashamed of my bare childish chest.

The rain had stopped when he closed the door behind him. My shirt was dirty, but I put it on again anyway. Stiffly, I crossed the lawn and made my way to the house. I told myself that my punishment was over. Soon I would be in my bed, the blanket pulled over me. The room I shared with Frankie had never seemed so attractive.

But the back door was locked. I stood on the porch, shivering. I thought about calling out. But Eleanor was away, I didn't know where. And my father would hear me long before Frankie woke. I went around to the front door and tried that too. I twisted the handle, pulled on it, but it was locked. Finally I went back to the alley. I was afraid to go back into the alley house, afraid my father would return. I made a place for myself on the damp ground and curled up among the cannas. I hoped it wasn't true, what Faline said, that rats nested there.

PAIN BLOOMED AT THE BACK OF MY HEAD. I didn't want to remember anything more. I stumbled out into the yard. Eyes closed, I crouched on the grass, retched and vomited into the flower bed.

The rain washed over me. I could hear it on the roofs and on the packed ground, steady now, predictable. I retched again, but nothing came up. Gradually I became aware of discrete sounds, water gurgling loudly where it ran from the gutter, rain sifting through the moving leaves. The green, soaked smell of the Island rose around me.

I heard footsteps on the porch and someone calling my name. I felt an arm around my waist, raising me, awkwardly at first. I moaned. Will pulled me to my feet, but my legs buckled and I staggered. Then he saw my face. "Jesus Christ," he said and reached for my knees, and in one easy movement picked me up. "Sweetheart." Already he was walking toward his house. "What? What is it?" he asked. I turned my face away, buried it in his shoulder. I felt the warmth of his body through my wet clothes, his wet shirt. As he held me, the feeling intensified until it seemed to have passed through my skin and into some other place.

Chapter 27

THE NEXT DAY, I MOVED INTO Stella's room. Will helped me carry my things across the yard and through the oleander hedge. Eleanor stood on the steps watching, her hands braced on her hips. She was wearing a yellow sundress with a full skirt that was unexpectedly girlish. Her face was stiff with strain. For the first time I could remember, she looked her age. "I don't know what this is supposed to accomplish," she said.

"El, please." Will turned to look at her, but she was already on her way inside. From the edge of the lawn, I heard the screen door bang shut.

The move didn't take long, I hadn't brought much to the Island— just enough clothes to fill a suitcase, my photo gear. Will handled everything carefully, as though my modest belongings were somehow precious.

He set the battered suitcase gently on a luggage rack and I laid everything else on the bed. "You have your own bathroom," he said, "as of course you know. What else?" He stepped back into the doorway as if to indicate that the room was now entirely mine. "Do you have everything you need?" He turned his gaze on me, and I noticed again how the effect of his attention was to convert a routine inquiry into something more. At that moment, I felt that I could ask him for anything in the world and he would give it to me.

Mary Liz said, "Someone might as well sleep in that room. It's not a goddamn shrine. House is full of people anyway."

Faline said, "I don't wash the sheets but once a week, so fix your bed in the morning."

Frankie wasn't around to comment, and I found, interestingly, that I was no longer sure what she would say.

Eleanor said nothing. She didn't need to. Her walk, the economy of her gestures, her shoulders, set as though she were preparing to lift something heavy, communicated her thoughts perfectly.

I wondered if Patrick knew. I was certain he had been in the house. I had encountered Faline hastily bundling up a pile of laundry—shorts, boxers, T-shirts—that could only have been his. That glimpse of his clothes called up a stream of familiar feelings. But to my surprise, they were now overtaken by others, larger and more compelling. I still longed for Patrick, but my sense of urgency about finding him was gone. Now when I thought of Patrick, it was mostly in his father's presence, a private acknowledgment of some similarity of looks or manner that made our exchanges even sweeter.

I told myself that it was a way of being with them both without ever having to take sides, to choose between them.

Will made it easy. He was playful, tender, thoughtful. He made small jokes. His benevolence encompassed the household. He was unfailingly patient with Mary Liz. He flattered and occasionally teased Faline. I saw their faces turn toward him when he came into the room like flowers bending toward the sun.

People said Will was charming, and that judgment was generally accepted. Still, if we'd been asked, I think each of us would have claimed some special understanding that set our relationship with him apart. Certainly, I felt this to be true. I had been waiting for Patrick, believing he would appear and make things right. But it was Will who had found me when I needed him.

Now I really could come and go as I pleased. Which meant that I spent my days at the archive. But every evening, I returned to Stella's room. I didn't open the albums or look at my notes. Instead I sat in the armchair by the window and listened for Will's step. I knew he expected me to join him and Mary Liz for dinner. The third night, he asked me to come down to his study beforehand.

"I want you to know you're welcome to any of these," he said, indicating the books and portfolios I had already investigated. I regretted then that I hadn't waited for him to offer me his things. Embarrassed, I examined the pattern in the worn Oriental rug. There was a pause. Will must have read my reaction as indifference. "Or they may not interest you," he said.

"Oh. Yes, they do," I said quickly. "I mean, I'm sure they will."

He smiled and took down a faded red volume with a leather spine. I don't remember what was in it. What I recall is the way he showed it to me, turning the pages slowly, offering the occasional comment, measuring my responses. At first I was afraid to say what I thought, afraid I might offend him. But I discovered that he liked me to have my own opinions and to express them, so that our conversations were less one-sided.

Our nightly visits in his study became a kind of ritual.

Once he found me with a large book open on my lap, one I'd seen him enjoying, *The Gardens of Italy.* "You're looking at Latham," he said, delighted. "I'm not surprised. Amazing photos." He gazed down at the open page. "The Italians did wonderful things with water. Water steps, like these, water organs, fountains. Or, if your host wanted to surprise you, a water jet hidden in a bench or between paving stones. Visitors never knew when they'd be in for a good soaking. I have to admit, the idea appeals to me."

"Didn't they mind?"

Will's eyes widened and he looked amused. "I'm sure some of them did."

I thought of him with his guests the night of the party. Who would he choose to startle? "Would you like to do that?"

"Why not?" His grin said I didn't need to worry, he would let me in on the secret. "You haven't been to Florence, have you?"

"No."

He nodded. "You will. One day. Your mother tells me you don't like to fly," he said. "But it might be worth it to see this."

He moved his hand across the page, almost as if he were stroking it.

I knew that later, he would leave and go to Eleanor. He didn't say so, but I knew. I believed Mary Liz knew. Faline and Otis, too.

Will sat down next to me. "So tell me, what do you think of this house?"

I didn't know how to answer.

"My grandfather built it," he said, "and I feel a certain responsibility. Toward the house and its contents. I know how it must seem to you. It can't compare to . . ." He gestured toward the open volume. "He was a self-made man. But the things Mary Liz said about him. You know, I don't believe any of that." He smiled. Clearly he wanted me to agree with him, to say there was nothing to the old rumors. I remember thinking it wasn't so much to ask. So I nodded.

What strikes me now is the precariousness of those days. The surprise wasn't that they ended, but that we were able to preserve that frail equilibrium at all. We were like the cast of a play that depends for its success on perfect timing, the actors entering and leaving the stage at just the right moment. I didn't think about what might happen if someone missed a cue. My only conscious desire was for things to go on as they were.

I didn't tell Will what had happened in the alley house. He hadn't asked for an explanation, and I hadn't offered one beyond the fact that I sometimes had terrible headaches.

"Migraines?"

I nodded. "I don't remember much afterward," I told him. It was a lie, but I didn't trust myself to say more. I didn't say anything about the photo I'd found either. The image of Stella with her father stayed buried behind some shoes and my camera bag, under the bed I now slept in.

I didn't think I could answer Will's questions selectively. I believed that one revelation would inevitably produce the other, that once I began to speak I would have no choice but to give up the whole truth, just as, remembering my disgrace, I had vomited into the plants and dirt.

DAYS PASSED, AND THE CALENDAR on Will's desk showed June 4. I had been on the Island a little more than two weeks.

It was hard to say what that meant in Galveston. The natural rhythm of the place was such that local people tended to think in terms of years, or even generations. To them, two weeks was nothing. The tourist perspective was different. Two weeks was a leisurely vacation. Like so many visitors to the Island, I found myself wondering where the days had gone. Was that what prompted me to go back for Will's note?

Almost immediately I'd regretted leaving it in the drawer when I could so easily have taken it. Since that night I had thought about the note many times. I wanted it for myself, for the pleasure of reading his words, also for the darker pleasure of knowing Eleanor couldn't.

I was in the kitchen. I had just opened the drawer and removed the silverware tray when I heard Eleanor at the front door. I knew she didn't expect me to be there. As she came into the hall, I heard Will's voice. Neither of them could see me.

"Consider it," Will said. "That's all I'm suggesting."

"I've had years to consider it. I haven't changed my mind." I'd never heard Eleanor so agitated.

"I just think we should have the discussion."

"Will, I know how this goes. We'll talk about it, and you'll behave as if you're listening, and at some point, later, you'll do what you want. Then afterward you'll say we talked about it. Just as if I'd agreed! As if what I said made no difference!"

I knew I should do something to alert them to my presence. I reached for the wall phone. Maybe I could say good-bye and hang up noisily. But how would I explain my presence in the house? I held my breath.

Eleanor's voice was unrecognizable. The woman I'd known, who never asked for anything, was pleading. "I thought you were happy. I thought we were happy."

"I am happy," Will said. There was no note of protest. It was a statement of fact. He sounded as though he meant it.

"Then why?"

"Because I think she should know."

"What difference can it possibly make, after all this time? There's just no good reason to do this now when everything is settled."

"I'm not sure she feels it is. Settled."

I dropped my hand. I slid the note back among the other papers and began to inch the whole pile slowly toward the drawer. I felt the old excitement and the ache that came with being invisible. They were talking about me. I tried to imagine what would happen if Eleanor, this new Eleanor I hardly recognized, found out I had heard them.

Will said, "I'd like to ask her to stay."

"And do what?"

"Finish the exhibition. Enjoy the Island. Take pictures. Eat! My God, I don't think she weighs a hundred pounds."

"And then what?"

"Then . . . we'll see."

"Admit it. This is not really about her. It's about you. And what you want."

"What I want is to take care of her. Is that such a bad thing?"

"You're already taking care of Mary Liz. And Catherine, and Patrick."

"What about you? What am I doing for you?"

He must have touched her. She sighed, then she made a sound low in her throat that I had never heard. "She's your child," Will said. "I would have thought—"

Eleanor cut him off. She had regained her poise, I recognized her voice again. "She's not a child. She's almost thirty years old. And she has a husband waiting for her at home."

"El, that marriage is over."

"Who is to say when a marriage is over? A lot of people would have said yours was, years ago. But you tell me no. Will, nobody can have everything, not even you. There's always something else to want. Do you ever think about what this has been like for me? What I've given up? The things I wanted? I sacrificed them for you."

I put the papers back in the drawer. Carefully, I picked up the silverware tray.

"Come here."

He must have approached her, caressed her again. The thought of it made me feverish. I could feel the heat in my face and neck. "No, don't," she said. "I know you too well. I can see what you're doing. Complicating things. Making them harder. I wish to God I knew why you must do this. Is your life so easy that—"

"I don't think my life is easy, however it may appear." I could hear pain in his voice.

"Don't talk to me about Catherine. You know that's not what I meant. There are things no one can change. But our lives could have been different. You could have made them different, but you wouldn't. You say you want to take care of Clare. Why? Why now? Be honest, Will. You love having people look to you for help and encouragement. You love that role. The more the better. And they do look to you. They don't know that in the end, that's all you'll give them—the blessing of your attention and more hope than anyone should have."

"Is that all I've given you?"

"You said we would go away. That we would be together."

"And we have. We will again."

"I don't want to go to Paris if I have to come back to this. I'm tired of it. I'm tired of fucking in the garage."

I thought of the space adjoining the tack room, the narrow bed, the table with its bowl of roses. Of Will and Eleanor meeting there. I fought the images that assaulted me—Eleanor on her back, her legs wrapped around Will's waist. Eleanor on her knees in front of him.

I thought of Will and Eleanor traveling together.

I wondered if she might have been away with Will the night I was locked out of the house. When my father looked up from his ruined pages and saw me, had he been thinking of her?

Will laughed, easily. "You could have fooled me." Then he said,

"El, I'm not an absolutist. I'm just trying to work things out. To get along. But you. You take no prisoners."

Eleanor's voice was hoarse. "Do I amuse you?" she asked.

"Is this really so serious?"

"Yes," she said. "It is. It was bad enough before. But now you want to bring her into it. I can't stand this."

Will's voice was calm. "Are you suggesting that I choose between the two of you? I hope not."

"I've never said that."

There was a pause. Then Will said, "You are free to go anywhere you want. You have the means."

"You say that because you know I won't."

"Is that such a bad thing? That we know each other as well as we do?"

There was a silence. Then Eleanor said, "You shouldn't be so sure of me."

I thought of Faline. *You can't say what a person thinking. Or what they might do.* I leaned into the drawer. I hoped that it would close smoothly. Slowly, slowly, I began to slide it shut. In a moment, when they left, I could slip out into the yard.

Then their footsteps came toward the kitchen. I pushed the drawer closed and spun around. As I did my hand brushed the kitchen table and knocked something to the floor, where it shattered.

I looked up. Eleanor stood in the doorway. "This has always been your least attractive trait. If it was unattractive in a child, it's much worse in someone who ought to be an adult." Her hands gripped the doorframe.

Will appeared in back of her. "She didn't know we were here."

"Oh yes she did." Eleanor's arms were shaking. "This is something she does. She sneaks around, listening, she pries." She followed my gaze to the fragments of green glass on the floor.

"I'm sorry," I said.

"She didn't do it intentionally." Will smiled briefly at me.

"What makes you think you know anything about her?"

He didn't answer. He just put his hands on Eleanor's shoulders. She twisted a little, resisting, then exhaled through flared nostrils and threw her head back. Will lowered his voice but he kept talking, his hands kept moving, as though she might be calmed by the right inflection, the right pressure. "Who knows," he said. "Maybe this is for the best."

She swung and would have hit him, but he caught her wrist and held it. Eleanor's arm was rigid. "Go. Just go." I stood staring for a moment before I realized she was talking to me.

Will said, "Maybe you'd better leave us for a bit."

I stepped forward, then hesitated. There was no way out that didn't bring me closer to them. I tried to pick my way past the shards of green glass, the stems of mint on the floor, turning my face so I didn't have to see that Will's arms were around Eleanor. That he was holding her firmly against him.

By the time I reached the Carradays' back door I was limping. A piece of the broken pitcher had worked its way into the ball of my right foot. When I sat down and pulled it out, I barely saw the cut. I felt nothing. My mind was full of what I had heard.

I crossed the threshold, moving the way you do in dreams—weightlessly, without even the small vibration that marks each step and fixes you in time and space. I passed smoothly through the house to the double drawing room where the tall mirrors set opposite each other amplified the already impressive setting. Their surfaces were mottled with age, so that I seemed to be approaching through a brilliant fog. I thought about what had been passed down through the Carraday family. Not just the house and its contents, the familiar stories, but the real legacy—Ward Carraday's overriding need, Stella's love and struggle.

In the gold-flecked glass I saw a young woman with an unruly mass of hair, in wilted, ordinary clothes that made her look out of place. Not tall, like Eleanor. Not blond, like her, with skin that turned an even biscuit color in the sun. Not athletic like Frankie. Not freckled like her or redheaded, like my father. I pressed close, closer until my own image looked back at me. The face of a stranger.

I had always believed that because I observed the world through the lens of my camera, because I looked at things in ways others didn't, I saw more. Now I understood that I had failed to perceive what other people with no special ability or training had seen at once. I thought back to the night of Will's birthday party, to Leanne's comment. *I thought you were part of the family.* I remembered Eleanor's reaction, *Did she say why?* Her visible relief when I told her I had no idea. I thought of Harriet Kinkaid's *I would have known you anywhere.* And then I thought all the way back to Aunt Syvvie trying to be kind. To Eleanor saying, *You'll give her ideas.*

"Clare, you're hurt!"

At the sound of Will's voice I turned and saw that I had left a trail of blood, red smudges on the polished floor. "Sit down and let me look at your foot," he said. I didn't move, and he took my arm and drew me gently to a nearby chair. The cut throbbed. "This is serious," he said. "You may need stitches." Kneeling, he might have been about to show me an especially elegant shoe. Then he looked up and I saw what everyone else had, the chiseled face, the long jaw, and under the brows that had been dark when he was younger, that were dark in all the old photographs, blue eyes very like my own.

"You're my father," I said.

His hands closed around my foot as though he didn't want to let go. "Yes," he said. I looked again at the crown of his head, at the hair that, if it hadn't been cut short, would have grown out thick and springy like mine.

Chapter 28

IT WAS DECEMBER, THE YEAR I TURNED FOURTEEN, when Patrick and I stole the car. All day the winter sky had pressed down on the Island like the lid of an aluminum pan. Later, fog moved in off the water and seeped into the city, muffling sound, blurring lighted windows. It was the kind of night when the Islanders, convinced already of their separateness, believe themselves alone in the world.

No one noticed when I went down to meet Patrick in the alley. Together we walked to the Liquor Mart, where I waited for him, leaning against the damp wall, trying to look unconcerned, while he went inside and flashed his fake ID. Finally the door opened, yellow radiance spilled onto the wet pavement, and Patrick came out smiling. He flung his arm around my shoulders. A piece of hair stuck out over his forehead and I reached to try and smooth it. We walked to the corner, his hip bumping my waist.

The car swam up out of the mist, a dune buggy with high seats and black roll bars, the keys still swinging in the ignition. "Someone's even more out of it than I am," Patrick said. He looked back.

"Who was in there?"

He shook his head. "Well, what do you think? Feel like going for a ride?" He dropped his arm and walked around to the passenger door. I felt the chill of the fog along the exposed side of my body, the place where he had been standing. "You're coming, aren't you?" he asked.

Patrick and I had been in and out of trouble for years. But the dune buggy was trouble of a different kind, trouble of a new order of magnitude. I think that was what made it irresistible—the feeling that what we were about to do together would change our lives.

Patrick put the car in gear and we lurched forward. The smiling face of a killer whale, black and enormous, loomed suddenly over the dashboard. I must have gasped. "You thought I was going to hit that wall, didn't you?" Patrick grinned. "Don't worry." He squeezed my thigh. "Everything is fine. Everything will be fine." He wedged the bottle, still in its paper bag, down between the seats. "Where do you want to go?"

I opened my mouth to speak and stopped. *Away* was what I wanted to say. *To the mainland.* Instead I said, "The Dairy Freeze?" It was only a matter of blocks away, but it was all I could manage.

"You sure? You've got goose bumps." I nodded. "Okay." He turned to me. "You wouldn't rather drive to New Orleans? Drink Sazeracs? Hear some jazz?"

I hesitated. Did he mean it? Had the thought of running away occurred to him too? The fog drifted in front of us like torn sheets.

"Sure," I said, hoping to sound casual, but the moment had passed. Patrick was reaching down for the paper bag. He unscrewed the top of the bottle and gazed fixedly into the night as if he were studying something I couldn't see. We backed up, turned, and left the parking lot. One wheel rose unexpectedly and bumped down again as we drove over the curb.

At the Dairy Freeze, strings of colored bulbs hung from the corrugated metal roof. There was music playing and the salt smell of french fries and hot cooking oil mixed with the other salt smell from the ocean.

"You need time to study the extensive menu or do you want the usual?" Patrick asked.

I nodded. Thinking about the two of us in some other place, maybe together in a hotel, had made me suddenly shy. Patrick ordered and paid and passed me a soda. "In New Orleans, they have a drink called a hand grenade," he said.

"Let's go." I thought of posters I had seen, the kind that have a flower in the foreground and the name of the place printed across the top. I thought of the smudged, black-and-white photos in Faline's newspapers. The foreign capitals, in my textbooks—Vienna, Buenos Aires.

They were all equally impossible. I couldn't imagine the two of us—Islanders born and bred specifically for that existence—in any of them, but I spoke quickly, not giving myself time to think about why it could never happen. "Let's go to New Orleans."

Someone banged the hood of the dune buggy. "Shit, man, what's this?" A face appeared—black hair that stood up like a scrub brush, a gap-toothed smile. Tony looked the same, only bigger, broader in the shoulders. Patrick nodded. Other faces appeared, boys mostly, a few girls, one with wings of green above her eyes. They surrounded the car. Tony slapped the windshield. "Your daddy buy you this?" His grin stretched tight. The others pushed against the sides of the dune buggy, first individually, then together. I felt drops falling from my drink onto my bare legs as the car began to rock.

Patrick smiled. "Quit that, we're eating." The rocking stopped.

The boy leaned over. "You're not eating." It was true, Patrick's hamburger sat untouched in its wrapper. He saw the hot dog with a bite out of it in my lap. "But she is. That girl likes weenies." He squinted and licked his lips. I flushed and looked down.

For a moment no one moved. Then another boy said, "Shut up, Tony," and elbowed him out of the way. "Look at her, she's a kid." The tension eased. The girl with the eye shadow smiled and blew cigarette smoke out of her mouth and inhaled it through her nose. She had round, heavy breasts and rounder hips and a little waist marked by a shiny snakeskin belt. I stared at my bony knees, humiliated.

"What do you want to do?" the second boy asked. His name was Lowell.

Patrick shrugged. He could behave worse than any of them, and that gained him respect. But there would never be any real penalty for him, not on the Island. Like his father, Patrick lived above consequences, but because he was less forthcoming, it seemed like an advantage he chose not to share. My father said Patrick was spoiled. I knew there were others who thought that too.

Someone mentioned the beach. "No, it's too wet," a girl said.

"That's why they call it the beach, genius. All that water."

"Asshole. I meant the sand."

"No such thing as too wet," Tony said. "Right, pal?" He was heavier than Patrick, broader in the shoulders.

"Try to relax, Antonio," Patrick said.

The breeze had come up and the strings of lights overhead swayed and cast splashes of color on the watching faces. Tony raised both palms and stepped back.

Over the speakers a country singer complained about his life on the road. I knew they weren't listening. Still, the group began to get restless. The girls dropped their cigarettes, pulled out mirrors and lipstick and gum. The boys swung their arms in halfhearted punches. Then all at once everyone standing around got into one car or another. Two boys climbed into the small backseat of the dune buggy, another perched above them. We left the Dairy Freeze and drove east down Broadway. The neon sign of the new Walgreens burst on us like a flare, but most of the buildings on either side of the street, the old houses, the windowed storefronts, were invisible in the dark.

"Hang on," Patrick said, and we swung around a corner.

I knew the place. Patrick and I had visited it before. Whispering and shoving, we went around to the alley, where one of the iron rails was gone. Someone had a flashlight. Its beam glanced off the dun-colored brick walls and the foliage that overran the boarded-up windows.

"Shut that thing off until we get inside," said Patrick. He was already shifting a piece of plywood that covered a window in the raised basement. It was not nailed, but propped artfully against the wall of the house, and it came away easily. Setting it aside, Patrick climbed through and reached back for me.

We were in the laundry room. There was a row of deep, zinc-lined tubs against the wall, and near them a mangle with wooden rollers and a white enamel basin underneath. A couple of ironing boards stood at careless angles, as though whoever had been using them had left hastily, intending to return. Hard work had been done there, but it was a pleasant space. The smells of soap and starch seemed to have penetrated the walls. I could imagine the smolder and hiss of hot irons, freshly washed linens swaying on the rack overhead.

We moved gingerly through the house. All the ornament had been stripped away. Only the high-ceilinged rooms remained. They echoed as though a hundred years of talk and laughter and the cries of children lingered there and resonated at our passing, the way a set of chimes stirs in the wind.

We trailed through to where double doors opened out into a glass dome. Whatever flooring had once been there was gone, and the room was an indoor forest. Wild plants and weedy, fast-growing saplings had shot up. In front of us stood a porcelain fountain, its base dry and discolored, its circumference littered with cigarette butts.

Patrick took the flashlight, held it to his chin, and grinned horribly.

People asked afterward, *Why did you go there? What did you do?*— and I didn't know how to answer. I said what any of us would have said. That I didn't know why we'd gone there, that we had done nothing, really.

In the days that followed, it seemed to me that the adults, with their questions, were bent on assigning some conscious motive to our activity. Theft. Vandalism. Sex. Drinking. The truth is, few of us ever acted with intent. There was little left to steal—even the doorknobs had been removed. Yes, we were messy, we dropped things and left them there. And, yes, some of the couples tunneled their way into the leafy corners of the room and did the same things they would have done under the bleachers by the football field or in the backseat of a car or at the beach. Patrick had his bottle, of course, and someone else had brought a couple of six-packs of beer. But none of what we did was purposeful.

I do know that the great house in its forlorn state was both sad and thrilling—that it spoke to me of loss and the inevitability of loss, but also of something else. When I leaned my head back and saw the iron ribs of the walls thrusting upward until they disappeared into the night, I felt a kind of release, as though my heart were rising with them.

What did the house mean to Patrick? Was it just another place that should have been off-limits? Or did it speak to him of something he secretly wished for—the collapse of family pride? The end of everything that came with it?

This is what I remember. The girl with the eye shadow stood close to me, so I could see the black patent-leather liner behind her lashes. She tapped my collarbone with a long, green fingernail and said, "You could be pretty, if you'd do something with yourself." There was a stump of holiday candle, half consumed, left from a previous visit. We set it on the edge of the dry fountain and Tony lit it with the girl's disposable lighter. He winked at me when he put the lighter in his shirt pocket.

Lowell asked Patrick about the dune buggy.

"We borrowed it," he said.

"From who?"

"I don't know. It was in the parking lot in back of the Liquor Mart."

Several of the boys were listening now. One of them let out a long whistle. "Holy shit."

"The keys were in the ignition."

Tony said, "You stole it?"

Patrick gazed thoughtfully at his shoe, as if it belonged to someone else. "I borrowed it." That was when Tony stepped away into the dining room. Later Lowell and some others called for him, but he didn't respond, and they concluded he had left. I remember feeling glad that he was gone.

When I smelled burning, the first thing I thought of was the irons in the laundry room, one of them scorching a pillowcase or a napkin. Then I saw flickers of golden light. It was neither the steady brilliance of electricity nor the wash of a flashlight beam but something else. Curious, I went to investigate. Below the tangle of wires the shredded remains of the dining-room curtains were on fire. Flames were racing through the old fabric, bits fluttered down onto the dark wood floor, where they continued to burn. It was beautiful. I stood transfixed as liquid flames poured upward onto the ceiling. The air grew thicker.

Patrick appeared beside me. "Shit. We've got to get out of here," he said, but instead of making for the laundry room, he turned and went back. At first, some of them thought it was a joke and refused to move from where they were lying or sitting, and I saw Patrick pulling at one, shaking another, until a girl saw the flames and screamed. Then everything became confused, and there was shouting and arguing. Someone grabbed my arm, hard, propelling me past the fire and toward the door. "Move," a voice said, "hurry," but of course we couldn't in the interior blackness of the hall. The flashlight was gone, and we had to feel our way. Haste made us clumsy. I fell against someone, felt his elbow in my chest and heard him swear. The girl who had screamed was sobbing, and someone else was saying, "Shut up, shut up." Somehow we reached the open window, climbed out, and lay panting on the grass.

I remember feeling the ground, cool and moist, under me. In a couple of hours it would be morning. Lowell laughed, and others joined in. We struggled to our feet and started toward the cars. Then someone asked, "Where's Carla?"

Lowell turned to a mousy girl with panels of brown hair framing a narrow face. "Where's Carla?"

The girl flinched, as though she had been hit. "She forgot her belt."

I looked around and realized that Carla must be the girl who had spoken to me.

"You let her go back?"

"Don't be like that. I told her not to." The girl's voice rose to a whine.

Flames had overtaken the roof when Patrick started across the lawn, walking fast, then running. I saw the back of his neck, his shirttail, his long quick legs. He was running toward the burning house.

One of the boys made to block his way, but Patrick stepped lightly around him, and I knew that my anxiety had been misplaced. Ever since we'd met up with Tony at the Dairy Freeze, I had been worried about what might happen between the two of them. The real danger was something I had not anticipated. I had never had any reason to fear a fight.

Chapter 29

A CLOUD PASSES, AND IN THE FIERCE Island sunlight everything appears different—the tops of the palms flash silver, the asphalt sparkles. Since the discovery that I was Will's daughter and Patrick's half sister, I had experienced something similar. My new knowledge lit up my surroundings.

It was, however, a private vision. There was no one for me to share it with. Not Frankie, who already knew and had tried to tell me. Not Faline, who had kept the secret for years. I thought of what Frankie had said—*There are only two sides, the Island side and everything else*— and I knew where Faline's loyalty would have to be.

Nor was there more to say to Will, who now held my face and kissed me gently when he said good night. Who clearly felt that all was well. How could I explain to him what my life had been like growing up, what his failure to acknowledge me had meant? How could I tell him what had happened to me without accusing him? When I imagined it, I saw his face close, saw him turn away.

So everything changed and nothing. Life in the Carraday house went on as usual.

One morning Faline stopped me at the foot of the stairs. "I got a whole tableful of silver to polish before dinnertime. You want to, you might could carry these over to Miz Kinkaid. She enjoy something sweet." She held out a plastic container.

"She's at home? You mean she isn't . . ." I stopped, not wanting to put into words what I had been thinking.

"Stand there with your mouth open like that, you going to catch a fly. Careful now. Hold it right. Lemon squares, so you don't need to be looking inside. You act nice, maybe she'll let you have one."

I placed the container carefully under the passenger seat of the jeep and drove slowly, easing my foot off the clutch, starting and stopping elaborately, as if I were taking a driving test.

Harriet Kinkaid was in her front yard when I pulled up. Her house no longer surprised me—I had become accustomed to its weathered exterior and the not-quite-wild plants growing in front of it. I wondered what the new owners would do to it. Paint it, surely, replace the garden with a flat green lawn that was cheaper and easier to maintain. Historically appropriate, too. Who would object? But I didn't want to see the house restored. I wanted it to stay exactly the way it was.

Harriet shook a spent bloom from one of the hibiscus. "This is what passes for gardening around here these days," she said. "What's that? If Faline made it, I know it's something good. Come. I'd like to rest for a moment." She took my arm and walked with me to her front steps. Although her manner was unchanged, her face alert, she seemed somehow slighter. Her hand rested on my arm as lightly as a bird on a branch.

She lowered herself and sat. "Now. You can stop looking at me as if you'd seen a ghost."

"I'm sorry," I said. I hoped I hadn't spoiled her pleasure in being outdoors among her flowers. "I came by before, but you . . . Your car was here. And there was no one home except your yardman. I didn't know what to think."

"Luis wouldn't tell you anything," Harriet said. "They don't like to discuss illness. It's the culture. You'd think, with the Day of the Dead and all. But no. The women get cancer and they won't see a doctor because they don't want to talk about it. Or be examined. Mexican women." She paused and inhaled, deliberately. "I was in the hospital for a bit. But that's done. We've all agreed. Now. If you could just open that for me, please. I have a little arthritis too."

I prized open the plastic lid.

"Ah," Harriet said. "Lemon squares. Faline knows how to make these. You'd better have one too. Good for the soul." She set the open container on the step between us. Her hand shook and powdered sugar drifted down onto the front of her blue chambray shirt as she ate, but she didn't seem to notice. When she saw me watching her, she lifted her chin and smiled, and I caught a glimpse of the young girl on the high, windy hill.

It was early still and for many people the day was just beginning. Newspapers lay uncollected. A battered truck pulling a trailer bristling with lawn mowers passed by. Then came a young woman with a boy alongside her, a boy about the age Bailey would have been if she'd lived. I waited for the feeling of emptiness to overtake me, along with the irresistible urge to move closer, to experience again, painfully, what I had lost. It didn't happen.

The mother wore shorts and sandals that laced up her legs. Her hair was wet, as though she had just stepped out of the shower. The boy would know the smell of her shampoo and of the sunscreen she wore that meant it was summer. He would know also the exact spot where his head would meet her waist if he should run to her, something he tried not to do anymore. As she walked, he circled her, dashing ahead sometimes, only to veer back and return to her side. She called to him occasionally, or gestured, but made no attempt to adjust her own pace. Her straw bag swung back and forth. I realized I was enjoying the way their distinct rhythms came together.

One day he would rush forward and not turn back. And she would will him to go. Somehow the sight of them gave me hope.

Harriet Kinkaid brushed at her shirt front. "My, that was good!" she said. "Now, tell me your story."

I began to speak about the exhibition, but she cut me off. "I want to hear about what's happened with you," she said.

"With me?" I repeated.

"Yes. It isn't a story, you know, unless something happens." Then her manner became serious. "I can see that something has. Happened. Do you want to tell me about it?"

I sat in silence for a moment, wondering what to bring forward first, where to begin. "Actually, there was something," I said. "It happened a long time ago. But I only just found out. Does that count?"

"Of course."

"I think you already know." I tried to sound matter-of-fact, but I couldn't keep the bitterness out of my voice. "Will is my father."

Harriet nodded. "You were bound to find out eventually."

"So everyone on the Island knows? Except me?"

"Your mother laid eyes on Will Carraday and—"

She stopped and placed one hand over her heart. Then she said, "In Spanish they compare that kind of love to an arrow wound." An image came to me suddenly of Eleanor, a thick shaft piercing her yellow cotton dress. I thought of the arrow's notched point, buried, impossible to remove. The effort it would take to conceal that kind of pain. "Will cares deeply for her," she said. "But he'll never leave Mary Liz. When you were born, and you and Patrick became close . . . I'm sure they thought of it as a solution."

"Until we got too close."

Harriet nodded. "Faline saw you kissing."

"What about Patrick? Does he know?"

"I can't be certain, you understand. But I believe he does."

"Why didn't he tell me?" I tried to keep my voice steady, but it came out thin and teary.

Harriet patted my knee.

"How long has he known?"

She shook her head. "You'd have to ask him. But I think part of his reluctance to see you at the party was not knowing what you would expect."

"I told you I tried to find him. I even went to a bar he likes." I hung my head. "How could I have been so stupid?" I stared at the space between my legs, at the stone pavers that made up Harriet's walk, the tufts of grass that sprang up between them. "All those years, all of us living here together, I never figured it out." My eyes welled, I couldn't bear to look at her, to see her pity me.

Harriet said, "You are not stupid. You must never think that. You know the saying 'Seeing is believing'? Well I think it works the other way around. Especially with children. Believing is seeing. And for a long time, children believe what they're told, especially what their parents tell them."

I thought then of Frankie, of how she had believed my father. How she had followed the course he laid out for her.

"My sister," I said.

"I was thinking of Stella Carraday."

"What do you mean?"

"It was peculiar, the way her father treated her. The way he behaved toward her. People used to see them together, on the street, in shops and restaurants, and comment. There was always talk. And she never had any friends. He didn't want anyone else in the house. Oh yes, everyone knew something was wrong there. But my point is, Stella didn't. She had no way of knowing. Until she met Henry Durand."

What would Harriet say about the photo I'd found of Stella naked? She didn't seem like someone who would be easily shocked. Still.

"I wondered if you would find out about Stella," she said. "I'm the only one who knows all of what happened, although Will surely has his ideas. They ran away together, the two of them. Stella and Henry Durand. They managed to cross the causeway before the hurricane struck. Afterward . . . It was a terrible time," said Harriet Kinkaid. "There was looting. Houses, those that remained unoccupied, were broken into. Someone came to him, to Ward Carraday, to say that Stella had left the Island with young Henry. Hoping for a reward, I suppose. There's always someone to play that role."

I began to speak, but she held up her hand. "You'd better let me finish." She closed her eyes briefly, then went on. "I hold him responsible, Ward Carraday. I want you to understand that. But no one tried to stop him. No one. Life here, on the Island, changes people." She gazed out at the street, but she seemed not to see it, her thoughts appeared to be far away. "I don't know why, I seem to be thinking in Spanish today. You know what the Spanish called Galveston?"

A magnolia stood not far from the steps, its moving leaves revealing rusty velvet undersides. The strong, sweet lemon smell wafted toward us. "Malhado," I said.

Harriet nodded. "Isle of Misfortune. Ward Carraday tracked them down. They were staying in a little flat with a few pieces of cheap furniture. He went through their rooms and smashed everything." She closed her eyes again. "You wonder how I know. I was a late-in-life baby, my parents had given up on having children when I came along. Maybe that was why my mother treated me like another adult. Told me what most mothers wouldn't have."

"It was different after her father brought her back."

"Yes. He gave away all her pretty clothes. Stella wore the same dress day after day, until it fell to pieces. She was no longer allowed to leave the house at all."

I thought of the notebook, of Stella, alone in her room, drawing the only flowers left to her, the ones on the wallpaper. Waiting and hoping that Henry Durand would return.

"My mother did what she could—called on her, sat with her on the veranda. She didn't like to go inside. But she worried about Stella, alone with him. Once she even took her a bird, a singing canary, thinking it would be company. When she saw it, Stella wouldn't even touch the cage. My mother said she'd never seen anyone so afraid.

"Then they began the grade raising. You know what that meant? Phillip Giraud had to go through the Carradays' downstairs to get to his house. Your house. And he saw Stella. She was changed. But Phillip Giraud was older. A good man. He went to Ward Carraday with a proposal of marriage. That was when her father took her away with him. On the European trip. They went alone. He said her mother was too ill to travel."

I thought for a minute. "Your mother helped Stella, didn't she? When she tried to run away."

"There. You are clever. You see? She did. She paid the groom. She never told my father. Or anyone else as far as I know. The Island is a small place. And they were all afraid of him. Of Ward Carraday."

I remembered the biography that mentioned his business ventures. His young wife. *He was not inclined to the pleasures of society.* Was that a way of saying no one liked him? I thought of Stella, alone with her father in a series of hotels, places where she had no one else, places where the servants spoke no English.

I sensed that Harriet was tiring. But I couldn't help myself, I had to keep asking. So much had been withheld from me for so long. Again I wondered if I should tell her about the photo.

"And then?"

"Stella's mother didn't live long. When Ward Carraday died, Franklin inherited. The bank, the businesses, the house." Harriet paused, as if considering, then went on. "Stella moved out. Her brother saw to her needs."

"She moved out? But why?" I thought of the big house, the image over the fireplace unaltered, perfect, while the real Stella had grown older, losing her looks, her clothes falling to pieces. Finally being made to leave.

"Franklin had a young family by then. And Stella. Well. She would go for weeks without washing. And she made strange remarks. Lewd remarks. Once she unbuttoned her blouse in front of guests. It's a sad story, I'm afraid." Harriet looked out at the street. "You've seen the Cartier-Bresson book?"

"Of course." I made an effort to hide my impatience. I didn't want to talk about photography. My mind was too full of other things.

"It's in the kitchen. On the table by the sink." Harriet closed her eyes and fell silent, and I understood that she meant I should go and get it. Reluctantly I rose and did as she wanted. When I returned she sat up a little and said, "You'll see. I haven't lost my mind." She turned the pages slowly, her fingers pale against the black-and-white images. "There. You wouldn't recognize her. Stella."

I knew the photo. It showed the interior of a once grand Galveston hotel. The carpet was worn, and many hands had rubbed the stain from what had been an elegant stair rail. On the landing was an elderly woman. She steadied herself with a cane. Her eyes, in shadow behind the frames of her glasses, were two black smudges. It was impossible to see what they held. It was the old woman in the boardinghouse.

Harriet said, "Poor girl." She set the book down and took my arm. "If you don't mind, I want my chair now. And a rest."

I helped her settle on the porch with the cushion at her back. She looked at me thoughtfully. "So now you know everything," she said. Her tone was gently mocking, and I blushed.

"It's just that . . ." I began.

"It's all right," she said. "I understand. Whatever you've found, you don't need to tell me. At this stage of my life, I'd just as soon not know."

The air was still and heavy in the garden. There was no lemon-scented breeze, not even the smallest leaves stirred. *Now you know everything.* I wondered. Was she really saying, *Now you know enough?* Once a photo is cropped, the image formed, no one cares what was left out. We accept the result for what it is.

It was just after ten when I drove away from Harriet Kinkaid's house. The brief, perfect calm of midmorning had settled on the street and the freshly mowed yards. Harriet had supplied a conclusion. I knew she wanted to give me some measure of peace. Instead, what I felt was the advancing edge of a new anxiety. With it came the certainty that I wasn't finished, just suspended for a moment, like the ballplayer with his arm raised, about to throw.

Chapter 30

A FEW MILES FROM HARRIET KINKAID'S HOUSE, but remote in every other sense, was the neighborhood that adjoined the Island's oldest cemetery, the place where, according to Will, Stella was buried.

Nothing grew around the small shotgun houses, no children played in front of them. Even in the heat of summer, the windows were shuttered and barred. Loud music thudded from the open doors.

In the gas station parking lot on the corner, a girl in shorts and a halter top waited near the pay phone. She strolled back and forth, her face expressionless. A pickup with a skull-and-crossbones decal circled the block and returned. The driver pulled in. They spoke briefly, he reached out to hand her something, and she climbed up into the truck.

I stopped in front of the entrance to the cemetery. A hundred years ago, this was where Galveston's elite had constructed miniature versions of their impressive residences. As the area declined, those with a choice had gone elsewhere. The dead and their memorials remained. A sign stuck in the ground said NO LOITERING. Where the grass grew long, it was carpeted with brilliant yellow daisies.

I had no idea where to look for the Carraday family, where to find Stella's grave. So I walked among the grieving figures, mostly women, that marked the larger monuments. The ground under them had shifted, and they leaned this way and that like commuters watching for different trains. There were angels too, their sloping, folded wings mottled with dark gray lichen.

It was well before noon, but the sun beat on my neck and back. I knew my hair wouldn't keep me from burning. I pulled at my shirt and felt sweat running down my sides. A grove of mature oaks clustered at the opposite side of the cemetery, and I made my way toward it. I hoped the Carraday monument might be under one of them.

I was halfway there when I saw someone sitting on the steps of a big pink marble mausoleum. The solid breadth of his shoulders and the relaxed way he sat, his legs splayed, contrasted pleasantly with the narrow, fretful stone figures. He was scratching the chin of a low-slung, brown mongrel. I realized I was glad to see Ty. As I approached, he raised the hand that wasn't busy with the dog and smiled.

"This might be what you're looking for." He stood and above his head, on the lintel, I saw CARRADAY in block letters. Behind him, set between marble panels, was a pair of bronze doors decorated with grillwork. The whole arrangement made me think of the elevator in an old-fashioned department store, the kind that was built as a sort of temple to commerce.

"Are there first names?" I asked.

"On the other side."

"Will said there was a stone. I wasn't expecting this."

"Maybe he was embarrassed. It's awfully pink. But even if it wasn't, would you want it?"

I shook my head. I remembered a story I had heard about a successful investor who spent a fortune while he and his wife were still alive to build an elaborate monument more than twelve feet high. By the time they both died, within a few weeks of each other, he'd lost most of his money, Island society had turned its back on them, and the only one who attended the funeral was the stonemason.

The dog grinned up hopefully. When it was clear that no more attention was forthcoming, he retreated to the cool earth at the foot of one of the oaks.

Ty said, "I've been looking for you. I followed you from town. I'm parked over there." He indicated the far side of the cemetery. "I wanted you to see me first, to know I was here. After the boat, I didn't know what else to do. I called. I left messages."

"I know you did. But I—"

"You don't have to explain." Ty shifted his weight, and I sensed his discomfort. He said, "There's something I think you ought to know."

"What?" I smiled, but Ty's face remained serious. He was not dressed for the office, he was wearing shorts and a polo shirt, and I wondered why. He'd made a point of saying he wasn't in Galveston for a vacation.

"After we talked at the ice-cream parlor, I got curious. I looked at some things closely, for the first time." Ty took a deep breath and exhaled hard. "I couldn't tell you that night on the boat, not with Will there. You know how he made his money?"

"He inherited it, mostly."

"He inherited a modest savings-and-loan and some land. It would have been enough for most people. But Will is ambitious. His real success has come from financing development. Real estate development. Some off the Island, some on. Not one house at a time. Big stuff."

My throat tightened. I remembered Mary Liz saying, *The tourists want condos.*

Ty looked away, as if he didn't want to see my reaction, but he went on talking. "It didn't hurt that he married Mary Liz Smith. The Smith brothers discovered the South Sooner Field. Big oil. So he's had plenty to work with."

I nodded. I knew how Mary Liz had been raised, the way she'd lived. I'd just never thought much about what it must have cost. "Are you saying the bank hasn't made money?"

"No, it has. That is, it did. The old way was pretty straightforward. Borrow money at three percent, loan it at six, hit the golf course by three. Or the boat dock. Will's not a golfer, of course."

"Why are you telling me this?"

"Because you were the one who made me pay attention to how things are here. I could say I didn't know. Probably it would be more accurate to say I wasn't looking for what I didn't want to see." He paused and regarded me thoughtfully. "This may not be easy for you to hear. I can stop anytime you want."

A man rode past on a rusted bike. The route through the cemetery must have been his regular shortcut. One of his tires rasped softly against a bent fender. I watched as he went by.

"Go on," I said.

"Real estate was booming in other places. People here wanted to get in on the action. Will helped them."

"Is there something wrong with that?"

"I guess it depends on what you do. And how you do it." Ty looked away over the clustered obelisks. "I don't know the whole story. I couldn't go into the details, not without being noticed." He grimaced, and I realized that it had been hard for him to give up the prospect of the burgeoning career that had brought him to Galveston. "Don't get me wrong," he said. "I like Will. How could anyone not like him? He made me feel so appreciated. So this is the part that's embarrassing to admit. I got to thinking how smart I must be. For him to have—"

"Singled you out?"

"Exactly."

Ty's neck and cheeks were pink, but he looked at me levelly. "I'm pretty sure the bank is going down. Not right away. But eventually. There will probably be an investigation." He went on talking. I heard the sound of his voice rising and falling, I heard *conflict of interest* and *bank fraud.* I heard my own voice too, now and then, but faintly, like a conversation in another room. Everything around me seemed to have faded slightly, as though the light had faltered. The man on the bicycle pedaled into the distance.

Ty was still talking. He said, "When this happens, if it happens, blame will be assigned. And it will be better for everyone here if much of it can be assigned to someone who is not an Islander. Some-one who doesn't count."

"You said, 'If it happens.' You're not sure."

"I'm as sure as I can be."

I wiped my forehead and felt sweat on my hand. "You think Will brought you here deliberately? I don't believe it." But as I said it, I saw Will at the party, greeting his guests, making introductions. At the boat dock, shaking hands. Had he introduced Ty, told the others about his responsibilities, before I arrived? I wanted not to believe it. At the same time it came to me that if what Ty said was true, Will might have introduced us with a purpose. He'd made certain we met at his party. He'd brought us together again on the boat. What exactly had he intended? Had he thought of me as a useful diversion? Something to keep Ty busy, preoccupied, while Will did whatever he had to? Once again, I knew what I'd seen and heard, but had no idea what it all meant.

Ty shrugged. "You don't have to believe me." Somehow his acquiescence was more convincing than any argument. "I've already let Will know that I'm leaving." He paused. "Was I wrong to tell you?" he asked.

"No." I spoke without thinking, the desire to know had been my guiding impulse for so long, it had never occurred to me that anything else might take its place. I had a sudden thought. "What about Patrick?" I asked.

"What about him?"

"Does he know? Is he—"

"I don't think Patrick knows anything about it. Your sister's right, he's hardly ever there."

This time I used the word. "So he hasn't done anything illegal?"

When Ty didn't immediately respond, I looked up. He said, "I can't answer that."

Chapter 31

SOMETIMES I WONDER WHAT IT'S LIKE to work only in black-and-white, like Cartier-Bresson. To forgo a whole class of images. I think about the shots of Galveston he must have considered and rejected because he knew they would only succeed in color. I wonder if some of them are still there, on the Island, waiting to be discovered.

Ty had offered no proof. I didn't have to accept what he'd told me. I could go on as if nothing had happened. I thought of my father saying to Frankie and me, *Believe what you want.* What did I want? I wasn't certain. In the meantime, it felt good to stand by the window, Stella's window, holding my Leica, thinking about light and composition.

I was planning to photograph the old palms in the Carradays' garden. To see if I could capture their moods, their postures, some waving, spirited, others bent and furtive.

I waited until the sun was low, then went out into the yard. I took a few shots of the trees, then decided their spiky shadows on the grass were more interesting at that moment than the palms themselves. I moved away, moved closer, considered using a filter. I was standing back, gazing toward the garage, when I saw that one of the doors was open.

Did I only imagine that I saw him disappear into its dark recess? Once I knew, it was obvious. He had even left me a sign telling me where to come if only I had been able to see it.

I went without hesitating to the tack room. On the round table was a bowl of roses. I could see, in the alcove, a canvas hat lying on the bed. I turned away, I didn't want to think about Eleanor and Will meeting there. I didn't want to think about Will at all. Thoughts of him led too quickly to thoughts of what Ty had told me.

There were the heavy collars, the harnesses on the walls. The smell of leather. The waiting carriages. I heard the wheeze of springs, saw one of the carriages move just a little. I walked closer.

"Patrick."

He reached out and I took his hand and stepped onto the running board. The carriage swayed, and he pulled me up. How many times had he helped me over windowsills, into cars, into any number of places where we shouldn't have been? Always, Patrick's strong arm was the thing I could rely on.

His hair was thinner and his body had settled. He had a little belly. The skin on his forearms was pale and ropey where he had been burned, and there was more of that pale skin along his chin. I saw and registered the changes. Still he was perfectly familiar, wholly dear.

"Hey," he said. He was holding the silver flask, the one I had seen resting on the carriage seat my first day on the Island. "Are you scrutinizing me?"

I smiled. "I wondered if you would be the same."

"Am I?"

"Pretty much."

"I'm giving you my good angle," he said. He grinned and turned his head and I could see where the scars stretched along his jaw and toward his ear.

"That doesn't matter," I said. "Not to me."

He set the flask down and took my hand and placed it against his, the way he used to. "You're pretty much the same too. At least, you haven't grown any." He sat back against the leather.

Patrick was never visibly drunk. He didn't slur his words or act out. He just became more detached. I could see that he had been drinking for a while. "You remember the time we poured Mom's bourbon down the heating vents?" he asked. "You remember how it smelled?"

I smiled. "Of course."

"Come here," he said, and I moved over and sat next to him.

We think we can't bear things. We say, *I'd die if he ever* and *I couldn't live without.* I used to say those things too and I believed them. That winter in Ohio, watching the ice form on the window in my bedroom, under the eaves of my grandmother's house, I was waiting to die. I believed it would happen, that it was just a matter of time. I felt sorry for my grandmother, that she would be the one to find me.

I leaned my head against Patrick's shoulder. When I began to sob, he pulled me close. "Hey," he said.

We sat for a few minutes like that. When I quieted, he turned my face to his and deliberately wiped my eyes with one knuckle. "How was Europe?" I managed to ask.

Patrick rubbed his chin, and I had time to conjure up things I'd seen in pictures—grand boulevards, cafés, people in colorful costumes. He said, "I learned to ski. I did a lot of skiing. They have real winter there."

"They have real winter in Ohio too. And skiing."

"Is it any good?"

"I don't know. I never went. I stayed with my grandmother."

Patrick nodded. "I guess not too many grandmothers ski. They drink wine in Europe."

I had nothing to say to that. But it didn't matter. Our conversations had always had an odd rhythm, lots of starts and stops. "You didn't come to the party," I said.

"I hate those things."

"But you knew I was here," I persisted. "I know you did. And I went out to the beach to try and find you. Why didn't you come and see me?"

"I started to, one time. I came by your house."

"You did?"

"I saw you in the window."

I remembered my first night on the Island. How I had gone to the window after my bath, looked out into the shadowy space between the houses. "You were outside?"

Patrick grinned. "I was kind of glad it happened. I never did get to see you with your clothes off."

I thought of the times we had kissed, my inexpert fumbling. Patrick's hand on my bare stomach. We had come close. "When did you find out?" I asked. "About us? Who told you?"

Patrick shook his head. "No one took me into their confidence or anything. Shit. It was Ernie. At the Liquor Mart. You were back east by then. And it was pretty clear I was done with school. Ernie didn't exactly tell me. I was in there one time, reaching for my wallet and he said, 'Where's your sister?' I told him, 'My sister doesn't live here,' and he said, 'No, I mean the other one.' I must have given him a look, because he handed me my change and went off into the back of the store. There was a curtain, and he ducked behind it." Patrick's mouth twisted. "He probably figured I knew. And then he saw I didn't."

"Everyone knew," I said. "Everyone except us."

"It wouldn't have changed things. Much."

"Maybe not for you. But my life could have been different." The words were out of my mouth before I realized that it was what Eleanor had said. *Our lives could have been different.*

"I don't know." Patrick shrugged. "Maybe you were the lucky one."

"How can you say that?" I felt a surge of anger, then I reminded myself that there was a lot he didn't know. "You left too," I said.

"I was only gone for a while. You stayed away. You did real things. All I did was ski. Up, down. Up, down." His expression didn't change, but something about the way he said it made me ache for him.

"You could have stayed away," I said. Patrick leaned his head back and said nothing.

I felt ashamed. What I'd told him sounded like the truth, but only if you didn't know Patrick. I was sure that other people, who didn't, had made the same argument many times, equally sure that it was futile. Patrick was living the only life he could. Wasn't that what the scars on his arms and face meant? That he was someone who would always go back, no matter how terrible the consequences? I had never judged him. There was no reason to start now. Surely it was beside the point.

I turned and took his face in both hands and kissed the scarred skin. "I bet you were a good skier," I said.

Patrick closed his eyes, and we sat for a moment in silence. Then he said, "Not bad. You know what a mogul is?"

I thought for a moment. "A powerful person?"

Patrick laughed. "You and me. We are definitely a team. Between the two of us, we've pretty much got it covered." He smiled, his knee bounced. "Well. What do you think? You want to go somewhere?"

I didn't care if we went or stayed. I just wanted to be with him, his body next to mine. He was tapping his foot and I could feel the vibration all along my leg. What we did, our conversations, were not important. They never had been.

"I used to think we might run away together," I said.

"I did too."

"I mean really."

"I mean really, too."

"Do you ever think about what might have happened?"

"God, yes. I thought about it when I saw you looking out that window." He pretended to leer and I laughed. I felt the tension surrounding that dark *what if* begin to ease.

"So tell me what you're doing now."

"I'm sitting in a funky old carriage with my arm around a beautiful woman who also happens to be my half sister. But, hey."

"I meant work."

"The bank."

"Is that all?"

"That's not enough? I wear a tie and everything." He mimed choking, and I didn't press him. There would be plenty of time to find out. Our shared future, not like anything I had imagined but still essential, lay ahead. We had always taken comfort from each other. For now that would be enough.

"You said you got cold feet."

"I wasn't sure you'd want to see me. You being a big success and all. I'm not anybody—"

"Stop it," I said heatedly. "Success isn't what you think." I recalled Harriet Kinkaid saying, *You must learn to take the credit too.* I knew she would disapprove, but I said anyway, "It's something that happens to you."

"Well, it hasn't happened to me."

That was the kind of remark Frankie would have tendered as proof that Patrick wasn't trying. I understood it as something else, his way of resisting other people's expectations. Not just his family's but the entire Island's. All his life everyone around him had had an idea about who he was or should be. I knew how it weighed on him. It was the thing I had been spared.

He saw me looking at him and said, "They wanted to do more grafts. But I said the hell with it."

I had told Eleanor that Patrick had no vanity, and I'd been right. What I'd worried about was that Patrick would be changed by time and living away. Turned into someone I didn't know. Instead the experience seemed to have driven him deeper into himself. I felt strangely disappointed. Wasn't that what I'd wanted? To have Patrick back? Himself, unchanged?

Then I had one of those flashes of insight that come only when they are too late to be useful. I understood that my wish had been granted, in the precise and pitiless way that wishes often are. Patrick had not changed, nor had my feelings for him altered. But I had. The girl who had roamed the Island with Patrick getting into trouble was gone, into another life, a dream.

Patrick sighed. His knee jiggled. "What about the beach?" he asked. "You want to go there?"

"Okay," I agreed. "The beach."

We drove out toward San Luis Pass and parked. It seemed like the most random stretch of sand imaginable, but we were only alone for a few minutes. Some men were wade fishing in the surf. When they saw us, they waved and greeted Patrick by name and brought over their cooler. Light was seeping over the horizon when we left.

Chapter 32

THE NEXT AFTERNOON, Patrick came to the archive. We whispered awhile in deference to the space—there were still no other readers. Then I put my work aside, and together we went to a park where a brass band was playing languid oompah music in a raised pavilion. Patrick pulled me through the crowd to the performers. When they saw him, the musicians stood and shook his hand and two foaming mugs appeared. Eventually Patrick said, as if the idea surprised him, "You want to eat?"

We drove to one of the old hotels, conceived in the mission style and meant to evoke the Island's largely nonexistent Spanish past. The new owner had spent a lot of money. The stucco walls were bright white and the tile roof gleamed. If the result was not "correct," it was convincing, and the restaurant was full. We were seated right away. The waiter ignored our shorts and T-shirts, shaking out my napkin and placing it in my lap. He produced Patrick's drink without asking for his order.

Clearly Patrick, like Will, knew people all over the Island, although I doubted somehow that they moved in the same circles. Wherever we went, he was recognized and greeted. I noticed that people wanted to do things for him, too.

Every day that week Patrick came to the archive and claimed me, much as he had when we were growing up. When we left, the man at the desk stared pointedly at the piles of photographs that had accumulated. Gwen hurried by looking anxious. I smiled at them both in a way that I hoped invited no comment.

Together Patrick and I toured the Island. Some places I had been to before, others I hadn't. His reception was the same everywhere—eager, friendly.

We were never alone. And finally I had to accept that we would never recover the place that had been ours, the private territory of our adolescence. It too was gone.

We did not go to Saint Vincent de Paul, and I didn't ask about it either.

I had seen and envied Will's ability to set aside anything troubling. I told myself it was a skill I could develop, and I made an effort to seem unconcerned. I believed that if I could achieve the outward appearance of calm, my state of mind would adjust itself accordingly. But I sometimes felt a burning in my chest as if the thoughts I refused to entertain consciously had taken form and lodged themselves there.

I saw Will only briefly, breezy passing encounters in the halls. Once he said, "You're going out again?" He looked preoccupied. He held a handful of papers, his reading glasses were pushed back on his head. He seemed pleased though, as if my new social busyness meant I was finding a way to be on the Island that was more than temporary. I could have told him I was meeting Patrick, but I didn't. He would hear about it from someone soon enough. I said as little as possible and let Will believe I was making new friends. Faline knew better, her face radiated doubt.

I no longer had a plan or felt the need for one. It was a revelation, the way life continued to unfold without my making the smallest effort. The sun rose through the pink mist, burned the unwary tourists, and sank again into the Gulf. The wind blew. The cruise ships came and went. The days rolled by in breathtaking, unbroken swells.

I have said that islands have a way of seizing the imagination. Of taking over. Did I think that because I'd been away for so long, it couldn't happen to me?

WE OFTEN STARTED OUT at Lafitte's. Once I knew some of the regulars, it felt different. There was Russell, the bartender, who lived with his mother in a double-wide trailer out by the mudflats. The woman in the muumuu was Edna, a former seventh-grade teacher. "She's harmless," Patrick said. "She's just used to hearing herself talk."

From what Frankie had said about Lowell Morgan, I hadn't expected to like him. But he turned out to be a big, sweet-faced man who had grown up the only brother of six girls. Maybe that explained the careful way he negotiated his surroundings, as if he'd learned early to be cautious of interiors. Lowell would nurse one beer for hours, picking the bottle up and setting it down again precisely on one of Lafitte's scarred tables. He built carved-wood porches for the owners of the Island's houses, old and new. They considered themselves lucky to be on his waiting list.

I left my Leica at home. I hadn't taken a photograph since Patrick and I had met in the tack room. The presence of my camera, whether I used it or not, seemed to remind him of his appearance and make him self-conscious in a way that saddened me.

Most of those nights run together in my mind—the images combine, like multiple exposures. But I do recall one evening—it was shortly after my first encounter with Patrick at the Carradays'.

When we arrived at Lafitte's, Patrick went straight to the shuffleboard table and skimmed a puck down it. Then he approached the bar. He patted Edna's plump hand and began flipping the channels on the ancient TV. No one seemed to mind. He adjusted the twisted coat hanger that served as an antenna. When the picture came into focus, he said, "Nolan Ryan. Having a good year." He sat down with his back mostly to the set.

"I see you're planning to watch the game," said Lowell.

The bartender came over with a beer for Patrick and a glass of wine for me. "Russell, my man," Patrick said. "You think the Rangers have a chance?" Patrick never seemed to pay attention to the games, but somehow he always knew what was happening. He turned to Lowell. "I don't like to let planning interfere with a good time. I'm keeping my options open."

Lowell said, "Well, I got to come up with a plan pretty quick. Darcie wants me to take her to the cat circus."

"The what?"

"It's only here for a couple of days, and she wants to go. Her car's in the shop again. She won't stop talking about it. Cats singing. Cats walking across a wire." He rubbed his neck as if it hurt.

Lowell's sister, Darcie, was the girl I'd met at the beach house. She had a summer job in a boutique on the Strand.

"You want to slip away? Go somewhere else?" Patrick asked.

"Sure. But what am I going to tell her?"

"Say you got confused and thought it was another night."

But it was too late. Darcie had skipped over the crack in the concrete floor and was coming toward us. She was barely five feet tall, and she was too young to drink legally, but I'd never seen Russell ask for ID.

"Hey, Patrick," she called out. He turned and picked her up in a hug, swinging her around so her sandaled feet flew and her flowered top rode up, exposing several inches of lean, tanned back.

"Whoa," Lowell said, "take it easy."

Patrick laughed. "You afraid I might break something?" He set Darcie down on one of the duct-taped barstools. "Want a drink?" he asked her. "One of those pink ones?" He slapped the bar to get Russell's attention and pointed at Darcie.

She grinned. "I may not have time. Did he tell you where we're going?"

Lowell sighed and stood up and wiped the place where his glass had been with a crumpled napkin.

"Look at his face," Darcie said. "You can tell he's excited. Lowell, I got good news."

"The tent fell down?"

"They're going to have the princess cat out so you can pet her. In a little tiara."

Lowell shook his head in disgust.

Darcie laughed. Russell brought her a drink in a tall glass with a straw. "Okay," she said, "I guess you've suffered enough. You're off the hook. We're going tomorrow, Mom too." She smiled and took a sip through the straw.

"Thank you, Jesus." Lowell sank onto a chair that was too small for him.

I sat back. Around me, the droning voices from the TV, the muttering of the men in the back of the room, the chink of glasses from the bar resolved into a murmur, as relaxing in its own way as the sound of surf. It filled your ears and quieted your worries.

Darcie leaned against Patrick, and he put one arm around her waist. Her long hair was straight and shiny, sun-streaked, and when she tilted her head to gaze up at him through her bangs, I saw her eyes widen. She squeezed his arm and they both laughed again.

Watching them, I felt suddenly like an outsider.

Darcie said, "You probably think we're pretty childish."

I shook my head, but it was what I'd been thinking, unfairly. Darcie was young. She believed the world was a good place, full of happy cats. If she lifted Patrick's spirits, why should I object? Hadn't I resolved not to judge him? I made an effort to look pleasant.

Darcie elbowed Patrick. "He brings it out in me. Partly because I've known him since I was ten. When I see him, I sort of revert."

As if to demonstrate what she meant, Patrick pulled at the little tie on the front of her blouse. "Quit that," Darcie said, pushing his hand away.

I wondered then what I was seeing. If theirs was a sexual relationship, it was easy, offhand, entirely without tension.

"Patrick and I go back a ways too," I said. Lowell looked away, and I understood that he knew about Patrick and me.

Darcie glanced around hopefully, as if she expected to hear some good stories. She wasn't jealous. She had no reason to be. I was older, someone from Patrick's past, important to him for a reason he hadn't explained, but not a rival.

"We used to pull pranks on Faline. And on her father. That kind of thing," Patrick said.

"Did you get in trouble?"

"We didn't get caught. That's the secret of life as a Carraday." He looked at me, and I saw that he felt my discomfort.

I was wearing the earrings Will had given me. Patrick reached out and touched one. "Did my dad give you those?"

I nodded and felt the pearls move. I wondered how he knew.

Patrick cleared his throat. "So," he asked Darcie, "how's work?"

"I hate it," she said cheerfully. "I want to get married and stay home. Watch *Days of Our Lives*."

Lowell said, "You don't finish school, the days of your life will be waiting in line at the welfare office."

Patrick said, "There's Joe over there. You could marry him. It's only been twenty-seven years since his last wife died. And he really enjoys talking about his hernia."

Lowell laughed and Darcie made a face. "You are so gross. Both of you." She took out a compact and dusted her cheeks. "So what are we doing tonight?" she asked.

"We're going somewhere," Patrick said. I saw that his knee was jumping. "Come on. You and Lowell follow me."

"What about my drink?"

Patrick picked up Darcie's glass, pushed the fruit to the side, and drained it. Then he swept an arm around me and turned for the door.

In the car, Patrick was quiet. He drove fast, swinging around corners and accelerating through yellow lights, the way he always did, but without any of his usual exuberance. Somehow Lowell kept us in sight without breaking any laws.

"So where are we going?" I asked.

Patrick didn't answer, and I didn't care enough to persist.

He pulled up in front of a pavilion overlooking the wharf, a steel-and-glass wedge that jutted over the water. Patrick gave his keys to the valet and we waited for Darcie and Lowell near the roped-off entrance. A handful of tourists stood nearby, gazing fixedly at the brightly lit space by the door. Patrick didn't retreat exactly, but he stepped away from the glare and turned the burned side of his face toward the building.

Darcie had put on more makeup in the car, and her cheeks sparkled. "I'm not sure I'm ready for this," she said, smoothing her clothes with her hands. I saw, all at once, how scruffy we were, except for Lowell, whose hair was cut short and who had tucked in his shirt.

"Well," Patrick said, "shall we go in?" His manner was curiously formal. I still had no idea why we were there, but Patrick's demeanor told me we'd come for a reason.

There was a broad-hipped man at the door with a list, but Patrick nodded at him and we passed through. We were early and the room was only partly filled. Against one wall was a raised, skirted platform with a microphone on a stand. There was no one near it except for a technician, who was taping a cord to the floor. Everyone else was over by the bar.

Darcie's instinct had been sound—it was a dressy crowd. Women in silk and linen, men in jackets. Patrick steered me closer to the guests.

That was when I saw Will. He was talking to a young woman whose back was toward me. Her hair was short, and her dark red strapless dress showed off her neck and shoulders. At first I didn't recognize her. But I did know the look on Will's face—intensely engaged, full of delight. He was using his hands to emphasize a point. I saw her fingers stroking the tanned skin of her upper arm. I heard the technician say through the mike, "Testing, one, two."

Will looked up then and saw me. Did I imagine it, or did he hesitate for just a moment before he raised his arm and waved us over?

The circle around him opened to include us, and I felt his energy. "You know each other, of course," he said, gesturing toward the woman in the strapless dress. It was the archivist, Gwen. She appeared as polished as ever. She said something, and the conversation went forward.

But I was thinking about other things. About what it must have been like for Patrick to grow up on the Island in Will's shadow. Never to be able to escape being his father's son, wherever he went. And I wondered when he had come to understand that whatever Will showed him of interest and affection was exactly what he offered everyone. Will's manner, like a fine instrument, could be tuned to any situation. But there was no real difference in what he gave of himself.

I recalled what I'd overheard between Will and Eleanor the night I broke the pitcher. Eleanor's desperate pleading. I wondered if Will was also taking care of Gwen, and what exactly that might mean.

I turned to face Patrick, but he was gazing out the window. He seemed to be looking for something beyond the gaily lit wharf, beyond the bay. The pale, rippled skin along the side of his face was drawn tight.

I understood then why he had brought me there. I stepped closer to him, until I felt the persistent animating vibration along his side. I slid my arm around his waist. He folded my right hand in his, raised it to his lips, and kissed my fingers. I still lacked the words to describe what we meant to each other. But in one way, at least, we were bound forever. Only he could know exactly how I felt at that moment. Appreciate that particular pain.

Chapter 33

IT SHOULD BE EASY TO TELL THIS STORY. I know what happened, and when. I should be able to put the events in order, line them up like beads on a string. But I think now that time is not a line but a spiral, bending back on itself, delivering us again and again to the same places.

When I woke around midday on the morning of June 17, the Carraday house was quiet. The door to Mary Liz's bedroom was closed. I leaned against it and heard her heavy, irregular breathing. She had said she was never alone, but the house seemed to be empty. I went downstairs and looked around, but found no one. Outside the front door, the newspaper lay untouched on the stone veranda.

I took the paper in its plastic wrapping and went back through the house and down the half flight of stairs to the kitchen. The room was in perfect order, the counters cleared. There was no sign of Faline. When I put my hand on the stove, it was cold. I sat and opened the paper.

It was Sunday. That knowledge made the surrounding air feel different and gave the room and the things in it—the basket of fruit, the stacked crockery—an added repose, like the elements in a still life. I closed my eyes and willed the stillness to include me. Instead the thought came irresistibly that something was wrong.

Where was Will? The house was too quiet. I got up and walked around, opened the refrigerator and peered inside. The sight of so much food waiting to be washed, cut, mixed, seasoned, and cooked one way or another was somehow oppressive. Where was Faline?

I stifled the urge to call out for her, and sat down again. Faline was probably with Otis. I looked at my watch and saw that it was past one.

I went back up the stairs to the front hall where the big chandelier hung dim and gray. The crystals shivered when the air-conditioning came on, and I felt a chill down my back. I understood then what it would mean to be alone in the house day after day, like Stella, waiting and hoping for what would never happen.

After a brief search I found the keys to the jeep. I climbed into it and drove without thinking past the rows of parked cars, past the restaurant with the shark, open-mouthed, rearing up from its roof. I turned onto Seawall Boulevard and saw long lines of heavy surf rolling in from the Gulf.

So that explained the change I'd felt in the atmosphere. Weather coming. I looked around and saw awnings and aluminum storm shutters closed, a car pulled up onto the patio of a restaurant so the plastic windscreen could enclose it—a gesture only, one that meant the owner was enjoying his preparations. *There's a storm in the Gulf.* I wondered why nothing had been done at the Carradays', why the tall windows hadn't been covered, the pots brought in from the veranda, but I had no desire to return to the house.

Instead I did what so many Islanders do when a storm threatens. I drove west toward the beach. At the pocket park, the gate was closed, so I pulled onto a nearby access road and bumped down through the dunes onto the sand. From this perspective the waves were larger, dark and heavy as beaten steel. Several other cars already sat in a row along the tide line.

Something had drawn us there while most people were putting up plywood and carrying their lawn furniture inside. Islanders who rode out storms in unlikely places were sometimes accused of thrill-seeking. To me the urge seemed more like a kind of bone-deep weariness, coupled with the hope that the unyielding surface of the everyday world might crack open and reveal something beyond it. *You are waiting for the world to end, and part of you wants to see it happen.* I headed east, digging my heels into the hard-packed sand, pushing myself forward. I tucked my head and kept my eyes down as I walked.

Above me the sky was vast and troubled. Everything else seemed diminished—the houses along the beach were small and indistinct, the park boardwalk a pile of weathered blocks among the dunes. This was where the continent poured itself out—here in this thin strip of sand. The expanse was so flat and open it seemed the wind might carry me away. I stopped and raised my arms and willed it to happen.

Instead, my legs began to shake. I remembered that I hadn't eaten anything that morning or much the night before. I turned back, but the breeze was against me. By the time I got to the jeep, the windshield was rimed with salt, the windows opaque. I rubbed at them, making long whitish smears. A woman passed me, her eyes wild, her hair a mass that whipped in the wind. She looked a little crazy. She glanced back at me, startled, and I realized I must look the same. Finally I gave up on the windows and climbed into the car.

The road back was two lanes and a narrow, gritty shoulder. I rolled down my window and drove slowly, hoping that the rain would come soon and clear the windshield. I had gone about a mile when I noticed a black pickup behind me, uncomfortably close. Two dogs hung out of the back, their tongues lolling. I took my foot off the accelerator and waited for the driver to pass. Instead he slowed too. I reached out and waved him on. Still the truck loomed through the streaky rear window. I could hear the noise of its engine. Wind buffeted the sides of the jeep.

We came to an intersection where the red overhead light bounced in the breeze. If I stopped, would the truck hit me? Thinking about it, I could feel the shock in my spine and legs. I glanced to the left, held my breath, and shot through.

We drove that way for about a mile, the jeep and the truck so close they almost touched. Finally the driver had enough and pulled past me. Then, just in front of my right tire it seemed, a rusted barrel appeared, bouncing in the road. I jerked the wheel to the left and the jeep swung into the truck's black side. There was a drawn-out scraping noise and I stopped, hard.

What happened next did not seem real. I saw the driver of the truck open his door and approach. I knew from the way he walked that he was carrying something heavy in his hand. Then he raised his arm and I saw the tire iron. The glass in front of me shattered and fell into the car, on me, on the seat, between my legs, and onto the floor.

I sat for a moment, stunned, disbelieving, as the truck accelerated loudly and drove off, the two dogs leaning out and grinning. That was when the rain came all at once, falling in a hard slant through the vanished windshield.

When I reached the Carraday house, all the first-floor lights were on. Through the rain and waving branches, the great rooms appeared warm and festive. I struggled out of the jeep, bits of shattered glass still clinging to me. Instead of my usual route to the kitchen, I went to the front door. I wanted to be noticed. I rang the bell, but no one answered. When I opened the door with the key Will had given me, I heard voices and laughter.

I went through to the drawing room. Will was there, standing by the fireplace, under the portrait of Stella, with some men I didn't know. They were holding drinks in their hands. They turned together and saw me.

What did I expect? I don't know, exactly. I know I wanted, childishly, to tell my story, to be comforted. Will glanced at me, at my wet clothes, laughed easily and said, "Well, look at you. How about a glass of wine? Or would you like something stronger? You can take it upstairs."

I stood still, waiting for him to see that I wasn't just wet. I shivered. A puddle formed around me, water and occasional bits of glass that dripped onto the polished floor. I didn't know what to do with my hands. I hugged myself and said, "I was . . ." Then I stopped. I was about to say, "I was in an accident." But there had been nothing accidental about it. Should I say, "I was attacked"? I opened my mouth, but couldn't form the words. Finally I managed to say, "Something happened to the car."

"Which car?" Will asked.

"The jeep."

"Otis can take care of it in the morning." Will turned away and spoke softly to one of the men. It was clear he didn't intend to include me in the conversation.

Had he been talking business before I appeared? I believe now that he had, that he and the men there with him had arrived at some kind of agreement and were celebrating. He was reluctant to break the mood, to lose the goodwill he had created.

I grew up in a doctor's house, and I think sometimes that love and sorrow and anger are like illnesses. We can't anticipate their arrival, we can't escape our portion. Love is a summer rash, hot on the skin. Sorrow the constant ache of a broken rib. Anger a contagion, passed on in an instant of contact. When Will turned his back, anger rushed through me, a gift from the anonymous stranger in the truck.

When Will approached, smiling, and held out a glass, I knocked it out of his hand. The heavy crystal landed on the carpet and rolled and the ice cubes scattered on the floor.

Will's jaw clenched. He looked over my shoulder. There was some movement of the men standing behind him. Feet shuffling, murmurs as they dispersed. After a while I heard the front door open. The sound of wind and rain. The door closing again.

Will and I were alone. My gaze never left his. I watched him until my own face was stiff with effort. I recalled our meeting four weeks before. I hadn't seen then the pouches under his eyes, the deep lines on either side of his mouth. Unsmiling, he looked tired and old, and I wondered if he minded. Time would be the thing he couldn't buy or win over.

Even then, it all could have gone differently. If he hadn't said, with some impatience, "What's wrong with you?" I had been asked that question, had asked it of myself, all my life. Now I thought I knew, and I told him. I described how the man I believed to be my father had treated me. The years I had spent crouching and hiding. The nights I'd lain awake, frightened, waiting. I flung the words at him and saw him wince. I wanted to hurt him, to know that I could. Finally I ran out of breath.

He covered his eyes with one hand. Then he rubbed his forehead, as though the thoughts he was having pained him. His eyes met mine again and he said, "I'm so sorry." It seemed to require no effort.

"That's all?"

"Clare, I don't know what else to say. It was terrible, I understand. But you're all right now, thank God."

I studied his face. I saw mild distress and something that might have been compunction. I thought of Frankie with Eleanor, the way she had pursued and cornered her.

Will turned and picked up the glass from the floor and began to reach for the ice cubes. I know I enjoyed the sight of him bent over. I thought how uncharacteristic it was for him to be cleaning up. But it wasn't enough.

I heard the door again and someone moving in the hall.

I said, "Remember when we talked about Colonel Moody? About his system? You have one too. But yours is different. Explain to me how it works. You do a good thing here and it cancels the ugly thing you did over there? Is that it? So it all balances out. And in the end you get what you want. Is that right?"

"I don't know what you're talking about."

"You're kind to Mary Liz, which makes it okay for you to sleep with my mother. You help Island people with money, which makes it okay to ruin the beach."

"Clare, you're hurt, I understand—"

I shook my head. "You're my father," I said. "And you never acknowledged me. What I want to know is this: What was the thing you did that made that all right? I'd like you to tell me. I'd like to understand what I'm worth to you."

"If I'd had any idea what was happening," he said. "You must believe I'm . . . appalled." From the way he said it, I understood that he was rendering judgment on someone else. As if what had happened to me had nothing to do with him.

"You had a grandchild," I said. "And you never even saw her. Doesn't that matter to you?"

"I had photos," he said. "Your wonderful photos. Your mother shared them with me."

The phone rang in another room and went on ringing. I realized Faline wasn't there. Will must have sent everyone away so that he could have the house to himself. So that he could have the conversation I'd interrupted without anyone to witness it. "Excuse me," he said. "I need to answer that." He left the room.

I recalled a party I had been taken to as a child. I knew no one, and I spent my time sitting under the dining-room table unraveling a crepe-paper ball I had been given as a favor. My fingers were sticky and clumsy, and the dining room was dark, but I persisted. Slowly I unwrapped the pink wrinkled layers to find at the heart of the thing a single plastic bead. Despair came over me as, holding it in my hand, I realized this was all there was.

I looked around the Carradays' drawing room, at the heavy chairs, the tall mirrors that reflected the same things over and over—multiple images receding into the depths of the old glass. I went out to the hall.

I smelled her perfume before I saw Eleanor standing in the shadow of the stairs. Her eyes glittered. Her shirt was partly untucked, and her damp hair hung in an untidy mass below her ears. There were long, watery streaks on her skirt. It was not like her to get caught in the rain.

"Oh those blue eyes," she said. "And you so observant. But you were busy with other things. With Patrick. With the camera." She made an attempt to smooth the front of her shirt and her hand left a wet smudge. "That was his idea."

"I know."

"You wanted to learn something. And you have. You understand now how he is. You can chase after him, but it won't change anything. You will never get what you want. What you need. Because . . ." She stopped, her eyes unfocused, and she seemed to withdraw into herself. I could hear her breathing. Her hand went over and over the same smudged place on the front of her shirt.

"You have no idea what I need."

Eleanor paid no attention. When she spoke, it was to finish her sentence. "Because that's the way he is. He says come and you come.

Happily." She smiled, but her mouth twisted. "He says wait, and you tell yourself it's only for a month, six months, a year. I believed him! There has always been a reason to wait. But our time, my time, never comes. What good is the money if it doesn't . . ." She looked around the entry hall. "I hate this house."

Eleanor's hand grasped the fabric of her shirt and worked it back and forth. She said, "You give up one thing. Then another. You tell yourself it doesn't matter. Your interests, your friends." Finally her gaze rested on me. "You give up your children. Because he says it's for the best."

"He never said that."

She looked at me and shook her head. "Time goes by. You find yourself in a room full of people. Always so many people. But you're alone." She shook her head again and the mass of her hair slid onto her shoulders. "They love that sureness of his, the way it makes them feel. *You* know. But he shouldn't be so sure."

I started up the stairs, my own hand on the banister, but Eleanor spun and caught my wrist and held me there. I could feel her trembling. Her face close to mine, she said, "You like to listen. Are you listening now? Look at me. Is this what you want your life to be? You think you have a choice. And maybe, for a little while, you do. But that won't last." Her eyes were suddenly wide and bright with unshed tears.

I don't know what made me respond then the way I did. Was it just for the pleasure of seeing her react? I'd like to think I was beyond that kind of reprisal. Then why?

I was already wondering when the rain would let up enough for me to drive to the mainland. Trying to remember if I still had a map in the car. Did I tell myself that I could wait until the morning to tell her I was leaving? So that she could suffer a little in the meantime? A few hours. Surely it was nothing compared to what she had done. "I don't feel sorry for you," I said. I wrenched my arm away, and Eleanor flinched as if I'd hit her.

On the landing I stopped. "I'm his daughter. He cares about me," I said. I felt no shame at my lie. If what I said wasn't true, it should have been. "We've been talking about Italy. About visiting the gardens." Buoyed by a strange sense of rectitude, I climbed up the big staircase and left Eleanor standing by herself.

From the landing I looked down. She was still grasping the stair rail. But her head was bent. A comb slid from her hair and bounced across the polished floor. No light came through the stained-glass window.

I'VE TRIED TO RECALL WHAT HAPPENED later that night, after the rain stopped. I stayed in Stella's room, gathering my things. I was exhausted, but too on edge to lie down. Someone left a plate of cold food outside my door. When finally I crept into the bed and slept, it was like stepping into a pool. Not a bright sparkling pool with a concrete edge, but the kind with a rocky rim and a black bottom you can't see. I remember nothing.

There must have been a noise, like a car backfiring, except that it came from the garage, not the street. Did I hear it and half wake? Would it have mattered if I had gone down?

I imagine how the alcove in the tack room looked the next morning, its austere calm disturbed by the night's events. I see the blue spread rumpled, pulled from the bed, the round table tipped on its side. Sometimes I see bits of broken china, flowers, leaves and stems and petals, water and blood on the stone floor. I know there was blood. Maybe that was all there was, after the first unbearable explosion of sound. A stain spreading across the floor, dust motes spinning.

I have to imagine it because I don't know. When I crossed the lawn to the garage, Faline was waiting, planted in the grass like a column. Her face was ashy. She shook her head. She stepped in front of me and took hold of my shoulders and held me with her strong, wiry fingers, and leaned down so that her forehead rested against mine. Her voice was just above a whisper. "No, baby," she said, "you can't go in there now. Your daddy been shot."

Chapter 34

I NEVER ASKED, BUT I BELIEVE that my grandmother saw each of her quilts before she ever picked up her scissors. That the arrangement present in her mind was something she could count on and return to. Watching in silence as she cut and pieced and finally hand-stitched the many-colored shapes, I was always surprised when the design announced itself.

That was her gift, the certainty of her vision, the way she saw her own modest life and its purpose laid out, whole and entire, like fabric on a frame. I don't believe she ever looked back or felt regret.

I live now in a place where the sky is never really blue, where I can go in any direction and feel myself surrounded by buildings. The slanting light is manageable. I don't miss the moments of sudden sun blindness, the hot wind on my neck. I prefer not to see into the distance.

I have a biography, an official history of my own. It doesn't mention my family or the Island, and when I read it, it seems to me like an account of someone else's life. I have a new agent too, a young woman with spiky hair who looks at me as if I frighten her and never calls me anything but *Ms. Porterfield.* Jules went to prison when it was discovered that he had appropriated several unsold paintings from an artist's studio. Security cameras in the building showed him entering and leaving not once, as he had claimed, but twice. One day, during the trial, as he stood on the courthouse steps with his lawyer, he called me over and asked if I wanted to take a photo. I said yes. "Good girl," he responded. "Always the pro."

Eleanor never had to face a trial. A grand jury ruled that Will's death was accidental. On the Island, it was the only possible outcome. After Will's funeral, Eleanor received the guests who came to express their sympathy at the Carraday house. In a black silk dress, her hair neatly arranged, she presided over the food and drink in the dining room. Mary Liz sat in the conservatory as usual. It was very much an Island event.

And for a time Eleanor remained part of Will's former circle. Then gradually that tide went out, and she was left to herself. The Carraday house now belongs to the Historical Society and is open daily for tours. I think about the lines of visitors moving through the rooms and up the stairs, fanning themselves with colorful brochures, about how different the experience must be without Will there to greet them, to press their hands and lead them on, envious and trusting.

I wonder if Eleanor even sees the crowds gathered in what used to be Will's rose garden. Her view is unobstructed. The hedge of oleander and the garden itself are gone, replaced by a wide walkway and a parking lot outlined with red reflective disks. The property teeters on the edge of shabby. The tourist season is short. There is a gift shop in the garage.

My mother possesses her own kind of certainty. I don't believe regret is in her emotional vocabulary. Perhaps the closest she ever came was the clothes, Frankie's and mine, hanging in her closet, reminders of a time when she still believed she and Will might have a life of their own together. I think about those years. I see her bedroom, the glowing lamp, the silver-topped jars laid out in its light. The flowers she appropriated. It still surprises me that passion leaves behind no visible trace.

Frankie used to call Eleanor selfish. Now the word she uses is *unnatural*. As if even she has to concede that the scale of an obsession counts for something. We ate dinner together recently when she came to the city for a medical conference. In her forties, Frankie has become the mother of twin boys. I think being the only woman in the family has changed her. Something has. She laughs easily, she has an assurance that has nothing to do with professional success. I suppose what I am trying to say is that she is happy.

"Show me," I said, as we sat together comfortably under a red paper lantern. And she got the snapshots out, a whole expanding plastic file. The two boys appeared together in every image, as though, after so much anxious waiting, their doubleness still amazed and delighted her. Two redheads in the sandbox, in the pool. She has answered her own question. *Is that what parents do?*

"Did you get the things I sent for their birthday?" I asked.

"You spoil them," she said, but her voice was tender. She sounded like a woman in love.

I see her joy and I pray that the charm will last, that she will never wake and listen for a cry that doesn't come, or stumble in the dark to an empty bedroom, or bend down, aching, to feel for a remembered wisp of breath.

When I think of Bailey, I remember that last year before the ad campaign, how she loved to run. It seemed she was always running—sliding on the wood floor, on the linoleum, dodging the furniture. At the grocery store, dashing ahead of me along the aisle. On the street, vanishing around a corner. Circling back to reassure me. She will always be a little ahead of me now, but I tell myself that she is there, just out of sight for a moment. That one day I will catch up.

Frankie and Stephen sold their condominium. Of our house and the Island, Frankie says she has put it all behind her, as if the experiences of those years, the nights we spent in our shared room, could be gathered together and placed here or there like the contents of a box. Like the boxes Harriet Kinkaid gave away. So the work of remembering has passed to me. Along with the stories, mine and Stella's.

I could claim to have discovered what Harriet didn't tell me in the photos I found, in the notebook and the album that I left hidden. But the truth is, it was there all along, in the Carradays' drawing room, for anyone to see. Henry Durand knew what had happened to Stella, but he was young and an outsider. There was no one he could confide in. So he told the story in the only way possible. It was Henry, I'm sure, who persuaded Ward Carraday to commission the relief portrait. Who set the image of Stella between the carved, hairy legs of a goat on the fireplace mantel.

I imagine that Ward Carraday drew the line at the broken pitcher, that he wanted it new and intact. Why would a man like him pay for an image of something broken? Henry Durand had to find another way to represent Stella's lost innocence. So he instructed the artist to add the lilies, symbols of purity, crushed at her feet.

His audience knew Ward Carraday's reputation. And they knew the language of flowers. Henry Durand must have hoped they would understand and sympathize when he and Stella ran away together. But he didn't know the Island. Or Ward Carraday. Of course she was brought back.

I was more fortunate. I understand that I have Eleanor to thank for that.

Mary Liz died not long after Will. It may have been coincidence, coming so soon after the shooting. Or it may have been one more proof of the mysteriousness of marriage, evidence that despite all I knew and observed, she and Will were bound in some way I would never understand.

I went into a bookstore yesterday. As I was checking out, the clerk asked me if I'd found everything I wanted, and I thought of Will, of the way his questions always seemed to mean more than other people's. What I thought next was *I don't know what I want until I see it.* See it and seize it, with my Leica. No comforting vision like my grandmother's guides me.

But there are images burned into my retina. Patterns. Bars of light and shade through old broken blinds, squares of carpeted floor. The black banding on a gull feather, a freckled hand holding a feather. The hands of the man I called my father.

He looked to history to explain things, to provide a precedent. Did he tell himself that my history, the fact that I was not his child, justified the things he did to me? He talked about facts and the truth, while he rearranged both to suit himself. In the end, for all his protests, he was an Islander.

Growing up, Frankie tried to know him. I tried too, for a time, to find a way into his world. Neither of us ever discovered the thought, the elusive act of imagination, that could show us the way or explain him to us.

I believe I know what Patrick was doing at Saint Vincent de Paul. Not long after I left Galveston for the last time, the *Daily News* ran a small article saying that Father James McAvity had been recalled from the parish and disciplined for creating a "situation" with the INS. Of course I can't be sure. The success of what they did—they would have called it providing sanctuary—depended on secrecy, something Patrick enjoyed.

Most people in Galveston probably still think of Patrick as an idle drunk who was bound to kill himself in a car sooner or later. But I believe Will knew what he was doing. That the knowledge was part of the complicated system of moral reckoning he used to justify to himself his different roles.

Eighteen months later, on a winter morning before daybreak, Patrick's car went off the Galveston causeway. The rising sun would have melted the thin coat of ice in a couple of hours. But he couldn't wait.

Ty called me once after he left the Island. More than a year had passed; whatever professional stature he might have lost on the Island, he seemed to have regained. His voice was the voice of a banker I didn't know very well, and our conversation was strained. He said, "I shouldn't have told you."

"That wouldn't have stopped it happening. You were right. About everything."

"I hope you know I don't take any pleasure in it."

Ty's prediction came true. Whatever was supposed to result from Will's last meeting, the outcome that would have resolved everything, or at least postponed the inevitable, never arrived. There was a civil judgment, a federal investigation. I saw the headlines, but I didn't read more. The process felt unstoppable, unavoidable, like the largest storm you can imagine, and in its way as necessary.

Every so often I get a postcard from Faline. The last one was a picture of an old-fashioned general store with a couple of pickups parked out front. The caption read, DOWNTOWN ACACIA. On the back she wrote, "Does it look to you like we need a golf course?" I always write back. Sometimes I send photos. They are worth a lot of money now, and I'm glad to have someone to give them to.

I don't think about the Island. Except when I've been too much alone. Or when I've attended an opening and listened to people talk and laugh. Or when I've walked for hours with my Leica under my jacket. When a sudden gust of hot air from a grate takes me by surprise, or the mist-covered moon appears, close and glowing, between two buildings.

Then I recall the summer nights, the heat that lay along the Island like another stretched-out body, the old-house air, the taste of damp wood and salt and aged lacquer in my throat. And it confronts me, the fact I can't escape. That air with its distinctive aftertaste oxygenated my blood, gave me breath.

In dreams I draw the salt breeze into my lungs, and my heart hums in my chest, the beats so quick they run together. I feel my bones grow lighter and I spread my arms.

I understand the wind in a new way, sensing its contours. Above the shaggy crowns of the palms, my field of vision explodes, and I see everything, all at once—the beaches and the brick-paved streets, the trash cans in the alley, the pointed spire of a church. A man watching. He stands in the yard behind his house, a white house with a porch. He raises one arm as if to stop me.

But I settle into a current and ride it higher, an ordinary bird, not one anybody would notice. I wing past the windows of the rooms where children play and read and fight and at night sleep undisturbed, to the water, the brown sand, the long lines of foam. I rise easily past the haze, into the blue, the sweet beguiling blue, that promises everything.

Acknowledgments

I would like to thank the generous friends who read and commented on early versions of this novel: Nisi Hamilton, Peggy Rhoads, and Marie Seidl. I owe a special debt of gratitude to those who persisted through multiple drafts: Faye Jones, Gail Siegel, and Lauren Silberman. I'm grateful also to Farnoosh Moshiri and the members of the Inprint Writing Workshop who read and commented on two chapters.

Photographer Mary Day Long kindly answered technical questions and reviewed the passages related to photography. Any errors that remain are my responsibility. Peggy Bush, who not only read several versions of the manuscript but also speared fish while I took notes, deserves a trophy.

Finally, my deepest appreciation goes to my daughters, Genevra and Francesca, the lights of my life, who have contributed in so many ways; to Nan Talese, the best of the best; to Ronit Feldman, wise beyond her years; to the stellar marketing and publicity team at Doubleday; and to my extraordinary agent, Mollie Glick.

* * *

Anyone interested in learning about Galveston's colorful past must begin with David McComb's *Galveston: A History* (University of Texas Press, 1986) and Gary Cartwright's *Galveston, A History of the Island* (Atheneum, 1991). First-person accounts of the Great Hurricane and its aftermath can be found in *Through a Night of Horrors: Voices from the*

Galveston Storm, edited by Casey Edward Greene and Shelly Henley Kelley (Texas A&M University Press, 2000).

The Galveston That Was (MacMillan, 1966), by Howard Barnstone, features Henri Cartier-Bresson's images of the island, including the old woman in the boarding house. She is not identified.

A NOTE ABOUT THE AUTHOR

Elizabeth Black was born and raised in Providence, Rhode Island, and now lives in Houston, Texas. *The Drowning House* is her first novel.

A NOTE ABOUT THE TYPE

The text of this book was set in Filosofia, a typeface designed by
Zuzana Licko in 1996 as a revival of the typefaces of Giambattista
Bodoni (1740–1813). Basing her design on the letterpress
practice of altering the cut of the letters to match the size for
which they were to be used, Licko designed Filosofia Regular as
a rugged face with reduced contrast to withstand the reduction
to text sizes, and Filosofia Grand as a more delicate and refined
version for use in larger display sizes.

Licko, born in Bratislava, Czechoslovakia, in 1961, is the
co-founder of Emigre, a digital type foundry and publisher of
Emigre magazine, based in Northern California. Founded in 1984,
coinciding with the birth of the Macintosh, Emigre was one of
the first independent type foundries to establish itself centered
around personal computer technology.